Beach Bummed

Travels and Travails of Maile Spencer

§

Kay Hadashi

Beach Bummed
Travels and Travails of Maile Spencer: Book Two
Kay Hadashi. Copyright © 2021. All Rights Reserved.
2nd Edition, April 2022.
ISBN: 9798782554736

Cover art by the author.
Original cover images from pixabay.com.

Chapter One

When Maile woke in the morning, she wasn't in a capsule, she wasn't in a convent, and she wasn't in the Cotswolds. She was in an unfamiliar bed anyway.

Opening both eyes, she recognized the room but wasn't sure why. Even with just a sheet over her, she was in a sweat. That's when it dawned on her that she was in the guest room at her mother's house. She was home, or at least in Honolulu.

She had her parents' house to herself for a few days, since they were visiting family on Maui. It was the perfect way to ease back into life at home after a long trip around the world. She had a quiet house, and no one was asking questions that had no answers. Maile was done sleeping for the day, but just couldn't bring herself to get up. The soft pillow and clean sheets wouldn't allow it. As much as she wanted to doze off again, she couldn't keep her eyes closed.

Her backpack was still leaning against the wall where she dropped it the night before, stuffed full of dirty laundry. That was something else to add to the list of chores. So far, that included going to church, cleaning the house, grocery shopping, and meeting her brother's girlfriend. She also needed to get some holiday shopping started. Christmas was a week away, the first one she'd celebrate at home with her family in several years.

The house was silent, too quiet. In many ways, she missed the noise and activity of military living, especially in far-flung locations. Or maybe it was all the men that were around those distant bases that made the military lifestyle so appealing. That was one of the few things she missed about being in the Army, the constant flow of men. But that ended a few months before, and she'd made a round-the-world tour since then. That had gone on longer than she expected, and being on the road for so long, and suffering a touch of Montezuma's Revenge, had taken its toll on her body.

She'd lost so much weight in the last few weeks, that she was sure she'd fit into her high school clothes. Her complexion was a wreck, and her hair needed the touch of a stylist's hand. Skinny, pale, and frazzled was not a good way of heading into the holidays, especially with so many phone cameras in the hands of devious people these days.

Being in Hawaii, she would get color back into her face with just a few sunny afternoon runs or a couple of trips to the beach. Eating her mother's cooking would pack a few pounds back on. Nothing but a pair of scissors would resolve split ends, though.

Yawning, Maile flapped air under her sheet to cool herself. It was going to take a few days to get used to the humidity of the tropics again.

The biggest chore of the day was having dinner with her little brother and his girlfriend. She hadn't met the girlfriend yet, not even seen a picture. That didn't bode well. It meant her brother Kenny was hiding something. He'd grown up while she'd been away, and become a semi-famous golf pro. According to their mother, anyway.

The girlfriend was turning out to be an enigma. While Kenny told one story of how nice she was, their mother told a different tale of how unnecessarily sophisticated the girl seemed to be. She talked too fast and liked to use big words while not always answering questions put to her. Kenny explained her the way Abraham Lincoln would've, that you could take the girl off her home island of Kauai, but you couldn't take the 'local' out of the girl.

Maile wasn't sure what Lincoln had originally meant with the expression, but she was pretty sure her brother wasn't going to be a statesman any time soon.

"What was her name? Ashley? No, Asher. Something Biblical. I wonder if they're going to church today or doing some other Biblical activity instead?"

She looked at the bedside alarm clock. Church service had already started. Not setting the alarm clock and waking up late was her built-in excuse for not attending that day. She turned onto her side and stared at the empty spot on the nightstand where a framed picture of a lover should be.

"I need to hire a barista. Just snap my fingers and a Roman gladiator would bring me coffee. Fluff my pillows, rub my feet, tell me how beautiful and charming I am. His name would be Domenico."

She daydreamed of the hiring process, searching Tuscany for the man that could pour milk into her coffee in just the right way.

"Gladiator laundry boy, gladiator chef, gladiator housekeeper. What good is being an Etruscan princess if there aren't gladiators doing things for me?"

That led to another fantasy.

"Naturally, they'd need uniforms. I suppose they could all wear the same thing the gladiator masseur would wear."

That led to the best fantasy yet.

"I wonder if gladiators get jealous of each other? If I worked it right, I could have them fighting over me."

Maile turned onto her back and flapped air under the sheet again.

"Oh, who am I kidding? The last time I had a date, it was a day pass to a water purification plant, and that ended rather poorly."

She reached for the backpack leaning against the wall and snagged it with a fingertip. That tipped the contents out. An energy bar tumbled across the floor, one of her travel meal staples.

"Done with those." She tossed that aside. "Somebody needs to invent poi-flavored energy bars."

Pulling more stuff out, she found what she wanted, a smutty romance novel about a football quarterback named Drake, something she'd been carrying around for months. She flipped from one page to the next, while sending telepathic messages into the cosmos, begging for someone to bring her a cup of coffee.

"I bet Asher brings coffee to Kenny."

She turned to a new page.

"I wonder what Asher does for work?"

She stopped to reread a page about the quarterback taking off his jersey and tossing it into the crowd at the end of the game.

"She's probably a dancer in a strip club."

Maile turned another page.

"That would be the event of the year. Kenny marrying a stripper in our little church."

She went back to the scene with the jersey being pulled off.

"That's why she doesn't want her picture taken. She's a famous porn star and can't risk being recognized. That would doom her smut career, discovered dating a nice boy from Manoa Valley."

She came to a scene in the book she knew well. It was off a blond cheerleader helping injured Drake take off his pads and cleats. Like every other time she'd read the scene, she tried replacing the blond with herself. As always, it didn't work. It seemed Drake was more interested in blonds than brunettes.

"I wonder if my Roman gladiator hairdresser could talk me into blond hair? I bet I'd be hot as a blond. My phone wouldn't stop ringing with calls from Drake. At least until the roots started to show."

The next chapter in the book was about two cheerleaders pressing their lips against Drake's face during a photo shoot of Heisman Trophy winners, the picture being used on a cover of Sports Illustrated.

"One blonde's not enough, he gets two of them? What's wrong with a nice Polynesian cheerleader from Honolulu?"

She found a page that had been bent over marking a spot where Drake had just broken up with the blond cheerleader made pregnant by the team coach. The scene took place in the weight room, where Drake was working his pecs on the rowing machine. Sweat ran down his body, his arms pulling, his legs pushing, his chest grunting, his muscles bulging.

Maile tossed the book aside.

"The real question is why am I so jealous of my little brother's girlfriend? That's beyond sad and downright pathetic."

When she heard her phone ring, she wondered who it could be.

"Mom calling to nag...no, ask if I've found a job yet. Or nag me about finding a man. 'When are you making me a grandbaby?'" Maile said, in a mocking falsetto.

Planning on going for a jog later, she got dressed in running shorts and a T-shirt, and went to the kitchen to fire up the coffeemaker. She stood with her hands on the counter, watching the machine.

"Snap it up, machine. You can be replaced by a gladiator."

Steam came out and fluid dripped into the pot. The room was quickly filled with the aroma of coffee.

"Forget Roman gladiators and bare-chested football quarterbacks named Drake. Someone with a job would do just fine. If he was somewhat conversant, that would be even better."

While the first pot brewed, she drummed her fingernails.

"Doesn't have to be smart."

She got a mug off the rack and went back to watching the coffeemaker.

"Doesn't have to be wealthy."

She got milk from the fridge and gave it a sniff.

"He just needs to be."

She gave the coffeemaker a swat to make it go faster.

"Didn't Schopenhauer say something like that? A man doesn't have to be smart; he just needs to be."

Unable to wait any longer, she poured the first mug as quickly as she could before replacing the pot on the burner.

"Maybe it was Descartes?"

She took her first sip of coffee.

"Is that a line from Shakespeare? To be or not to be the quarterback in Maile's bedroom."

Taking sips in rapid succession, she added milk. Ancient images from high school floated through her mind of being a cheerleader, and of the quarterback that had spurned her interests.

"Nope, done with them. No more gladiators, no more quarterbacks. No more Maile's stupid flashbacks."

She refilled her mug.

"Who am I trying to kid? I'll never get married, or have kids. I'm a nurse. That's what I'm good at."

Maile finally checked her phone. A message had been left from her dad to call him right away.

She was still having a hard time thinking of Reverend Ka'uhane as a father figure, rather than the pastor at the church. When he retired, he married Maile's mother, only days before Maile left for her commission in the Army Nurse Corps. Nine years along, she still thought of them as newlyweds, and him as her pastor and spiritual confidant.

She took her mug to the table with her phone. It would be easier to call him first to get the scoop about what her mother wanted, before entering the lion's den and calling her mother directly.

Maile opened the fishing magazine that had been left out by her dad. She didn't know anything about deep sea fishing, but knew it was popular. She'd grown up eating every imaginable fish that was pulled from the waters that surrounded Hawaii. Looking at the pictures, she was able to see what the fishermen that caught those fish looked like.

"Probably a dumb question to ask a retired minister, but how was church?" she asked when her dad, Ka'uhane, answered.

"Oh, fine. The minister here draws a good crowd." He launched into a one-sided conversation, while Maile sipped coffee. "What are you plans, Hoku?"

"Do some laundry."

"I was thinking of long range plans."

Maile flipped from page to page in the magazine, looking at pictures of caught fish. "I know. That'll take the rest of the morning, which is as far ahead in time as I can think right now."

"You must've been giving the next chapter of your career some thought in your time off?"

"Of course. I need to find a job that I'll like for more than twenty minutes. I might go to grad school. Then there's the tour company. It would be nice to grow that a little more. I have some ideas about that."

"Knowing you, Hoku, you'll try doing them all at once."

Maile chuckled. "And make a giant mess of everything."

"You should be able to get any nursing job you want, anywhere in Honolulu, right?"

She looked at a picture of a marlin that was bigger than the fisherman who caught it.

"Yep, but I'd like to be selective, you know? The idea of taking the first job that's offered isn't appealing. I'm looking for something more challenging."

"Write your own ticket? That's the right idea. Just don't wait too long. What about the tour company? I heard you might sell it?"

"May as well. What do I know about running a business? I'm hoping Brian has some money saved up, enough to buy the place from me, lock, stock, and barrel."

"If you don't mind me meddling in something I know nothing about, why not hang onto that until you're settled into your new job as a nurse? It would be money coming in."

"Yeah, not much, but something," she said.

"You have your law suit settlement from the hospital, too."

Maile found an ad for charter fishing and left the magazine open there.

"That's for my retirement. I had David Melendez put that into a long term annuity."

"Governor Melendez."

"Oh, yes, I forgot he's our governor now. And his cousin Melanie is our Lieutenant Governor. By the time I got the absentee ballot where I was based in Khashraq, the election was over. How are they doing?" Maile asked.

"You know how the media treats politicians. One day they're the best thing since chopped liver, and the next they're stray dogs having rocks thrown at them."

"Yep. Anything else going on in Honolulu I need to know about?"

"What do people say? Same ol', same ol'."

"How's Mom?"

"She's fine. She's waiting for you to call her."

"I just got home a few hours ago, and most of that time was spent sleeping."

"Eat breakfast and give her a call. She has a couple of things to talk to you about."

"Any hints about what she wants to nag...talk to me about?" she asked.

He laughed. "I've been sworn to secrecy."

Maile got a call from her mother, and put off breakfast to take it.

"Hi, Mom."

"You didn't go to church this morning, Maile girl."

"How'd you know that?"

"You know how. Coconut wireless."

"Just got off a long flight and I needed some sleep. Church will still be there next week."

"Long flight was last night."

Maile did her best to withhold her first sigh of the conversation. "Mom, I'm dead tired, and haven't got much sleep and even less food lately. Can your interrogation about the lack of men in my life and the absence of grandchildren in your house wait until tomorrow? Please?"

"Of course."

"How's Maui? You and Dad having fun?"

"Thinking of moving here. Kelani has been showing us condos."

"You're seriously thinking of buying a condo? You'd leave Honolulu?"

"Nothing carved in stone."

Done with the fishing magazine, Maile got the phone book and turned to the Yellow Pages. "When are you coming back here?"

"Tuesday. You'll pick us up at the airport?"

13

"Better for you guys to take an Uber."

"Just drive your dad's car."

"That's a good idea, if he wants paint removed from the fenders. It looks new. I could break it in for him, with emphasis on breaking it."

"Don't forget to go to Keneka's house for dinner tonight."

"I was hoping to find a way out of it." Maile scanned down the listings in the phone book, looking for a hair salon in Honolulu with an Italian name. When she found one, she bent the corner of the page. "I might be busy later."

"Doing what? Too busy for dinner with your brother?"

"Maybe I'll be lucky and be in a horrific accident instead."

"Don't talk like that. Those things come true."

"So I've heard," Maile said. She kept looking the Yellow Page listings for her gladiator hairdresser. "Who says the cottage is his house?"

"You're never there."

Maile stifled her second sigh. "I'm not moving in with you and Dad. You can get that out of your head right now."

"You'd rather live with them?"

She needed to change the subject. "What do you know about Asher?"

"Not much. Has a job some place. Can't cook."

"Not pregnant, is she?" Maile asked.

"I didn't ask."

"Is that why Kenny's in such a hurry to marry her?"

"None of my business, Maile girl."

"Since when are weddings and grandbabies none of your business?"

"Since you're not making them."

"That makes no sense at all, Mom."

"I have a list…"

"Of eligible bachelors at church, yes, I know." Maile went back to the listing for the Italian salon and read it again. Good news, that the owner was a man. "Can you give me another week or two to find a Roman gladiator on my own?"

"Gladiator?"

"I met one a while back in Italy. I was thinking of sending for him."

"That's why you liked it so much there?" her mother asked.

"Just daydreaming. Anything else?"

"You're not getting any younger, Maile girl."

"And when you were my age you already had two kids, and one of them was in school. Yes, I know the story well." After allowing her mother to pry impossible to accomplish promises out of her, Maile begged off the call. She didn't give herself the chance to back out of making the call when she tapped in the number for the Italian salon.

If there was one piece of wisdom that was obvious, it was not being humorous when dealing with bankers, plumbers, or hairdressers. Too many things could go wrong.

"Hi. I'm looking for a new stylist and have time to come in today. Is someone available?"

"You haven't been in before?" the girl asked with a sweetly youthful voice.

"Unfortunately, no. I've heard you guys are great, though. Is Antonio available?"

"He's the owner. He doesn't do hair."

"Oh. Who is available?"

"Jim has time later."

"Jim? Is he Italian?"

"Not even close," the girl said.

15

"Where's he from?"

"Kansas."

"I don't suppose he's built like a quarterback?" Maile asked, giving up hope.

"Kinda skinny," the girl said quietly. "He has time at one, at two, at three, and again at four."

"What about at five?" Maile asked.

"We close then."

"Not very busy, is he?"

"Not very good," the girl said in her quietest voice yet.

"Do any of the Italian men stylists have appointment time, even later in the week?"

"We're not really Italian. Bella Donna is just the name of the place, and Antonio isn't even a real guy."

Maile slapped the phone book closed and tossed it back into its cubbie. "That's disappointing."

"You might want to find another place."

"Yeah, a place in Rome," Maile said, ending the call.

Tossing her phone aside, she dug a pair of running shoes out of her backpack for a run. Before she could get out the door, her phone rang again. It was from Brian, the manager of her little tour company. "Must be signs up all over town, announcing my arrival home."

No message had been left. She waited for a text, but never got one. She wondered if that meant he was so swamped he was too busy to send a text, or if it was simply a call to welcome her home. They'd been holding regular calls on the first day of each month, to discuss the business, the hiring of new employees, the purchase of a new tour van, and how they wanted to steer the company in the coming year. Christmas and the New Year holidays were coming, and bonuses would need to be paid. Decisions needed to be made but could just as easily wait.

She called him anyway.

"Are you coming in today?" he asked after welcoming her home.

"I've been home for six whole hours. Amazing how tiring sitting still on an airliner for eight hours can be."

"Better than those endless military transport flights, right? Just come in for a while. I have something to talk to you about."

"It's Sunday. I wasn't planning to do anything more than eat a meal and take a nap. If I could think of a way of doing both at the same time, it'd be perfect. Can it wait until tomorrow?"

"Tomorrow's too late. Remember that idea we were tossing around about multi-day tours?" Brian asked.

"Yeah, camping, festivals on other islands, deluxe tours. So?"

"I just got a call from a Girl Scout troop master, or whatever she's called. She said she leads a group of Girl Scouts from Kauai. They're here for their winter break from school and want to hire us to take them on a three-day campout here on Oahu."

"Why did she call us? We've never offered that sort of thing before," Maile said.

"Word of mouth, all the way to Kauai, I guess. Multi-day events and tours are something we've talked about a few times. What do you think? Are we ready to try it?"

"That would be a great way of seeing if it's something we want to do. Not so sure about Girl Scouts, though. What did you tell her?"

"I said I needed to talk to you," Brian said.

"Well, if they want to camp, we'll need to rent tents and camping gear, which wouldn't be cheap. We'd have to haul along food and water, and whatever else Girl Scouts need to survive. That'll cost them extra. It'll also take some time to figure out the logistics, and the legalities, of something like that."

"From what the scout leader told me, they've borrowed everything they need from a local troop. Tents, bags, stoves, everything. They even have a route and campground picked out. All they really need is an adult to go with them."

"An adult?" Maile asked. "What about the troop master, or whatever she's called?"

"From what I understand, there're two of them, but neither have much experience with outdoors stuff."

"And we do?" Maile glared at the phone screen for a moment. "You and I have been in the Army, but we lived in plywood structures built by engineers. The only campfires I ever saw were MRAPs that got blown up and the tires burned all night."

"You've never been camping?" he asked.

"Sure, as a kid with my mom and brother. We'd go to the beach and set up our tent, cook wieners over a little fire. There were restrooms with plumbing, picnic tables, and a car to take us home when Kenny and I began to fight. I think Girl Scouts like to rough it a little more than that. They have to pass merit badges, or whatever they're called."

"The thing is, I might've made it sound like we'd take the job," Brian said.

"What?"

"Sorry, Mai."

"How many are there?" she asked.

"Eight."

"Well, have fun, brah. Teenaged girls are an experience like none other."

"Why me?" he asked.

"We don't have anyone else that can do it. All three of our guides are city girls. They wouldn't know one end of a tent from the other. They'd get lost without their drivers. And no, I'm not sending Lopaka or Daniel out with a pack of Girl Scouts. That means you and Amelia are taking them."

"Troop of Girl Scouts. Why can't you?"

"I have job interviews to go to. I also have year-end job evaluations to do, including yours. You can take Amelia. I bet she'd love to get out of the office for a couple of days. I can cover sales calls while she's away."

"Two little kids, remember?" he said.

"Oh, yeah." Maile rubbed her forehead for a moment. "Did you give the scoutmaster a price?"

"I said that it would be comparable to three full-day tours in a row, paid per kid. The good thing is you wouldn't need a driver the whole time, just one to drop you off at the trailhead and pick you up again. That would save a lot of money, not having to pay for fuel or driver time."

"That's true. When do they want to go?" Maile asked.

"I think I mentioned they're visiting here from Kauai and have limited time to use the tents and gear they've borrowed."

"When, Brian?"

"Well, tomorrow."

"Tomorrow? We're supposed to just slap something together in one day?" she asked.

"She might've called me a while back about this. I back-burnered it, until she called back yesterday. I was hoping she'd find someone else. Apparently, no other tour company in town wants to take little girls on a hike."

"Because they're smart." While her stomach grumbled for food, Maile's legs ached for a run. "Hey, I gotta go. Text me her name and number and I'll give her a call to see if this idea is realistic."

Knowing she was stuck between a rock and a pack of little girls, Maile admitted that taking them on a hike was the perfect opportunity for growing her business. It would also be a way of getting her body used to the tropics again, by going on a long hike in the humidity. She needed to stretch her legs and burn off some pent-up anxiety, and even if teenagers were involved, the sooner, the better.

Wondering if his number still worked after several years, she called her old lawyer.

It was a heady thing, to have the phone numbers of the Governor and Lieutenant Governor in her phone list. In the past, one had done some work for her, and the other had been only a passing acquaintance when Maile took her kid on day tours. Somehow, they'd progressed in life to becoming important leaders, while Maile was still looking for her dream job.

"Maile Spencer!" David Melendez said enthusiastically. "Welcome home from the war! I've been watching the news and wondering if you were okay. There were a few rumors going around town a while back about you. Any of them true?"

"Lies, David, I mean Governor Melendez."

"Please, it's still David to my friends."

"Am I interrupting anything?" Maile asked.

"Just got home from some sort of fundraiser. They all blend together after a while. Is there something I can do for you?"

"Maybe you remember I have that little tour company?" She explained about the idea of the multi-day tours, and how she might need extra releases and disclaimers, especially for something like camping or hiking. "The problem is that the first trip happens tomorrow. Is there some sort of standardized form that I can use to cover my butt? Sorry, protect me from unnecessary lawsuits?"

"You had it right the first time. There is some standard language used, but my office can write up a few things specifically for your needs. When do you need them?"

"By tomorrow morning. Sorry. I just learned about it a few minutes ago."

"No problem. I can have something printed up and couriered to your office this afternoon. I'll make sure they use office stationery, From the Law Offices of Melendez, etcetera. People pay closer attention when they sign something like that."

"Send me a bill..."

"It won't be much. An hour or two of paralegal time. I can cover the courier, since we send things out all day, every day."

"This isn't beneath your practice?" she asked.

"I love doing things like this, Maile. These are the kinds of things all lawyers should be doing. We'd have better reps if we did. I have to go, though. There's a Christmas pageant somewhere that I can't miss."

After the call, Maile realized all over again Christmas was only a few days away, and wasn't even close to being ready. With Christmas shopping on her mind, she set off on her run.

Chapter Two

It had been nine years since she'd run these streets, and Maile had a hard time deciding where to go. One direction took her up into the Manoa Valley, known for its cool breezes and frequent showers. Another direction took her toward downtown, pointless to visit on a Sunday. If she ran far enough in another direction, she'd get to Waikiki, where much of her business was conducted. Waikiki was always open for business, and she figured at least one of her guides was giving a tour there that day. Indecisive, she took off down a street that could lead to anywhere.

It wasn't long before she was at a sporting goods store she'd known all her life. It had been twenty years she'd been inside, and when she went in to look for camping things, she discovered it had turned into hunting and deep sea fishing gear. Pistols were locked in glass cases, and rifles in every size and shape were chained to the walls. One of them was an M-4 tactical rifle, general issue of the US military, something she'd been forced into using once. She still shuddered at the memory of that moment.

"Everything I could possibly need to blow away a platoon of Khashraqis," she muttered while walking through the place.

"Gun or ammo?" a salesman asked when he came over to her.

"Neither. I'm just planning a campout for tomorrow."

"Outdoors?"

"Where else?"

"In your little girly's bedroom?"

Already with the sexist stuff. Looking at him, she figured he'd never been anywhere near a military uniform, but pretended he was a soldier by running through the woods in hunter's camo with a rifle, looking for something to kill. "Outdoors with Girl Scouts."

He seemed to find that funny. "Mountains or beach?"

"Beach. We're hiking from Waimanalo Beach to Bellows and back again."

"That'll be fun." He took her to the camping gear aisle. "Assuming you already have the big stuff, you might be able to find a few things to make yourselves more comfortable. You can find ladies' products at…"

"I know where to find them, thanks."

Maile looked at what was on display. Picking a few things that she knew she didn't have, she filled a basket. The last thing she grabbed was a package of flashlight batteries. That's when he showed up again.

"Know what you're looking at?" he asked.

"I've been able to figure it out. Those little labels on the packages help a lot."

"Being a wise guy?" he asked.

"No more so than anyone else in the store right now." Maile made a show of scanning the store over the display rack. "Oh, look. You're the only other one here."

"My ex over on Kauai was a Girly Scout leader. Real piece of work."

Maile moved down the aisle, trying to ease away from him. "Sorry you suffered so much."

"You remind me a lot of her."

"Lucky for you to have a flashback to the good old days."

She took her basket of items to the checkout, hoping another clerk would be there. No such luck.

"Where you going with the girlies again?" the salesman asked.

Maile knew better than to tell him exactly where they were camping. Paying with a credit card could be a mistake, but she had no cash. With the card, he'd have her name, and a way of finding her, if he decided to continue being a jerk. He looked smart enough to get in trouble, but not bright enough to avoid it. "Windward."

"Oh, yeah. Waimanalo side." He handed her the bag. "Have a nice campout, Miss."

"Have a nice campout, Miss," she said mockingly after she left the store. "He's up to something, I can feel it in my bones."

Running with a bag of merchandise was clumsy, so she rolled it as tightly as she could and carried it like a football as she ran. She wondered if she looked like a shoplifter fleeing the scene of her crime.

Before she got home, she'd have to run past the office of her tour company. She was trying to grow the business, or at least her manager Brian was. Her main role in that was okaying his plans and allowing him to write checks for larger expenses. She knew leaving him alone to run the business would be wisest, but meddling in things was a part of her genetic code. She just couldn't help herself.

His latest big idea was to offer multi-day trips to other islands. Hiking, camping, and exploring remote areas was growing in popularity, known as 'adventure travel'. They might even be able to develop an eco-tour service, if they found an appropriate place for it. They were still just grand ideas, though, and she had no way of knowing if her guides and drivers would be interested. Her guides were city girls, all of them from Honolulu. The drivers were satisfied with their lots in life, of driving from one place to another, and reading fishing magazines while they waited to drive to the next location.

If they took on the new line of tours, there would be hotel rooms to manage, campgrounds to find, and tour vans to rent on short notice. Drivers would surely get lost on lonely roads, guests would have meltdowns, and guides would miss flights. Last minute cancellations, insect bites, sunburns, guests lost in the woods, and broken bones to set.

"What a nightmare," she muttered when she rounded the corner to the parking lot of her business. All three vans were there that day, the newest one positioned prominently next to the office entrance. That was the one she'd never seen but had okayed its purchase from ten thousand miles away. She had also approved of Brian's recommendations for hiring the new guide and driver to run the bus, people she hadn't met yet. All Maile knew was how much they were being paid, which was more than she was earning as owner of the business each month.

She'd seen pictures of the new paint job on the outside of the building, and laughed at how much brighter it was in person. Giant hibiscus and bird of paradise flowers had been painted over a green base, and along the top was a maile flower garland, maybe a secret nod to her as owner.

Maile went to the window and peeked in to see who was answering phones and making sales calls that day. It was Amelia, someone she'd hired right before leaving for the Army. She was blind, likeable, a runner like Maile, and married to Brian, the office manager. They'd started a family while Maile was away, two kids she still needed to meet. Month after month, almost without fail, Amelia was the top booking agent for the company. That wasn't saying much, since there were only four sales agents, and whatever time the guides spent on making calls.

Brian wasn't there, maybe out on errands, or taking the kids somewhere. One thing Maile needed to check on was if the releases and disclaimers David promised had arrived.

"May I help you?" Amelia asked cheerfully when Maile went in.

"It's just me, Maile. How are you, Amelia?"

"Hey, our world traveler! Welcome home, at long last." Amelia reached her hand out and Maile gave it a squeeze in return. "We weren't expecting you until next week. Lopaka has a welcome home party planned for you."

"Tell me the day and place so I can avoid it. But congratulations on the kids! Sorry I haven't been here to see them earlier. They're three and five now, I think?"

Instead of using the keyboard, Amelia used a voice prompt to ask the computer to bring up 'pictures of kids'. A new window opened, which displayed two children at various ages. They were the usual pictures, of a mom and dad playing with youngsters at the park, at home, in a pool somewhere, and at the beach.

"So cute! The girl looks just like you."

"Really? People keep telling me that, but I think they're being nice."

"She really does. The boy looks more like Brian."

"I can tell his face is shaped the same."

Maile felt for her friend then, a mother unable to see the faces of her children except by feeling with her hands.

"Do they look okay? Healthy?" Amelia asked.

"As a nurse, I think they look fine. Your daughter is kinda skinny."

"She only eats orange stuff. Cheese, oranges, Goldfish crackers, mac and cheese. If it's not orange, don't bother putting it in front of her."

"Four food groups in one?" Maile asked. "Orange, orange, orange, and orange?"

"That's about it. Did you stop in to see if I'm working? Or did you want to book one of our glamorous tours?"

"Just to check in. It's easier with just you here. Hopefully, you're not expecting me to make a speech?"

Amelia reached her hand out again to take Maile's for a moment. "Just glad to have you home, safe and sound."

"Thanks."

"You're wearing a new scent," Amelia said.

"Some lavender hand lotion from Italy. I'll bring some in for you."

"I'll have to remember. It's how I recognize people."

"Did those forms from the Melendez law office get delivered yet?" Maile asked.

Amelia pointed vaguely toward another desk. "Something was dropped off a few minutes ago. I didn't know we were expecting something."

"They got here fast." Maile looked at the bundle and found the forms she'd requested. She picked out a few that looked best for the Girl Scout hiking trip the next day. "Brian will need to get these signed by the kids' parents, along with everything else that needs to be done in the morning."

"Yes, the big adventure on the beach. It sounds like fun."

"I wish you could come along. From the sounds of it, I'll be outnumbered. There're only three adults for eight girls."

Amelia smiled. "Yes, that's outnumbered."

"Well, I need to go and jam everything that eight teenagers might need into my backpack for tomorrow, and then go meet my brother's girlfriend. Rumor has it she's my future sister-in-law."

Amelia smiled. "A wedding to plan!"

"And fortunately it's not mine."

Chapter Three

Maile spent Sunday afternoon doing laundry and reminiscing about a few of the travels she'd just come home from. There was something about seeing a new place for the first time, and meeting the people who made that place so special. While the Cotswolds had been fun, and Tuscany had been educational, floating down the Nile River had been the strangest. There was a limit to escapism, though, and that came while mopping the floor of a convent in silence.

Wearing an outfit assembled from the odds and ends of clothing she'd found while on the road, Maile felt more like she was going on a date than she was having dinner with her brother and his girlfriend. Her hair seemed hopeless, the fashionable asymmetric style she'd got in Rome now truly lopsided. The best thing about it were the split ends.

"Forget it," she muttered, tossing down her comb. After getting the salad she'd made and the flowers for Asher, she went to her dad's car in the driveway. "I really have to drive his nice new car? It still has all the paint on it."

Maile got to the little cottage that Kenny shared with his girlfriend without having a fender-bender along the way. She parked behind a late model SUV. Seeing that, she hoped it wasn't something else she was financing in Kenny's life. He and the girlfriend were waiting at the door for her.

Maile was surprised when Kenny was able to conduct the introductions without goofing them up. Instead of his usual grubby T-shirt and cutoffs, he was wearing expensive clothes that were ready-made for the golf course, and looked suspiciously handpicked for the event. Asher looked sophisticated, not that his past girlfriends had been known for that. She wore what could only be called a complete ensemble of a colorful dress, with a batik waistband and matching scarf. Her makeup and hair were, well, enviably flawless. Even her nails were perfect. One thing that wasn't on her hand was an engagement ring. Without that, Maile had less to gossip about, but provided more questions to ask.

"I've been looking forward to meeting you, Maile. I've heard a lot about you."

"Good or bad?" Maile said, taking her salad to the kitchen.

Asher seemed taken aback with the question. "Good, naturally."

"Kenny said something nice about me?"

"Of course. Why wouldn't he? Anyway, I've heard from others as well."

"From who?" Maile asked as they sat at the small dinner table. The first thing she noticed was that there was new dish and stainless ware, replacing the old plastic dishes she'd known since she was a kid. It was the same table she and Kenny had grown up at, in the same cottage that had been their lifelong home. It truly was a cottage, with three tiny bedrooms, a small kitchen and living room, and a bathroom that doubled in size when the window was open.

When Maile thought of 'home', it was this little house with her mother in it. Now her mother lived in a different neighborhood with Maile's 'new' dad, and a strange woman was living in the cottage with her brother, who was now well dressed. Her family had changed while she was away.

"Your parents, mostly."

"Yes, my cheerleaders. I pay them quite well to spread interesting gossip about me."

29

Asher chuckled. "They said you have a dry sense of humor."

"I do?"

"It that what it's called?" Kenny said.

"Be nice, Kenny," Asher told him. "Your sister has been away for a while. We're just trying to get to know each other."

"Try the teriyaki chicken, Mai," her brother said, handing her the platter of meat.

"Thanks." She passed it along to Asher. "Maybe later. They look good, though."

"Your job in the Army sounded fascinating," Asher said. "I bet you have some great stories to tell."

"Some of them. I generally keep them to myself, since the only people that might understand are ones who've had the same experiences."

"What about your travels last year? Kenny said you spent a lot of time in Italy?"

"Mostly picking grapes, but did some sightseeing. Fall's nice there, if you ever go. Great weather for wandering around the countryside. And if you're a wine drinker, it doesn't get any better than Tuscany."

"You drink wine?" Kenny asked with a mouth full of teriyaki. Now his true colors were beginning to show.

"When in Rome, as they say."

"Oh, wow, Rome," Asher said, sitting back in her chair. "Kenny and I are still trying to decide of where to spend our honeymoon. It's down to either Rome or Paris."

Maile looked back and forth between her brother and Asher. "Honeymoon?"

"Someday!" Asher said cheerfully. "What're the fashions in Rome like right now?"

"Maile knows about fashion?" Kenny said, snickering.

"Shut up, Worm," Maile shot back. As hard as she tried, she still couldn't view her younger brother as a grown-up, or that their relationship might have proceeded in growing up. She decided to focus on Asher and the girl talk she insisted on having. While Maile considered herself to be a world-class gossip, her girl talk rarely included fashion trends. She'd rather hear about the latest screaming match in the war between the sexes, or who was secretly loitering in the obstetrician's office. "This scarf is from Rome. So is this hairdo, or what's left of it. That reminds me, I have something from Tuscany for you."

She got the bottle of hand lotion for Asher, who was already done eating her half plate of food.

"I love lavender," Asher said, giving it a sniff. "You got that style in Rome?"

"It was a lot nicer than this originally. Being on the road for a few months since then hasn't helped. What finally did it in were two weeks in a Buddhist convent, using only lye soap."

"Did it in?" Kenny said, snickering again. "More like slaughtered it."

"Kenny, I'm warning you…"

"I know someone that might be able to work with it," Asher said.

"Oh? There's hope?"

"I work at Koni's in Kahala as a massage therapist. There are some super talented hairdressers there," Asher said.

"They just got an award," Kenny said. "Don't you know Koni?"

"She did everybody's hair and nails for my wedding. You would've noticed something different on us if you hadn't dozed off in the middle of the ceremony."

"You've been married?" Asher asked Maile.

"Unfortunately."

31

"Don't ask for details or she'll give you her life story before freaking out," Kenny said.

"Worm, this is the last time I'm warning you…"

"Maybe she'll freak out first, and then…"

"Anyway…" Asher said to interrupt. "Make an appointment with anybody at Koni's. They're busy but do amazing work."

"It'd have to be amazing to help Maile," Kenny said quietly.

When Maile started to glare at him, Asher interrupted again. She smiled this time when she took Kenny's hand. "It's where Kenny goes to get his hair done."

Maile grew a smile. "Well, isn't that sweet. Kenny goes to a lady's salon to have his hair done."

"Other guys go there," he said, when biting into another chicken wing. "You went to Don."

"Not much choice at the time, and he did a nice job on it, too," Maile spat back. "Maybe I'll go back to him to have it evened out. That's all it really needs."

"Needs a team of Nobel prize winning experts," Kenny said.

Picking up her fork as though it were a weapon, Maile shot him the same glare she had all her life. "Brah, part of my training in the Army was learning how to kill people, and you're really close to having a target on your forehead." Maile blushed when she looked at Asher, who looked thoroughly stunned. "Asher, if I was serious about killing Kenny, he would've been dead twenty years ago when he was still in diapers."

"I'm twenty-seven. I wasn't wearing diapers twenty years ago," he said, looking cross.

"No, I'm pretty sure you still were."

"Why don't you take a diaper and…"

"Kenny, you agreed…" Asher began saying.

"Asher, I promise there won't be any bloodshed at your dinner table." Maile blotted her lips. "I've learned how to hide it."

Asher guzzled her wine to finish the glass. "Well, if you come in to have your hair done, ask for a facial, and have one of the girls do you nails for you before you start your job search."

Maile looked at her nails. "I can chew them off on my own, thanks."

"What kind of job will you be looking for?" Asher asked after bringing out dessert.

"In emergency services, maybe in surgery. The Army crossed-trained me for surgery. That might be a refreshing change."

"I'm sure a hospital will snap you up in a heartbeat. No pun intended," Asher said.

"That was funny. You'd fit in well with us at the hospital. Right now, I'm thinking more about how to grow my business."

"Oh, yes, you own a tour company. Any ideas?" Asher asked as the others ate leche flan for dessert.

"We're thinking about offering multi-day adventure trips to other islands. Whenever I think about it, I get excited. Then reality sinks in when I think of the logistics involved with schlepping strangers to another island and back again, without losing any of them." Maile looked at her empty bowl of flan and wondered if there was more in the kitchen. Then she calculated the number of miles she'd have to run to work it off her hips. "In fact, I have a group of Girl Scouts that I'm taking on a campout tomorrow."

"I think I know who they are. Is it a troop from Kauai?" Asher asked.

"How'd you know that?" Maile asked.

"I know the woman that's making all the arrangements. The girls want to have more camping adventures, but their leaders aren't very outdoorsy. They've come to Oahu during winter break and were hoping to find a tour company that could manage something for them."

"Apparently, they found me. How do you know them?"

"Asher's from Kauai," Kenny said.

"Oh?"

"You might've heard of my family, Maile. The Kawika'kamaole family?"

"Really? I've met a couple." They talked about who Maile had met in Asher's family, and how they were related. "I didn't even pick up on the fact you're Hawaiian."

"Hawaiian, but just barely. With this blond hair and hazel eyes, most people thing I'm haole."

"What color is your hair supposed to be? I thought you were a blonde anyway?" Kenny asked.

"Uh, yeah, Kenny, it's naturally blond."

He shrugged and went back to eating flan.

"How long have you been in Honolulu?" Maile asked.

"Not too long. As soon as I graduated high school, bam! I went to the mainland for cosmetology school, which included massage training. When I came home, Kauai felt too small, kinda claustrophobic, so I came here. I had one job interview before I was working at Koni's."

"That's why she hired you?" Maile asked. "Because you're part Hawaiian?"

"Probably because I trained at a fancy place on the mainland. My job interview was to do massages on a couple of her stylists. Boy, was that ever stressful! But they were happy and she hired me on the spot. I was working the next day. Six months later, I'm working independently using her massage room."

"She earns a lot," Kenny said.

"Probably more than what I'll make as a nurse."

"Maybe twice as much," Asher said. "Sorry, not polite to talk about that stuff at the dinner table."

"By the way, are there any Roman gladiators working at Koni's?" Maile asked. She instantly regretted it when Kenny snickered.

"Gladiators?" Asher asked.

"Never mind. Lame question." Maile wondered how much a massage from Asher would cost, and if getting time alone with her for more gossip about her brother would be worth the cost. "Okay, so tell me about the Girl Scouts I'm dealing with tomorrow? Any raging lunatics that I'll have to dart with a sedative?"

"I was in the same troop a long time ago. I know some of the families, and one or two of the girls might be a little troublesome."

"What exactly is troublesome in Girl Scouts?"

"Oh, maybe they're not quite as energetic as they could be," Asher said. "They have the same leader that I had. She's okay, but I heard she might turn the troop over to someone else."

"Well, she's not my problem," Maile said, watching her brother finish Asher's flan. "She's an adult. It's not my job to motivate her. I'm just taking some kids from point A to point B and back again, hopefully without losing too many in the process."

Asher filled in Maile about a few of the girls that would be going on the hike, and something about their families. It sounded like they were all well-heeled, and because of that, Maile was busy thinking of extra fees and charges that could added in the morning before they set off.

"What about you, Kenny? How's the golf gig going?" she asked her brother.

"I told you. I got my PGA card a couple of years ago and I'm one of the club pros at the Upcountry Golf Club near Moanalua."

"That's a paying job, to be a golf pro?"

"Money's going into my bank account."

"Somehow not into mine," Maile mumbled. "What about the pro golf tour, or whatever it's called? Don't they win a lot of money in those?"

"I've only been in weekend tournaments on Oahu so far."

"Kenny's in a big tournament on Maui next month," Asher said. "I keep telling him he needs to go over and practice at the course a few times first."

"Might be a good idea, Kenny," Maile said. "You could stay with Auntie Kelani."

"Golf pros don't stay with their aunties," Kenny said.

"Okay, pay for an expensive room in a resort. Whatever winnings you get will be chewed up by that." By then, Maile was done with family dynamics, but she still had one more question to ask. "When Mom gets home from Maui, she's expecting me to move in here with the two of you. Is that going to work?"

"We have your room fixed up for you, Maile," Asher said.

Her room? It was supposed to be her cottage now that she was home, and Kenny would be her roommate. In Maile's way of thinking, Asher would be tolerated as an overnight guest, even if it was one night after another. "Okay, well, Mom and Dad get home on Thursday, so I guess I'll move in on Friday."

"What about that apartment you used to live in?" Kenny asked. "You can't go back there?"

"Mrs. Taniguchi's Flophouse, Bordello, and Cockroach Refugee Center? No, thanks. I'd rather live in a box at the park."

Asher laughed. "I gotta see that place!"

***

Once she got home with her dad's car safe and sound, Maile put the bag of food she'd got from Asher in the fridge. Unfortunately, more leche flan hadn't been sent along.

She gave Brian a call. "I've agreed to take the little...the kids on a three-day campout. They're each supposed to pay for three full-day tours. Make sure you charge them for the deluxe package."

"I didn't know we had a deluxe package."

"We do now. Just make it twenty percent more and let them negotiate down ten percent. That'll make everyone happy."

"That's what we want, happy campers!"

"Funny, brah. If anything goes wrong with this deal, it's your head flying off the chopping block."

"It'll be fine."

"It'll be fine because they're all going to sign waivers and releases before going anywhere near a hiking trail with me."

"I found the forms. Pretty snazzy stuff. You really know Governor Melendez?"

"He's helped me with some legal stuff a couple of times. And no, we're not dating, so don't even start that rumor."

"Why not? It would be an interesting one."

"Because if my mother got the idea that I even know David, she'd explode."

"She doesn't like his politics?"

37

"I doubt she even knows his political party. She'd have wedding bells ringing and a church decorated long before she ever knew anything about his politics."

Brian laughed. "Before you get ideas about him, he got married while you were away, and has kids of his own."

After the call, she tossed aside her phone. "Dang, that's too bad. I wouldn't mind living in the Governor's house. He even looks like a Roman gladiator."

Chapter Four

Maile took the bus to the office on Monday morning, her backpack overflowing with anything she could imagine a group of teenagers might need. Eight noisy girls were almost vibrating with excitement, while a woman who already looked tired waited outside. Inside the office, parents were signing forms that Brian was sticking in their hands.

Somehow, it didn't seem enough, that the preparations had been hurried, and something was going to go wrong. It had to. As it was, one of the two official leaders hadn't shown up yet. They hadn't even got to the trailhead and things were already coming unraveled. They waited for as long as they could, until the troop leader gave the other one a call.

"Ms. Mahoe won't be joining us today," Michelle told the others after the call. "Apparently, she's caught a cold."

"Lucky her," Maile muttered, as she loaded the last of the gear into the tour van.

Once the parents had hugged their kids and left, she introduced herself as someone that would be helping their leader. She kept the meeting formal, by checking that their packs fit properly and weren't too heavy. Each girl needed a sleeping bag, enough food for three days, a couple bottles of water for that day's hike, and a change of clothes. That would have to be good enough, considering Lopaka was taking the rest of the gear to the campsite later. First, he needed to drop them off at their starting point.

It wasn't a long drive to get from town to Waimanalo Beach, but it turned into an endurance test for Lopaka and Maile both when the girls began singing old-fashioned campground songs while they drove. Maile wondered if there was half as much blood on his mind when he finally parked as there was on hers.

"Okay, kids! Let's check our packs one last time before we set off!" she told the group. With any luck, they'd tire out in a hurry and keep quiet.

"Maile, I think I twisted my ankle when I got off the bus," Michelle, the troop leader, told her. She was doing a pretty good job of faking a limp when she went to a curb to sit. She must've known Maile was a nurse, because she didn't let her come anywhere near examining it.

"Will you be able to hike?" Maile asked. She and the girls stood in a circle around Michelle, waiting for an answer.

"You have to come with us, Miss Jones," one of the girls said. Not only was she the youngest, she was also working on the award for being the most enthusiastic.

"I better not carry one of those packs."

"That's what I figured. Want me to wrap your ankle?" Maile asked.

"I think I can walk okay," Michelle said. She reached her hand out for help up. Maile watched as a new performance was made with a fake limp. She wasn't sure, but she thought the woman was favoring the wrong leg.

That left Maile on her own at keeping the girls corralled and moving forward. Deciding it was best to let Michelle take the lead and set the pace, Maile brought up the rear, keeping everyone in front of her. She counted heads every five minutes, anyway.

They were barely away from the parking lot when Maile's phone chimed. It was an email with a heading about *nursing position*. When she opened it, it was from a name she didn't recognize, with a job offer as a flight nurse on a local medical helicopter transport service that was owned and operated by the statewide Emergency

Medical Services department. It would be a job working for the state, with good pay and excellent benefits. The only other provider in the state that offered emergency airlift services was the Coast Guard. Figuring it couldn't be that much different from emergency nursing, she decided to call him.

First, she needed to get out of the wind so she'd be able to hear him, and get the girls in one place so she could keep an eye on them. That meant stopping for their first rest break.

"Okay, kids! Time for a breather! Take your packs off and have some water."

Once they'd found spots to drop their packs, she noticed the woman leader that had come along looked miserable, and she wasn't wearing a backpack like the rest of them. That wasn't Maile's problem, so she called the man with the job offer.

"You have a few years of experience in civilian nursing and spent eight years in the Army Nurse Corps, experienced with combat injured patients. That seems perfect for my needs, Ms. Spencer," Dan Sink said.

"I'm not familiar with being a flight nurse, though."

"Not much difference between taking care of airlift patients than ones in the hospital, except that you'd work independently. The longest distance you'd have to transport them would be from the Big Island to here, before turning them over to paramedics for ground transport from the airport to the ER at Honolulu Med. That's where you used to work, right?"

"Ten years ago. I doubt many of the same people are still there," she said, wondering what her reputation was like there. After she'd been wrongfully fired for the mistake another nurse made, her lawyer had been able to get a substantial settlement out of the hospital. Hopefully, it would be forgotten by now.

41

"The only thing is that you'd be on your own during the flight, with only another nurse backing you up."

"That's what I figured. I received a lot of those patients back then, and those flight nurses were on the ball."

"From what I've seen of your service record, you're on the ball, too."

"Miss Spencer!" one of the girls shouted to get Maile's attention. Maile put her finger to her lips to quiet her.

"How did you come across my application? I've barely sent any out."

"When your digital app went into the system, it was statewide. I got an alert about you and I couldn't pass it by. But I need you to come in for a formal interview and then go on a flight with another nurse. You don't get airsick, do you?"

"Not on airplanes. Never spent much time on helicopters, though."

"Auntie Maile, Nancy needs to go shi-shi!" another girl announced.

Maile pardoned herself from the call, looked at Michelle for help, who was staring off into the distance. "Which one is Nancy?"

"I am," the youngest one in the group said. She stood knock-kneed with a look of desperation on her face. "Gotta go really bad, Auntie."

"How do Girl Scouts go shi-shi on the trail? Is there an official way of doing that?"

"Dig a hole."

Maile got a plastic trowel from her pack and handed it over. "Start digging."

She tried going back to her call, but was interrupted again.

"I gotta go, also!" another announced.

"Stand in line. Maybe all of you should go? And stop drinking so much water." She went back to her call. "Sorry, just having a little crisis here."

"I think we were talking about air sickness?" he said.

"Airplanes and boats are okay, but who knows what might happen on a helicopter."

"Mostly we use a fixed-wing aircraft for transport from one island to another. Most of the patients are brought here to Oahu. Is that something you'd be interested in?"

"As long as someone else does the flying, I'm happy." She quickly added, "Sir."

"I like you, Ms. Spencer. When can you come in for a formal interview?"

"I'm busy for the next three days with Girl Scouts. I could find some time on Thursday or Friday, though?"

"You're a Girl Scout leader, too?"

"Hopefully just this one time." She turned her back to the group. They'd formed a human fence around whoever it was that was crouched over a hole. "That's my little crisis, of where to find a place for them to, you know."

"Sorry I'm missing all the fun," he said, chuckling.

She got his location, jotted it down on her calendar, and put it in her phone. She had a solid feeling about the position, that it wasn't simply going back to the same old job she'd had years before. It offered some new challenges, too. Careful not to start celebrating too soon, she got backpacks on the girls again. While they got their straps adjusted, she filled the hole with beach sand.

"Probably just broke half a dozen public sanitation laws."

They hiked for another hour, with Maile playing goalie with some of them, trying to keep them out of the surf and dry.

"Okay," she announced when she was having a hard time keeping a couple of them moving forward. "We're halfway there. Let's take another breather."

"Oh my gaw…" most of them said in unison when they dropped their packs to the ground.

"I am sooo tired!"

"Whose idea was this, anyway?"

Maile felt good, that her legs were finally getting some exercise. Figuring the morning hike was the most physically tiring thing they ever did in their lives, Maile took pity on the girls. She made sure they all had a snack to eat and a small portion of water while they sat in the shade of a tree. Seeing the other woman sitting alone, she joined her.

"I didn't get your name earlier."

"The kids call me Miss Jones. You can, too."

Talk about a mood breaker.

Maile tried again. "Kinda fun, huh?"

"Save your rah-rah for the kids," Jones said. "Got a cigarette?"

"Sorry."

"How much longer till we get somewhere?"

"We're somewhere right now, aren't we?" Maile asked.

"You know what I mean."

"Probably just another hour to the campground. I wanted to get a little more than halfway before taking this break."

"Who put you in charge? I'm the leader of their troop," the woman said.

"Then start acting like one," Maile said, leaving Jones behind to rejoin the girls. After a few minutes, more singing started and that meant the girls were ready to hike again. Like she predicted, it was a little more than an hour before they came across the end of the old runway at the shuttered Bellows Air Force Base.

There was more sand and gravel than asphalt on the long-forgotten runway. A man and his son were out flying a kite in the steady breeze that came from offshore, and a family was playing in the surf. It wasn't so much of a trip into the wilderness, but more of a relocation from one end of a continuous beach to the another.

They slowed to a stop one at a time and dropped their packs with thuds. With renewed energy when they saw the bathroom at the far end of the campground, they all went off to there. Once they regrouped, Maile had an idea.

"You know what? I bet sleeping on the beach would be fun, right up until high tide rolled in. Personally, I don't want to go swimming in the middle of the night. How about you girls? Where do you think it would best to pitch our tents?"

"Where else are we gonna sleep?" Jennifer asked. She seemed to be the leader of the girls, being the tallest and oldest.

"Can't sleep in the bushes," another said.

"No, sure can't." Maile picked up her backpack again. "But there's plenty of space on that old runway. Flat and level too, not lumpy like the sand."

"Not gonna be planes landing all the time?" someone asked. Maile still didn't know all their names.

"They haven't used this landing strip in decades. Who's joining me?"

"I am."

"I am."

Michelle, who'd not worn a pack for the hike, got out her phone. "Must be a bed and breakfast around here."

Maile ignored her. Once she had the kids assembled and clearing rocks from the part of the runway they planned to use, she took half the group with her to find Lopaka and their tents.

"How's it going?" he asked. He wore a mischievous grin on his face.

"What're you up to, brah?"

"Nothing! It's just so sweet to see you leading girls around like a mother duck."

She held her fist up to him where the kids couldn't see. "Say one more word and you better be ready to duck this mother."

He laughed. "Seriously, is everybody in one piece?"

"That troop leader they have could use an attitude adjustment, but the girls are doing great. I hope the one with the horrible cold is surviving."

"When I talked to her on the phone, I distinctly heard the sound of a cork coming out of a bottle."

"Good for her. The one I'm stuck with is busy looking for a B and B."

He gave her a sack. "Thought you might want something more than oatmeal for dinner."

"Who said anything about oatmeal?"

"I asked the one at the hotel when I called her if they had enough food. Nobody likes camping if there isn't enough to eat. She said all the girls brought was oatmeal. They figured it would be easy to make, just boil some water and stir."

"They need more than that. What kind of scout leader sends kids on their first big hike, and all they get are oats? They're not horses, for goodness sake." Maile looked in the bag and found instant meals designed for camping that needed only hot water to make. There were several different meals, enough for two dinners each, along with pancake batter and bread. "You're a life saver, brah. I owe you."

"Forget about it. I'm just glad to see you back leading tours."

"Don't get used it," she said, catching up with the kids who were carrying tents and gear back to their campsite on the runway. "I can't do this forever."

It took a while to learn how to assemble and put up the tents, but once one was figured out, the others went up quickly. They made a ring of rocks in the middle of their campsite, and gathered sticks of driftwood for a campfire after dark. One thing they did have was a camp stove, courtesy of Lopaka.

If there was one thing Maile had learned during her time in the military, it was to keep a positive attitude. That was most important when things got rough. Seeing Jones continue to jab a finger at her phone screen, thoroughly ignoring the others as she searched for better accommodations, she decided to focus on the girls having a good time. That meant she'd have to take over as their leader.

"I was a captain in the United States Army," she muttered while watching the girls decide who was sleeping in which tent. "I was in command of an entire department in a military hospital. Surely I can deal with a squad of Girl Scouts."

Maile tried to keep things light-hearted by telling them to sing while they built their campsite. To do that, they relied on their official handbooks. One task that needed to be done was the construction of a table from driftwood, and the collection of rocks and chunks of wood to sit on. Once they had their campsite arranged, it almost looked as though they knew what they were doing.

By the time dinner was done, Maile was as tired as the girls. The sky had gone dark, and she tossed a couple of larger sticks onto the fire to get the blaze going. When she assembled the girls around the fire, she saw Michelle going off on a walk. She also noticed the glow of a cigarette.

"Gonna make S'mores?" one of the girls asked.

"I've never had them," Maile said. "How are they made?"

"Need Graham Crackers."

"Melt some marshmallows."

"And gooey Hershey's chocolate bars."

"Then what?" Maile asked.

"Squish them altogether into a weird little sandwich," the youngest one said.

"They sound very sweet. Is there insulin that goes with them?"

"Huh?"

"Never mind. I'm pretty sure we don't have any of that tonight. Maybe another time," Maile said. The last thing she wanted was eight girls high on sugar right before they were trapped in their tents all night. "Okay, who knows a ghost story?"

"Nancy does. She knows all kinds of stuff like that," one of them said.

"Sorry, which one of you is Nancy?"

"I am," the youngest said. She was the only one that didn't look like a teenager, maybe only nine or ten at the oldest. Built like a stick, she had large eyes and the longest hair in the group. Maile wasn't sure, but she might've had some Hawaiian blood in her. She'd had a hard time keeping up as they hiked, but had given out as much encouragement as she'd gotten from others. "What kinda ghosts do you want to hear about? Real kind or fake kind?"

"Ooh, I want to hear about real kind ghosts," Maile said. She figured whatever story a girl dreamt up would be pretty mild.

"Okay, once upon a time..."

"Hey! Ghosts, not fairy tales!" the one named Melody said.

"It's about ghosts and you better be ready, because it's super-scary, too," Nancy said defensively.

"I bet it is," Maile said quietly.

"Once upon a time, there was a dead guy on the beach…"

Maile wasn't sure, but she thought she heard a fart toot, and hoped it hadn't come from one of her tentmates.

Nancy kept going with her story. "There was a lady and a bunch of girls that were camping. One of them was named Melody."

"No way!"

"True story. Anyhow, Melody spent all night farting in her tent and nobody liked her anymore."

"Let's stick to ghosts," Maile said. "What about the dead guy on the beach?"

"The dead guy was the town meanie, always picking on little kids and kicking dogs. They say he even ate a cat once, when it was still alive."

Maybe the idea of having a little kid tell a ghost story wasn't such a good idea after all, Maile started to think.

"Well, one night, he went to the campground where the lady and the kids were camping."

"What'd he do to them?" Melody asked.

"Nobody's sure what happened, but when they found them in the morning, not all their parts were still attached to them."

"Is there a ghost in this story?" Maile asked.

"Yeah, that part's still coming up," Nancy said.

"I thought you said the weirdo died?" Melody asked.

"He did. That was worst of all. They found him on the beach with both his eyeballs missing."

"Can't die from that, can you, Miss Spencer?"

"Sure can't see too good without them. I'm still waiting to hear about the ghost."

Nancy continued. "Well, when the police looked closer at the dead guy's eyeball holes, they saw his brains were missing. Somebody sucked all his brains out until the inside of his head was hollow."

"Is there an end to this story?" Maile asked. Seeing the girls' faces in the flickering light of the campfire, a couple of them were close to freaking out. In the dark, she wasn't feeling too good about the story herself.

"Guess what they found under the dead guy when they picked him up?"

"What?"

"A gun?"

"Snakes?"

"No snakes on the island, silly."

"What'd they find?" Maile asked. At that point, she just wanted the story to end so she could hide in the tent.

"The hatchet that he used to chop up the lady and the girls."

"No way!"

"Yeah, way. Totally true story, too."

"Where'd that happen? Kauai?" Melody asked.

"It happened really close to this beach. That was a long time ago."

"Oh, well, that makes it okay," Maile said. "How long ago was it?"

"Like really super long time, maybe even ten years ago."

"Did they ever find his eyeballs?" Melody asked.

"Never. They say his ghost still walks on the beach, late at night, looking for his eyeballs. If he ever finds them, he's gonna pop 'em back into his eyeball holes so he can find ladies and little kids to chop up with his hatchet."

Maile pretended to look back and forth, even flashing her flashlight into the dark space around them. "Well, I don't see anybody walking around looking for his eyeballs. I think we're safe. Who knows about tomorrow night, though?"

She watched Michelle open a tent and go in, zipping it closed again. Apparently, she'd had enough of the great outdoors for one day and was going to bed in a tent of her own.

"Okay, who has to go shi-shi one last time before bed?" Maile said, stirring the embers to death. "If you don't go now, you have to come back outside the tent later. By yourself. With the man carrying a hatchet looking for his eyeballs."

All of them went as a group to the campground restroom. On the way back, they decided with an elaborate game of rock-paper-scissors of who was going to sleep in Maile's tent, and who had to sleep in another tent 'far away'. Keeping one flashlight for herself, they put another on the driftwood table they had constructed for anyone that did need to go in the middle of the night. A special hole was dug in the bushes nearby, and a stick with a handkerchief flag was stabbed into the dirt to mark the spot.

"Okay, good," Maile said once their little latrine was done. She doubted anyone would use it, though. "Just don't step in it when you're done."

Once they were settled into their sleeping bags in the pitch-black tent, one of the girls asked a question.

"Aunt Maile?" Nancy asked. "How could the man without eyeballs look for his eyeballs if he had no eyeballs?"

"I don't know, but hopefully he won't find them."

"Why?"

"Because if he finds them, he'll use them to look for us," Maile said.

"How will he find us?" Nancy asked. "Too dark out there."

"He'll hear all the talking we're doing."

With that, there wasn't another peep from any of them. Barely a minute of silence passed before Maile felt the girl next to her snuggle up to her side.

***

Maile never dreamed that three girls could snore so much as the ones in her tent that night. Wishing she had a tiny flashlight and a book to read, she lay on top of her sleeping bag, thinking of how she could pull together more trips like this one, without being so intimately involved. So far, it had been a moneymaker and hadn't been as difficult as she expected. That's how things went, though; if she thought the worst of something, it always turned out better. She was just drifting off to sleep when there was a noise outside the tent.

"Probably someone going to the restroom," she whispered. The only problem with that idea was that the only restroom was located at the far end of the campground, and the few other campers there that night had set up closer to it than they were. When she heard a dog growl, she got her answer to what was making the noise. A stray dog had found them, following the scent of cooked food, and was looking for leftovers.

But when the dog's growling turned into the sound of a roaring bear, she sat up and turned on her flashlight.

"What the heck?"

"Miss Spencer!" called someone from another tent. "A Monster!"

"Aunt Maile," Nancy whispered. "The man with no eyeballs found us!"

"Stay in the tent, girls," she told them, trying to keep her voice even. By then, her tentmates had each turned on their flashlights and were waving them around.

There were no bears in Hawaii, the biggest animals being deer in the mountains and humans in the city. And horses and cattle on ranches, but they didn't roar. When there was another roar, and something started shaking their tent violently, she shouted back at it.

"Knock it off!"

That's when she heard some laughter.

Zipping open the tent flap, she told the girls to stay put and went out to confront the 'bear'.

A man shook another tent and growled, and when he saw Maile's flashlight beam land on him, he stopped and laughed.

"Hey, Scoutmaster! How's your little girly campout going?"

She walked toward him, aiming her light in his face. A few of the girls had joined her, but not Michelle. In Maile's way of thinking, Girl Scouts didn't pose much of a show of force while in their jammies. "Who are you? What do you think you're doing?"

"Giving you and your little brats a thrill!"

"You can take your thrills and shove them. No reason to scare kids like that."

"What're you gonna do, Missy? Beat me up?"

That's when she smelled liquor on him. "No one's going to beat up anyone else. Why don't you go sleep off whatever bender you're on and leave everyone else alone?"

"One night can be a long time when you're all alone, Missy!" he said while walking away. "We're not done with this!"

"I am." Maile shooed the kids back into their tents. Taking her flashlight with her, she followed him for a couple of minutes, just to make sure he was leaving. That got them to the middle of the runway and halfway to the parking area and restrooms. At least he didn't try any confrontational stuff on the way. Hopefully he'd got the idea in his head that she wasn't playing around.

Maile stopped to watch him retreat into the dark. Once she no longer could see him, she headed back to the campsite. When she got back, flashlights were still on in each tent, including Jones, their real leader. Her tent flap was partially open, fluttering in the wind. Ignoring her, Maile told the girls in the other tents to turn off their lights and go to sleep.

Once she got back to her tent, she eased back and turned off her own flashlight.

"Was that the hatchet man?" one of the girls asked.

"No."

"How do you know?"

"Didn't have his hatchet," Maile said.

"What if he comes back with one?" Nancy asked.

"We'll call the police. But I doubt he'll come back."

"Why?"

"No more eyeballs in his eyeball holes," Maile said. "Go to sleep, please."

Maile was thinking of calling the police in the morning, just to report the disturbance. Maybe a patrol car could swing through the small parking area once or twice the next night, just to be a presence. With that thought on her mind, she dozed off.

Chapter Five

In the morning, Maile was first up, mainly because she needed coffee. She was just getting her sleep cycle adjusted to Hawaii time, but somehow her caffeine cycle was lagging behind. Getting a kettle of water going on the camp stove, she dug out packets of instant oatmeal and arranged enough for everyone. Except for Michelle, who was busy smoking in her tent.

"Couldn't be bothered with sitting at the campfire with us, but is perfectly happy being in her private little rebreather chamber," Maile said, stirring her first cup of instant coffee.

Some of the girls were getting up, complaining about being hungry or needing to go to the restroom.

"Everybody survived the night?" Maile asked, looking them over. Jammies were disheveled, hair went in every direction, and yawns were wide enough to fly an airliner though.

"We didn't get chopped up," Nancy said. Last night's ghost story teller looked almost disappointed about it.

"Yeah, that's a shame. Once you put on regular clothes, you can all go to the restroom together. After that, we'll have oatmeal and maybe even pancakes for breakfast. And there's Tang! So, take kettles for more water."

"We can make pancakes here at a campground?" Michelle asked. She'd finally joined the rest of the group.

"Not so hard. How would you like to be chef this morning?"

"You're assigning chores now?"

"You haven't done anything else."

"Who put you in charge, anyway?" Michelle demanded.

"You did, since you're not pulling your weight."

"Well, lah-di-dah!" Michelle said, going off in the direction of the restrooms. Unlike the kids, she followed the beach instead of the runway.

"Whatever." Maile put on more water to boil while waiting for the girls to come back. Whoever returned first would get the job of mixing pancake batter.

The entire group returned at once. They all had worried looks, and a couple were close to tears.

"Miss Spencer, there's a problem."

"Restrooms are still locked?"

"Worse."

What could be worse than not having access to a pot to sit on first thing in the morning? Maile figured they could rough it by using their little latrine. It would give them a story to tell later. If they got desperate enough, they could even walk to a small business area nearby to use the restroom at a fast food place. But they couldn't get by without water to cook or wash with. That would bring a sudden end to the trip. "Broken water pipe?"

"Never got to the restrooms."

"What is it, then?" Maile asked.

"You know that story Nancy told last night about the dead guy?"

"You found his eyeballs?" Maile asked kiddingly.

"Found more than that."

"I wish someone would get to the point," Maile said.

Melody looked nervous when she answered. "We found a guy sleeping back there."

"I think he's dead," Jennifer said.

"We found the dead guy in Nancy's story," another girl said.

"Still got his eyeballs in his eyeball holes," Nancy added.

Maile refilled her cup of instant coffee, doubling up on the amount of freeze-dried powder. They hadn't even had breakfast and they were already cooking up games. "What are you guys talking about?"

Jennifer pointed down the old runway. "There's a dead guy."

"For real?"

"Go see."

"It's just a guy sleeping," Melody said again. "Gotta be."

"Why?" Nancy insisted.

"They don't let dead people sleep at the campground."

"What do you know about dead people?" Nancy asked.

"Can we stop talking about dead people, please?" Maile begged.

Maile looked down the length of the broken runway and saw a hump of some sort. She figured it was just a pile of rocks she hadn't noticed the day before, but decided to go look anyway.

"Melody, I want you to make pancake batter, and someone else needs to find a pan to cook them. Someone else can start making oatmeal, and we need to make a kettle of Tang. That's four jobs, with two girls per job."

"Where's Miss Jones?" someone asked.

"I think she went to chain smoke some cigarettes."

"Still gotta go shi-shi, Miss Spencer."

"Yeah, me too. Anybody not cooking can follow the beach to the restrooms, but come right back. No playing okay?"

"What if…" one girl started to ask.

"This is the schedule for the morning," Maile said. "Bathroom, breakfast, wash the dishes, wash ourselves, straighten our tents. Chores first, then fun, just like at home. Then we'll find something more fun to do."

Once a few of the girls were on their way following the beach, Maile went down the runway to see what the hump was. The steady breeze coming off the ocean that morning was strong, and fluttered something white. The closer she got, the more it looked like a pile of laundry. Closing in, she saw it was a man lying sprawled out and face down, his shirt flapping in the wind.

"Probably a drunk that went looking for the restroom in the middle of the night and got lost. Instead of him sleeping it off in his tent, I have to wake him up and send him on his way." When she got up to him, she gave him a nudge with her toe. "Hey, time to get up. People are camping here. Sleep it off somewhere else."

When he didn't wake, she bent over and gave his shoulder a shake. That's when she noticed a smell that wasn't booze. He had a cool feel to his body.

"Oh, come on."

She felt for a pulse at his wrist, and then his neck. Rolling him slightly, she saw the unmistakable pale blue of death in his face. His eyes were half-open, staring past her. One cheek was flat from where his face had been resting on the ground.

Maile took a few steps back but kept an eye on the body.

"Well, this sucks. Their first time camping, and they find a real live dead body."

As much as she just wanted to walk away, Maile knew she needed to call the police. Dialing those three numbers that nobody liked to call, she waited for an operator.

"I need to report a death."

"Are you in a safe location? Is there risk to you from others, Ma'am?" the operator asked.

"Everything's fine. I just need someone to come deal with a body."

"Is it an expected death in a home?"

"No, entirely unexpected and outdoors in a public place."

"Your location, Ma'am?"

"The beach at Bellows Air Force Base."

"That base is no longer operational, Ma'am. Are you sure of your location?"

Maile's patience was already being tested. She was standing over a dead body, the scoutmaster of the kids was AWOL, the kids needed breakfast, and she needed more coffee. Now she was waging a contest of wits with a 9-1-1 operator. "Absolutely certain. I'm standing right in the middle of the old landing strip at Bellows, looking down at the body of a dead man."

"You're certain he's dead and not sleeping?"

"No heartbeat, no breathing, no response, body stiff, and his skin has turned a sickening color of white. Yep, pretty darn sure he's dead."

"I'll send EMTs along with the police. Your name, Ma'am?"

"Maile. They can find me when they get here. I'm the one with the Girl Scouts camped out at the end of the runway. But right now, I need to go supervise oatmeal."

"Was he dead?" Melody asked when Maile got back to the campsite.

"Dead, huh?" Jennifer said.

"Yes, I'm pretty sure he was. How're the pancakes coming?"

"First one got burnt, so we made another. That was runny, so we made a third. Nancy ate that one. She hasn't croaked, so we're making more."

"Good idea. What about the oatmeal?"

"Sorta lumpy."

"Tastes funny."

Maile looked in that pot. They'd put all the oatmeal packets together, but not enough water. "Maybe we can stir in more water to thin it out a little."

"Is there milk?" someone asked.

"See any cows?" Melody said.

"What do cows got to do with anything? Milk comes from bottles."

"Comes from cows first, dummy."

"No name calling, please," Maile said. By adding water, she got the right consistency in the oatmeal but needed the stove to heat it up again. When she finally got a pancake of her own, it was soggy on one side and burnt on the other, with a giant lump in the middle.

"Where's the syrup?"

"Don't got none," the redheaded girl said. Maile was still trying to learn her name, but at least she never asked for much.

"Seriously? Is there sugar?"

"No more."

"How's your pancake, Miss Spencer?"

"Delicious," she said, washing down dough with cold instant coffee. "Reminds me of MREs."

"Huh?"

"Never mind."

By the end of the meal, everyone had either a pancake or oatmeal and a couple of the girls had both. Good enough.

"Where's Miss Jones?" Jennifer asked. Even though she was the oldest, she was turning out to be the least useful with food preparation.

"That's what I'd like to know. Has anybody seen her since she went to the restroom?" Maile asked.

"She said something about taking a bus somewhere," a girl said.

Maile had something to say about that.

"We don't use those words in the Girl Scouts, Miss Spencer."

"Sorry. I guess you learned a new one today."

"I think we already knew it," Jennifer said.

"Is there a merit badge for cusswords?" Maile asked. "If there is, I could get you checked off on that today."

Nancy giggled. "Melody already has that one."

"Shut up, brat."

"No name calling, please," Maile said again.

"You just called Miss Jones a..."

"I know, it was wrong, and I've already apologized. Who's doing dishes?"

"Not me. I cooked."

"You call burned pancakes cooking?"

"You ate one."

Maile saw a police car come into the campground parking lot, the lights on the top of it flashing. As contentious as the morning already was, it was going to get worse in mere minutes.

"Okay, everyone that didn't cook, start cleaning pots and pans. Leave one kettle of water on the stove. The rest of you, start straightening your sleeping bags and tents."

The dispatcher must've told the police where to find the body, because the car hopped a curb and drove the length of the runway. When they got near the body, they stopped and got out. With pistols in their hands, they slowly approached it.

"Cool, the cops are here," Melody said.

"Yeah, swell," Maile said with a sigh. "I need to go talk to them, since I was the one who reported it. Can you guys do me a giant favor and do your chores? Please?"

Getting a few nods would have to be good enough. As much as she was trying to protect them from the reality of death, she knew the kids were going to get involved somehow.

By the time she got to where the police were looking down at the body, an ambulance had shown up. The police told her to stay back, that it was a crime scene.

"I'm the one that reported it, Officer."

"You did? Someone down at the parking lot said they reported it."

61

"I'm the one that called earlier."

"Your name?"

"Maile. I told it to the 9-1-1 operator."

The officer checked his notes. "Yeah, that's the contact name we were given. You're sure your name is Maile? Because the woman back at the parking lot said she was Maile."

"I have been for thirty-some years now. How could someone at the parking lot identify themselves as Maile if I'm here?" she asked.

"When we rolled in, a woman waved us down. We asked if she was Maile and she said yes. She aimed us down here to the body."

That didn't make sense at all. Maile could only figure Michelle had sent them to the campsite looking for her. "Well, that wasn't me, was it?"

"Your ID, please?" the officer said.

Maile got out her coin purse and retrieved her driver's license to give him.

"Hokuhoku'ikalani Spencer. That's a different name than what you just told me."

"Maile's easier to spell."

"You're from Texas?" he asked.

"That's where I was when I needed to renew my license. I live here."

"Why were you in Texas?"

"I was in the military. Are we discussing me or do you want to know about the body?" she asked.

"Both, if possible." He flashed a large Samoan smile. "Start with the body. What time did you find it?"

"A minute or two before I called the operator to report it. That was maybe an hour ago. I didn't notice the time."

"I can get it from dispatch. Why are you out here so early in the morning?"

Maile pointed toward her group. "Girl Scout campout."

He looked past her toward the tents. "You're their leader?"

"Unofficially. More of a glorified babysitter."

"Who's the official leader?" he asked.

"Someone named Michelle Jones. I haven't seen her since we got up this morning."

"Have you performed a search for her?"

"Not really. She's an adult. She can take care of herself."

The cop looked toward the ocean. "Did she go for a swim?"

"The last I saw her, she was walking along the beach toward the restrooms. Anyway, I never got the idea she's into athletics."

"I'm more concerned there's been a water mishap."

That startled Maile. As much as she was learning to dislike Jones, she didn't want her to drown. They went to the beach and walked up and down it, the officer staying a few steps away from the water.

"I don't see any recent footprints leading to the water," he said. He rubbed his chin while scanning the ocean surface again. "Nobody's floating."

"Seriously, I doubt Jones had any interest in going for a swim, but go ahead and call for the water search team, if that'll make you feel better."

She listened as he made the call to his beat sergeant, and then to the water search and rescue team. "It won't be long before they're here, along with a Coast Guard helicopter."

"Whatever. My money's on that she found a restaurant." Maile looked back at the campsite, trying to see what was going on. "I should get back to the girls."

"Just a couple more questions. Did you touch the body in any way?"

"I felt for a pulse in his wrist and neck. I tried turning his head, but that's when I found he was already stiff."

"Okay, good. Has anyone else been around the body?"

Maile sighed. She was afraid of this. She could lie and protect the kids from being drawn into whatever investigation might come of it, but that could easily unravel if he started asking them questions.

"Yes, the girls. They found the body when they followed the runway to the restroom and came back to report it to me. At first, they thought it was just a man sleeping there, and that's what I thought also. I figured a drunk had wandered away from his tent in the middle of the night and got lost in the dark."

He kept writing notes. "They reported it to you, and then you came down to see it for yourself? And then you reported it to dispatch, is that right?"

"Exactly right. The operator said she'd send the police and EMTs, and here you are. Anything else? Because I really need to get back to my group."

"I'll go with you."

By then, the officer's partner was stringing yellow crime scene tape around the body, securing it to the ground with rocks. The ambulance was driving away, with nothing to take with them.

"You said there was another woman who's the actual troop master? Is that what it's called for Girl Scouts?"

"I have no idea what they're called. All I know is that I hiked with eight girls in green uniforms from Waimanalo Beach to here yesterday, along with their crappy leader, who has since disappeared. We told a ghost story last night around our little campfire, and this morning we had the most god-awful pancakes you've ever eaten."

He laughed. "What was wrong with them?"

"No butter, no syrup, no sugar, just hunks of dough that were gooey inside and burnt on the outside. Truly amazing how bad they were. But don't tell them I said that."

"Of course not. What exactly is the purpose of the campout? Are they working on a badge?"

"Again, I have no idea. They're actually from Kauai and came here during winter break from school. They wanted to go camping, so here we are."

"Who are you to them?" the officer asked just as they were getting back to the campsite. The girls were listening to what the cop was asking Maile. "A parent to one of them?"

"She's Miss Spencer," one answered.

"Aunt Maile!"

"We're gonna make her our honorable leader," Nancy said.

"Honorary leader, dummy," Melody said.

"Dork," Nancy spat back.

"Nerd."

"Please stop calling each other names," Maile begged. "This is Officer Tagaloa. He wants to ask us as a group what we saw with the body earlier. Can someone help him?"

"Would you like some coffee, Sir?" Jennifer asked politely.

"How could I say no to authentic Girl Scout coffee?"

Maile gave him a smile and a shrug as a warning while Jennifer mixed a shovelful of instant coffee into a metal mug and stirred in some water that wasn't hot enough to have steam rising from it. Maile watched his face for a reaction to its flavor. He did well at hiding it.

"Okay, most important, did anybody touch the body?"

"Not me," most said, while others simply shook their heads.

"How did he die?" Nancy asked.

"I'm not sure," Officer Tagaloa said. "The coroner will need to determine that. I didn't see any blood. Did anyone else?"

"Not me."

"Me either."

"Still had his eyeballs in his eyeball holes," Nancy said.

Maile wanted to clamp her hand over the kid's mouth.

"Eyeball holes?" Officer Tagaloa asked.

"She means eye sockets. We had a ghost story last night about a man with no eyes."

"Never heard that one before."

Officer Tagaloa got each of their names. At the end, reassured Maile that he doubted investigators would need to talk with them. Maile wasn't sure, but a couple of them might've been made up names. As far as she was concerned, that was a good idea.

When a plain car showed up at the scene, Maile figured it was a detective there to start the investigation before the body was removed by the coroner.

"I need to check in. How much longer are you camping here?" Tagaloa asked.

"Tonight and then we hike back to Waimanalo Beach tomorrow morning."

"They can go home, but Ms. Spencer, please don't leave the island."

"Wasn't planning on it."

"One more thing. You might want to find more cheerful bedtime stories to tell," Officer Tagaloa said as he left them behind.

Chapter Six

After a morning of running races on the beach, with Jennifer being crowned as Victor Beyond Belief, and Nancy being named Most Inspired, Maile had the girls figure out what to eat for lunch. While they made bread sandwiches, which consisted of a slice of bread pressed firmly between two other slices of bread, Maile kept an eye on what was happening with the dead body. A CSI team had arrived and erected a canopy over the body to keep it in shade. They were taking their sweet time in poking around the runway and bushes alongside, looking for something that Maile could only guess about.

The police divers with the water search and rescue team had been there and gone, and after making a few sweeps from above, the Coast Guard helicopter had also departed. Both apparently found nothing. Another vehicle had shown up at one point. A man looked at the body briefly, had something to say to the officers, and got a report from the crime scene techs. He too poked through bushes and kicked at sand, looking for something.

Eventually, the plain-clothes investigator came to their campsite.

"Troy Silva, HPD Investigations, Ma'am," he said to introduce himself. He referred to his notepad. "You're Ms. Spencer or Ms. Jones?"

"Spencer."

"Interesting first name. Hokuhoku'ikalani. I think that means something about a star?"

"Shining Star in the Sky. I was born during a meteor shower. What's that got to do with your investigation?"

"Nothing. Just an ice breaker."

"This is the tropics. We don't need to break ice here." Maile was still feeling protective of the girls, and continued to wonder where Jones had gone off to. She didn't like being thrust into having sole responsibility for the kids, and needed to discuss with Jones if they should continue with the campout or quit early. The whole trip had been just a little too bizarre, with troop leaders pulling disappearing acts and a dead body showing up in their place. "Is there something I can help you with?"

"Maybe you can help me clear up a few things with the body. Now, I've already got a detailed report on your activities with and around the body from the responding officer, so there's no need to go over all that again."

"Thank you."

"There's some question about the manner of his death," Detective Silva said.

"I have no idea about that."

"I'm sure you don't, but tell me what you witnessed anyway."

"When I first saw him, I got the impression he'd been drunk and lost his way in the middle of the night, that he couldn't find his way back to his campsite," she said. "Or that he's homeless."

"Yes, with so many people living on our beaches these days, it gives a whole new meaning to beach bums."

Maile crossed her arms over her chest. A few of her friends over the years had fallen on hard times and had lived at the beach for a while. "Not all of them are bums."

"Bad joke. Getting back to the point, he's not a beach bum. He had a wallet with ID that matches his appearance, along with cash and a credit card. I've already checked with the other campers at the campground, and they all deny knowing him. Also, all campsites had someone at them, so that means to me he's neither living nor camping here at the beach."

"Who was he?" Maile asked.

"I'm just waiting on fingerprints for positive ID. There is evidence of foul play, though."

"You guys actually say that? Foul play? I thought that was just a TV thing."

"We say it, when there's been foul play."

"I didn't see any blood, if that's what you're going to ask me," she said.

"There shouldn't have been. According to the coroner that just left, he suffered a catastrophic blow to the head, or blunt force trauma to the posterior cranium, as he put it. That means..."

"I know what it means. Someone gave him a whack in the back of the head? Or was he in some sort of accident and wandered in here to die?"

"From what we can determine, and this is still preliminary of course, was that he died where he dropped, and from a purposeful blow to the back of his head."

"I'm sorry to hear that. But on behalf of these girls, we had nothing to do with that. All we know about him is that the girls found him on their way to the restroom in the morning, and reported finding him to me. When I went down to see him and determined he was dead, I called the 9-1-1 operator."

He looked at the girls. "That was the exact right thing to do, to report something wrong to your scoutmaster."

"Miss Spencer's not our scoutmaster," Melody said.

"Oh? Who is? Is someone else here that I haven't met?"

"Miss Jones," Jennifer said with a tone of derision.

"Oh, yes," Silva said. "I heard about her. Where is she? I'd like to have a talk with her."

Jennifer was talented at wearing her derisive tone on her face. "She left already."

"Left?"

"Early this morning. The other officer already knows about her," Maile said. "From what I understand, she's not the outdoors type, so the troop hired me to lead the group on this campout. I got the idea she's not very athletic. She didn't bother with a backpack of her own, but had our driver deliver it for her."

"I thought you hiked here from Waimanalo Beach?"

"We did. Each girl carried their own pack, and did a great job of it, too. But we weren't able to carry the tents or all the food and water we need, so I had my driver bring it here to the campground."

"Oh yes, that's right. You're a tour guide, not a scout leader. About what time did Ms. Jones leave?"

"Maybe half an hour after sunrise?" Maile offered. "We were all up by then, trying to figure out who was going to the restroom first, and who would get breakfast started. Do you suppose that was the person who the responding officers talked to in the parking lot?"

Silva looked up from his notepad. "I didn't hear about that."

"Officer Tagaloa said something about meeting someone in the parking lot who said they were Maile, the contact name he had. I was wondering if that was Jones?"

"I have no idea. Was that before or after the body was found?"

"After, of course," she said.

"Yes, of course. Did Jones leave before or after the body was found?"

"Before."

"Maybe she reported the body also?" he asked.

Maile scratched her head with thought. "I'm not sure, but when she left, she went along the beach rather than the runway."

Silva looked at the beach and the runway in turn. "Not sure why she'd do that. The runway goes straight to the parking lot."

"She said something about going to the restroom, but never came back," Maile said. The more she thought about Jones, the more confused she got over her. All Maile knew was that she was glad she was gone, but she also wanted her to come back and take over responsibility for the kids again.

"Did she have access to a vehicle of her own?" Detective Silva asked.

"Not that I'm aware of. We're on our own until we get picked up back at Waimanalo Beach tomorrow."

"She said she was going to look for a bus," Melody said.

Silva scratched his head. "Seems awfully early for a bus."

"The first number fifty-seven bus leaves Waimanalo Town at five in the morning and goes over the Pali. It takes about an hour to get to downtown. Unless something has changed with bus schedules lately."

He looked surprised. "How'd you know that?"

"Been riding the buses all my life. But I've been out of town for a while, and some of the schedules may have changed."

"Yes, in Texas. What took you there?"

"Military transport aircraft."

"Okay." He scribbled on his notepad. "Back to Miss Jones. Why would she decide to abandon the campout?"

"She doesn't like exercise," Jennifer said.

"She doesn't like us," Melody said.

"She doesn't like anybody," Nancy said.

"Abandon might be a strong word," Maile said. "I don't know her very well, and she might be a very good leader, just not outdoorsy."

"She gave no indication that she was planning on leaving?"

"She moaned and groaned a little about the conditions, but I thought she was going to stick it out with us," Maile answered.

"Conditions?" he asked.

"Roughing it in a tent at the beach."

"She's a..." Nancy started.

Maile glared down Nancy before she could say anything further.

"All of you are from Kauai, including Miss Jones?" Silva asked.

"We are, but Miss Spencer is from here," one of the quieter kids said.

"No she's not. She's from Honolulu."

"Manoa Valley," Maile added. She gave him a business card for the tour company.

He stuck it under a paperclip on his notepad. "Thanks. What I'd like to do, with your permission of course, is take a quick look in your tents."

Maile crossed her arms. "For?"

"Just being thorough. To make sure I cross my Is, dot my Ts. You know how it is."

"You got it backwards, Sir," one of them said.

"I do?"

"You dot Is and cross Ts. Gimme your pencil and I'll show you."

"Just making a joke," he told the girl.

Maile had nothing to hide, and figured neither did the kids. She hadn't made an inspection of their tents yet, though.

"Well, girls, can he look at our stuff? Or will someone be embarrassed?"

"Maybe my stuff is still messy?" Nancy admitted.

"Well, I don't mind too much, if you don't? In fact, I'll look in your tent last," Silva said.

Maile sent Nancy to straighten whatever was messy while the detective looked in the other tents. It really was a cursory look, and Maile figured he was looking for their scoutmaster that might've been hiding. When he backed out of Michelle's tent, he zipped it closed.

"That's her tent?" he asked.

"Yep. She stayed in there alone last night," Maile said.

"I'd appreciate it if everyone stayed out of it for now. Your tent, Ms. Spencer?" he asked while putting on a fresh pair of rubber gloves.

"The blue one. My sleeping bag is in the middle."

Maile waited outside while he searched inside, and the girls tidied their campsite. Five minutes later, he backed out, bringing her flashlight with him. He had it in a plastic evidence bag. "Whose is this?"

"Mine," Maile said. "Why is it in that bag?"

"Potential evidence."

"My flashlight?"

He continued to label the bag. "See the dent on the edge of the rim?"

"Yes. What about it?"

"And how the plastic lens is cracked?"

"It's seen better days. So?"

"Just from my cursory exam, the damage on this could potentially match the wound on the back of the dead man's head."

"Oh, come on! You really think I had something to do with that man's death?"

"I found it beneath the sleeping bag you identified as yours. I'll have the CSI techs check it for fingerprints before they leave, and collect yours for comparison."

"They won't need to get mine. I'm already in the system."

"Okay, good. That's helpful."

"Are you taking her in?" Jennifer asked.

"You're going to arrest Miss Spencer?" Melody asked.

"Don't take our auntie!" Nancy said, looking close to tears. "We can't sleep out here all by ourselves!"

Maile put her arm around her shoulder. "I'm not going to leave you."

"I'm not going to take her away." Detective Silva smiled at Nancy before scanning his notes again. "Tell me about Miss...what was the scoutmaster's name again?"

"Michelle Jones."

"She's your scoutmaster but she doesn't like camping, but she also agreed to come on this campout, and then she left early this morning without saying anything to anyone about where she was going?"

"I'm right here," Michelle said, walking up to them.

"Where have you been?" Maile demanded.

"Out for a walk, okay?" Michelle glared at the detective. "Who's this? And what's going on back there?"

"Ma'am, there's been a suspicious death," Silva said after identifying himself. "I'm investigating, and since Ms. Spencer here called it in, I'm starting my investigation with her and the kids. Do you have some ID to show me, please?"

Michelle performed a flawless eye roll as she took her driver's license out. "The kids had nothing to do with it. Her I'm not so sure about."

"Her who?" Maile asked.

"You."

"Me?"

"You're the one that got out of the tent and chased someone away in the middle of the night."

"That was just some clown messing with us," Maile said.

"What's this?" Silva asked.

"A rabid maniac attacked out tents!" Nancy said.

"Quiet, twerp. Let Miss Spencer answer the questions."

"A maniac?" Silva asked.

"Oh, somewhere around midnight or a little after, someone came here and started growling like a dog and shaking our tents. When it escalated into him making bear sounds and almost collapsing one of the tents, one or two of the girls started to cry. Then I heard laughter, a man laughing. That's when I went out to confront him."

"In the dark?"

Maile nodded at the flashlight in his evidence bag. "I took that so I could see who was making the noise."

"And did you?"

"He was gigantic!" Nancy said. "He had foam coming out of his teeth like maniacs do!"

Maile got the girl's attention. "Nancy, maybe you should let me answer his questions, okay?"

"I got something to say about it, too," Michelle said.

"I'm sure you do, but let's have Ms. Spencer have her say first, okay?" Silva said. "Back to the man. You saw his face?"

"I was aiming my flashlight right into his face from just a few feet away."

Pressing the button, Silva turned on the light and aimed it at his hand. "Strong beam."

"Put in new batteries right before the campout."

"Girl Scouts are supposed to be prepared, just like Boy Scouts," Jennifer said.

"Yes, that's good." Silva seemed to feel the heft of the light, maybe guessing at its weight. "Pretty heavy. Looks long enough for four batteries."

"It's old but it works. I used to keep it in the trunk of my car, when I had one," Maile said.

"Okay, when you confronted him, you were alone?"

75

"A couple of the girls came out of their tents, also."

"After you saw his face, what happened?" he asked.

"He laughed a little more, then growled and shook one last tent as he left. Real wise guy stuff, you know?"

"Then what?"

"I followed him for a moment to make sure he actually left."

"How long is a moment?" the detective asked.

"One or two minutes? Not any longer than that."

"And did he leave?"

"I guess. I figured the girls would need some reassurance, so I came back to the tents and talked with them for a moment."

"Good, thanks." He turned his attention on Michelle. "Ms. Jones, since you're their official leader, why didn't you confront the man, also?"

"I, well, was busy in my tent."

"With?"

"I couldn't find my flashlight, and I was trying to put on my clothes. These tents are small, you know."

"Yes, they're always smaller on the inside than they look from the outside," Silva said. "You eventually came out?"

"I came out at one point. That's when I saw her chasing after the man, so I went back inside."

"Chasing?" he asked.

"Yeah, she was running after him."

"Running after him?" Maile said. "I was not running. All I did was walk about twenty feet behind him for a moment and then came back. Certainly more than anything you did."

"Hey, I'm the girls' leader and everyone knows that. I don't know why you had to come along and make a mess of everything," Jones spat back.

"Mess? They had something to eat, last night and again today, because I was here watching over them."

"Nobody invited you."

"You hired me," Maile said.

"That was a mistake."

Maile looked at her nemesis in the argument. "Look, Jones…"

"Everybody relax, okay?" Detective Silva said. "Where's your flashlight, Ms. Jones?"

"I never did find it."

"It was the flashlight we left on our little table, with TP, in case someone needed to go in the middle of the night," Maile said. "She knew that. She even offered it to us."

"They were supposed to go all the way to the restroom by themselves?" he asked.

Maile felt embarrassed, and wondered if they'd broken any campground rules. "We dug a little hole, you see…"

"Miss Spencer had it all figured out," Melody said.

"She's a good camper," Nancy added.

"It sure sounds like she is," Silva said. "Where's that flashlight now?"

"I don't have it," Michelle said quickly. "It was taken away from me."

After the girls looked for it, Maile asked, "Did anyone use it last night?"

"Not me."

"Me neither."

"I wasn't going out there with rabid maniacs running around with hatchets!" Nancy said. Maile was a moment too late with getting her hand clamped over the kid's mouth.

"Hatchet?" Silva asked.

"Part of her ghost story last night."

"I hope so. Just to dot another T, do you have a hatchet or axe here at the campsite?"

"We didn't bring one," Maile said. "We used driftwood for our campfire and rocks to pound in tent stakes."

"That works," he said while jotting more notes. "We've been sidetracked from Ms. Jones' statement. You said you came out and saw Ms. Spencer chasing after the man. How was she holding her flashlight while she ran?"

"I wasn't running," Maile said quietly.

"She was carrying it like a runner in a race with baton, swinging it all over the place."

"Did you see her hit the man in any way?"

"Well, maybe not. I was only out of the tent for a moment."

"Did you see the man's face at all?" he asked.

"No. He was being chased away by her by then."

"Wasn't chasing him," Maile muttered.

"Ms. Spencer, you must've got a good look at him with your flashlight in his face. What did he look like?"

"I'm not sure. White, maybe in his thirties, early forties?"

"Eye color, hair color? Facial hair?"

"Maybe my light was a little too bright? I couldn't see much detail except that he was a man."

"I guess I can understand that," Silva said. "What about his clothes?"

"Light-colored shirt, jeans."

"Height, weight?"

"Average and slender."

"Everybody's average and slender, or average and fat. Just once I wish I could get a decent answer from someone."

"Okay, let's say five-eight to five-ten, and around one-fifty to one-seventy."

"Excellent! You base that one anything in particular? You know a lot of men in that size range?" he asked.

Melody giggled.

Maile crossed her arms. "Know?"

"Have seen?"

"I'm a nurse, detective, I've seen thousands of men in many sizes and shapes, including soldiers while I was in the military."

"You're a nurse?" Michelle asked, looking surprised.

"You were a soldier?" Jennifer asked.

"I'd like to hear a little more about that, too," Silva said.

"Officer in the Army Nurse Corps until a few months ago," Maile said. "Before that, I worked at Honolulu Med, downtown."

He continued jotting notes. "Impressive."

"That's why you're such a good camper!" Nancy said. "And so brave when the maniac attacked!"

"I wasn't being brave," Maile said. "I just wanted to get rid of the guy so we could get back to sleep."

"You were being braver than you realized at the time. Or dumber," Detective Silva said.

"Why?"

"When the CSI techs checked beneath him, they found a .357 magnum revolver. Loaded, by the way."

Chapter Seven

When Detective Silva consented, Maile sent the girls to collect more water for cooking.

"Well, that would've sucked," she said, once they were gone.

"You had no idea he was armed?"

"Not at all. It was his gun?" she asked.

"Checking prints on it, which I hope don't come back as a match to yours."

"They won't."

"Not mine either," Michelle said. "Can I go to the bathroom also, please?"

"I should be finished with you for now. Just don't leave the vicinity of the campground. And once I'm done here, I want neither one of you to leave the island."

"I'm supposed to go home tomorrow with the girls," Jones said.

"You might be here longer than that," he said.

"But Christmas is on Sunday! You can't keep me here for that!"

"Do you have a husband or kids waiting for you on Kauai?" he asked.

"No, just my parents."

"They've had other Christmases with you. You can miss one for a change, if need be."

"But…"

"What hotel are you staying in?" he asked.

"Kuhio Palms, on…"

"I know where it's at."

"I'm not sitting in there all by myself for Christmas!" Michelle demanded.

"Rather get parked in a cell downtown?"

"I know people," she said, stomping off. "On this island, too! This isn't the end of this, not by a long shot."

"No, sure isn't," he said. Silva smiled at Maile. "If I had my druthers, she'd be on the next flight back to Kauai."

"Me, too. I thought I was the only one that said druthers anymore."

"Couple of old farts, I guess."

"Old?"

"Old beyond our years."

That didn't help. Maile was beginning to wonder if a trip to Koni's salon was needed more than she realized.

"Do you need anything else from me, Detective?"

"If you don't mind, I'd like you to take a look at the body. It sounds as though you have the same idea about him that I do."

"What's that?" Maile asked.

"That the dead man is the same one you chased away last night."

"Okay, first of all, I didn't chase anyone. All I did was…"

He turned Maile to walk to where CSI techs were still working with the corpse under the canopy. "Yes, I know. You followed him until you thought he was gone, and then came back to your tent. You're absolutely certain that was done at a walking speed?"

"Yes. He even out-paced me slightly. When he got to about thirty feet in front of me, I gave up and turned back."

"And you never saw anything in either of his hands?"

"Like a gun? No, never. Not at the campsite, or while walking behind him."

"Good enough. Where exactly did the two of you walk?" he asked.

"Right down the middle of the old runway. Yes, this one where the body was found."

By then, they were at the canopy over the body, and Silva had one of the technicians lift the plastic sheet that covered the man's face.

"Not squeamish?" he asked as the sheet was lifted.

"Seriously? After eight years of military nursing, I think I'm beyond that."

"You can go closer, if you like."

The body had been rolled over onto its back. Maile looked down at the man's pale face. His expression was locked in place, one cheek smooshed over slightly where it had been on the ground. His dark hair was messy but looked like it was usually combed back from his face. He had a shadow of whiskers. He wasn't particularly good looking, but dead people rarely were. Even so, something seemed familiar about him.

"Can I see his shirt?"

The tech lifted more of the sheet to expose a pale blue, informal buttoned shirt, now open. She looked at his feet and saw the cuffs of blue jeans below the end of the sheet.

"Pretty sure that's the same guy."

"How sure?" he asked.

"Eighty percent."

"Good enough. What's bothering you?"

"I don't know. There's just something familiar about him, but I can't put my finger on what."

"More familiar that from seeing him in the dark last night?" he asked.

"Sure seems like it, but I just don't know from where."

"Is he a neighbor? An old acquaintance? Someone you dated once a long time ago?"

Maile shook her head slowly, still trying to place the face. "No."

"You were away for eight years while in the service, right?"

"And then a few more months while I traveled. I just got home last week. I haven't really met anyone new since I've been home."

"Well, maybe something will come to you." He handed her a business card. "Give me a call if it does."

"Does that mean the kids and I can finish our campout?"

"Okay with me. We'll be wrapping up our activities here pretty soon."

"Thanks."

"Ms. Spencer, if you don't mind me asking, what prompted you to serve?"

"In the Army? Just inspired by a couple of friends. I was between jobs and decided to do something that was bigger than me. I wasn't going to miss out on anything by leaving town for a few years, so I went."

"You're not married?" he asked.

"Not even close. Been there, done that, as they say. Not in a hurry to do it again."

"As a comparison," he said. "Would you rather serve in the military or be married?"

"No contest. The worst day in the Army was better than any day being married." She gave her answer some thought. "To my idiot ex-husband, anyway."

He made a motion like he was tipping his hat and left to go talk with the CSI techs.

The girls were back with their water buckets and were standing quietly, with worried looks on their faces.

"Are you going to the slammer?" Nancy asked.

For the first time all day, Maile chuckled. "No, nobody's going to the slammer. But I think we should put on some sunscreen and then look for seashells."

"Nobody in our troop named Shelly," Melody said.

"Why is that important...oh, I get. Shelly sells surfboards at the seashore."

"That's not how it goes!"

"They sell seashores at the..." Nancy said. "They serve horseshoes at the...oh, darn."

By the time they were done searching for the Biggest Seashell in the Entire Universe, and had a few races through the waves that were tumbling ashore, the CSI van was gone, as was the body and Detective Silva. Maybe their campout could finally proceed.

"Hey, girls! I have good news!" Maile announced.

"Going to McDonald's for dinner?" Jennifer asked.

"No, even better. I have a surprise for you." Maile dug to the bottom of her backpack and got out a watermelon. "It's not cold, but it should be tasty."

"Oh wow!"

"Cool!"

They cut it up with a careful eye to making ten equal portions.

"Why ten?" Melody asked. "There's eight of us and Miss Spencer. That's nine."

"And Miss Jones," Maile said. "She's on this trip, also."

"She said mean things about you."

"No reason to be mean back. Trying to include her is the nice thing to do, isn't it?" Maile asked.

"Maybe."

"Isn't that a part of the Girl Scout code, to be nice to each other?"

"Guess so," several said in unison.

"Easier when she's not around," Melody mumbled.

"Maybe the most important time to be nice is when it's not so easy."

"Can we go look for more dead guys?" Nancy asked. She'd been glued to Maile's hip since the seashell search.

"No."

"Why not?"

"There won't be any more to find."

"Might be something."

"Don't listen to her, Miss Spencer," one of them said. "Nan's a little ghoul."

"Am not."

"Why do you like dead stuff so much?"

"Do not! Take that back!"

"Don't hafta, and you can't make me."

"Another good reason not to go looking for trouble is that it's almost time for dinner," Maile said. "I think we should make a giant feast that none of us will ever forget. How does that sound?"

"With Miss Jones?" Melody asked.

"If she shows up again. She's been gone for a while. She was supposed to go to the restroom when you guys were there."

"We never saw her," Jennifer said.

"I saw her going to the parking lot," another said.

"She was going to the bus stop," Jennifer said.

"Going to buy more fire torches of burning death," Nancy said, pinching her nose.

"What're those?" Maile asked.

"Cigarettes," Melody said. "Nan hates ciggies as much as she likes dead stuff."

"Do not!" Nancy shouted. "Wait a minute…"

"Well, if Miss Jones comes back, she can eat dinner with us," Maile said, assembling all the packages of freeze-dried meals.

"Maybe you should call her," Jennifer said.

"I never got her number."

"I have it," several of them said.

"I don't," Nancy said.

"Because you're a little squirt and don't have a phone yet," Melody said.

"Getting one for Christmas," Nancy said with a pout.

"Can I get Miss Jones's number, please?" Maile begged. Once she got it, she walked down the beach to talk privately. "Where are you?"

"You're running the show there. You obviously don't need me."

"You're their leader. You need to be here for them."

"Give it a rest, will you? How am I supposed to compete with an Army officer?"

"By learning what needs to be done on a campout ahead of time, and then carrying your fair share of the weight."

"I have bad shoulders. I can't carry one of those backpack things."

"Not that weight, but forget it. You did more than the other one that bailed out before we even got started. Tomorrow, you get your troop back and will never see me again."

"Probably won't be their leader much longer anyway."

"Why not?" Maile asked.

"Doesn't matter."

"Have you made it back to your hotel room yet?"

"Pretty soon. Why?"

"Take the night off. Regroup. Consider this trip a learning experience, and make a new start tomorrow."

"Easy for you to say," Michelle said, right before the call ended.

**

Once dinner had been eaten and the evening grew late, Maile dug another surprise out from her backpack.

"Who wants to roast marshmallows over the campfire?" she asked, showing the kids a bag of them.

They found sticks and twigs to use as skewers, and Maile limited the number of marshmallows to three per kid, just so they wouldn't get too wired on sugar right before climbing into their tents. It was Melody's turn that night to tell the ghost story, which when compared to Nancy's the night before, was rather tame.

Just as she was getting to the end, there was a *thump thump thump* droning sound in the sky. Maile knew right off what it was from hearing the same sound of helicopters coming in for landings while in the military.

"Now what?" she muttered as she peered into the night sky. She felt the girl on each side of her lean in close.

"That a flying monster?" Nancy whispered.

"No, they're helicopters."

"Coming for us?"

"I hope not." When Maile finally saw the red blinking lights on them close together, and heard the heavy drone of their powerful engines, she figured they were military craft from one of the bases on the island. There was just enough ambient light to make their silhouettes show up.

"Giant grasshopper monsters," Nancy said quietly, snuggling in closer to Maile.

The group of them watched as the two helicopters stopped and hovered over the ocean. Within seconds, rafts were dropped into the water, followed by the plunges of several men.

"Miss Spencer, are we being invaded?" Melody asked.

"I think it's a training drill being performed by the Marines from their base at Kaneohe. They do that on this island."

"Why are they invading our campsite?" Nancy asked.

Maile put her arm around the girl's back. "They're not. It's just practice."

"Practice for war?" one of them asked.

"Yes, but not a war here in Hawaii. It's nothing to worry about. Just watch what they do."

After another moment, Maile could see two rubber inflatable rafts being paddled by soldiers dressed in black come ashore. As soon as they were on the beach, they hopped out, and in unison lifted the rafts and ran up the shore with them, disappearing into the brambles and shrubs that were growing wild. When one last man ran up the beach, he seemed to notice their campfire and ran to them.

Maile stood to greet him. "Sorry if we're in your way. Is this a training drill?"

"Yes, Ma'am. This beach was supposed to be evacuated several hours ago. Why are you still here?"

"I didn't know anything about that. Is this going to be a live fire exercise?"

"Only flash-bangs at the heads, Ma'am. You know about live fire exercises?" he asked. Water continued to drip from his soaking wet uniform and gear.

"You're gonna shoot someone in the head?" Melody asked.

"They're not going to shoot anyone," Maile said. "Flash-bangs are fake grenades that make noise but don't do any damage. It's just a training exercise. No one's going to get hurt, because they're not going to use any of them near us. Right, Sergeant?"

"Copy that, Ma'am."

There was something familiar about his voice. His face was covered with black face paint, only his eyes and teeth showing up in the dark. She glanced at the small patch on his chest that identified his rank. "Gunny, do I know you?"

"Gunnery Sergeant Gustafson, Ma'am."

"Gus!" Maile wanted to hug him. "I'm Maile. Captain Spencer, from Khashraq."

She recognized his bent smile when a few more of his teeth showed. "Sight for sore eyes, if I could see you, Ma'am. But my boys are waiting to recon the campground. We'll be gone in no time."

"Gus, I still have the same phone number," she told him as he turned to leave them behind.

He turned around and ran backward so he could face her. "So do I, Ma'am. And we still have some beach activities to wrap up!"

Once her old friend from the military disappeared into the night, Maile sat down again.

"Miss Spencer?" Melody asked.

"Yes?"

"Do you know everybody?"

Maile chuckled. "Seems like it sometimes."

"Is he your boyfriend, Auntie?" Nancy asked.

"No. Why do you ask that?"

"He was looking at you like he wanted to be."

Maile closed up the bag of marshmallows. "I think we've had enough sugar and it's time to go to bed."

After only a few minutes, the squad of Marines took their rafts back down the beach and pushed their way through the waves, before paddling out to sea again. Just as the rafts were disappearing into the dark, the helicopters returned.

Once the girls were settled in their tents, Maile walked down to the beach. The tide was out, and she went to the edge of the water. The wind was steady, fluttering her clothes and tossing her hair in every direction. She watched for breaks in the clouds that floated overhead until she could see the stars.

In the dark, the sky was indiscernible from the sea, the horizon lost in the moment. Gentle waves washed past her legs; sand and tiny shells pecked at her shins. She walked in deeper. Once she was in up to her waist, she raised her hands to the sky.

"Ua ho'i mai 'o Kamali'i-wahine Hokuhoku'ikalani. Pomaikai ma na kapakai o Hawaii."

***

Maile was sitting on a low bluff just above the beach in the morning when the girls got up. It was the first sunrise she'd seen since coming home, and had been glorious. Even with all the sunrises and sunsets she'd seen in her life, Maile never had understood why they looked different from each other. The act was the same, only reversed. It wasn't that the colors were different; it was the sense of the moment that seemed the same, only different.

"Miss Spencer?" a girl asked, interrupting the mood. "It's time for breakfast."

"Morning, Melody. Is there hot water?"

"Not yet."

"Need hot water for oatmeal. Take all the girls to the restroom, and make sure everybody washes their face and hands. Then boil water for oatmeal."

"Are you mad at us?"

Maile looked at Melody. "Who thinks that?"

"Nancy. You never came to bed last night and she thinks you're mad at her."

"I'll talk to her later. You just tell whoever is making the pancakes this morning that they had better be good."

"Yes, Miss Spencer."

With that, the moment of listening to the ocean during the night while sorting through her life came to an end. About all she learned was that sunrises and little girls brought new problems to be solved.

***

The group decided at breakfast that they'd break camp and leave for home when the morning chores were done. Maile gave Lopaka a call, who came for the tents and the heaviest of gear to drive back to town. That allowed the girls to carry the minimal amount of stuff they'd need on the hike back to Waimanalo Beach.

"Well, are we done here at our campsite?" Maile asked.

"I'm ready to go."

"So am I."

"I hope eyeball hole man doesn't follow us," Nancy said.

"So do I," Maile mumbled. "There's one last thing we need to do and that's clean up our site. That means everybody lines up about five feet apart and walks across everywhere we've been. Pick up anything that doesn't belong on the beach."

"What about the..." Nancy asked, while pinching her nose.

"I'll fill in the latrine. You kids just make sure the place is spick and span before we leave."

"What if something blew here during the night and it wasn't ours?" a girl asked.

"Pick it up anyway."

"But we didn't put it there!"

"Just like everything else in life, leave a place in better condition than when you got there." Maile looked down the runway where the trouble had been the day before. "Sure wish we could do something nice for the man we found yesterday."

"We did, Miss Spencer," Melody said.

"We made a little shrine for him on the beach," Jennifer added.

"Oh?"

"We picked some flowers and found shells for him."

"I found a crab, but he ran away," Nancy said.

They led Maile to where flowers had had been arranged on the sand. Shells that they'd collected had been carefully placed, and sticks had been arranged spelling RIP.

"That's very nice, girls. I'm proud of you for doing that."

The return hike to their starting point went fast, with Melody and Jennifer setting the pace at the front, and Maile and Nancy bringing up the rear. Maile carried anything heavy that would slow the girl down. To make it look like she was doing her share of the work, Nancy carried mostly clothing in her pack.

Lopaka was already there waiting for them with the van, with bottles of cold juice for the girls and a large cup of coffee for Maile.

"Lifesaver, brah," she said, taking several sips in a row.

"Where's the other lady?" he asked.

"Who knows? She left us yesterday."

"Dang, Mai. You took on eight girls all on your own?"

"It was fun. I'd do it again. Not this week, but maybe someday."

"It went okay?"

"Not entirely." Maile smiled about something. "I got a little help from the Marines."

"Huh?"

Maile told Lopaka about the body they'd found, and the girls talked about the police that showed up.

"Yeah!" Nancy shouted. "And Auntie Maile called for Marines to protect us from the weirdoes last night!"

After getting a curious glance from Lopaka, Maile finished the story about the helicopters.

At the office, parents were waiting in rental cars for the girls. It amazed Maile at how tired they pretended to be in front of their parents, when just an hour before they were playing in the surf while wearing backpacks. One that didn't need to pretend was Nancy. She dragged her pack behind her as she went to her father, who was there by himself.

"How'd it go, punkin?" he asked.

"Dad, don't call me that in front of other people," she said dropping her pack in the trunk of his rental.

He grinned. "Oh yeah, you're too old for that now, aren't you?"

"Dad, please!" Nancy implored, with a dramatic combination of eye roll and sigh. "You need to meet our new scout leader. She's nice. Go talk to her."

Maile decided to give Nancy a personal goodbye. Nancy did the introductions.

"Dad, this is Auntie...Miss Spencer. She saved us from a maniac. Miss Spencer, this is my dad."

"Maniac?" he asked.

"Long story. Nancy can fill you in later. She has a great imagination."

"You're telling me. Where's their leader?"

Maile explained how Jones needed to return to her hotel room early.

"None of us figured those other two would stick it out for three days," he said. "That's why we were glad to pay a tour company to help out."

"Well, everybody got home safe and sound, and that's what matters. I think they had some fun along the way."

Maile took him and the other parents aside and told the crib notes version of the dead man they'd found, and reassured them that the girls could go home the next day and never have to worry about it again.

Once the kids and parents were gone, she went into the tour office where Amelia was working alone. After filling a mug with tea, she drew up a chair and sat. She kicked off her boots and started rubbing her feet.

"Tired?" Amelia asked.

"I'm more tired from playing mother hen than I am from hiking. We found a nice place to camp, though."

"I heard something about a dead body?"

"Nice place to camp except for that." Maile chuckled. "And an invasion by the Marines."

Maile told the story about finding the dead body, and then the landing by the Marines, and how the girls took it all in stride.

"No wonder you're tired," Amelia said.

"I still have a few other things to process before I can decide if I'm tired."

"I'm impressed with how you stuck it out. Anybody else would've packed up and left when the rabid dog started barking, or whatever happened with that," Amelia said. "You're not going home?"

"I have a giant favor to ask, and it's a little sneaky," Maile said, scooting her chair closer to the desk.

"My favorite kind! Can I be a part of your conspiracy?"

"I need you to make it work. I want to do the year-end employee performance evaluations on the guides and drivers, but I don't want them to know about it." Maile explained about her idea to wear disguises while going on tours with her guides and drivers, to see how they were doing.

"You don't think they'll spot you?"

"When the guides see fake names on the tour guest list, I'll have an edge. I can wear big hats and sunglasses, different clothes, and not talk much."

"Can you speak with an accent?"

Maile used the British slang she'd learned in England and faked an accent for a couple of sentences.

"Don't do that one," Amelia said.

"Not so good?"

"To be politely blunt, please don't ever talk like that again."

"Maybe French," Maile said before speaking the few words of French she knew.

"Maybe mute. Sorry."

Maile chuckled. "Yeah, mute doesn't work any better for me. Somehow, I'm unable to keep my big trap shut. But let's book a basic Waikiki tour with each guide."

After a voice prompt, Amelia began touch-typing. "Christy and Daniel have a Waikiki tour tomorrow morning, and Leah and Ed have one at noon. You could get their evaluations done in one day. Susan and Lopaka have one on Friday morning. They might be the hardest for you to fool."

"That's what I was thinking. How do you keep all the tours straight if you can't see the screen?" Maile asked.

"I keep them all memorized. Great system, until I start getting cancellations or changes. That really messes with my head."

"I would guess so. Put me down for a basic Waikiki tour with all three."

"What names?"

"Oh boy. Gwen Wickerstrom on Thursday morning, Agatha Philpot that afternoon…"

"Philpot?"

"It's a real name. And Brigitte Lavigne on Friday."

"Good. A librarian from Nebraska, a logistics consultant from Canada, and a fan dancer from Paris," Amelia said, laughing. "Can't wait to see you pull this off, Maile."

While Amelia answered a call, Maile made them cups of tea. Somebody had been pinching pennies by buying the cheap stuff for the office, and there was no coffee, not even instant. That needed to change.

"Still running?" Maile asked after the call.

"One or two days a week. That why I like to work Sundays. I can run here in the morning without Brian having to worry about me getting run down by a car. Then he takes me home again in the afternoon."

"How can you run through city streets like that without being able to see where you're going?" Maile asked.

"I've memorized the number of strides from one intersection to the next, to the next, to the next. Traffic signal walk signs make those funny sounds, and by running so early, there's not much traffic." Amelia took a sip of her tea. "Every now and then there's a close call. Don't tell Brian that or he'll be driving me around everywhere."

"I guess I shouldn't tell you to be careful."

"I wouldn't know it if I wasn't!" Amelia said, laughing. "Otherwise, Brian takes us to the high school where I can run laps around the track while the kids play."

Maile checked the time. In the past, she could've run a marathon in the heat and humidity of Honolulu, but her body was still in a sweat over the short morning hike that had ended two hours before.

"Speaking of running, I need to get going before I melt. I'll be in on Friday afternoon for a team meeting."

Amelia chuckled. "You sound like Brian, gathering the troops to hold a team meeting."

"Keep it under your hat about my tours on Thursday and Friday. I don't want them hearing about my little conspiracy."

"If they do, they won't get it from me. They'll be too busy the next couple of days to spend much time in the office."

"Good. Wish me luck in pulling it off." Maile sat up straight. "Hey, when you see Brian, let him know I have something important to talk to him about."

"Firing him?"

"Nobody's being fired. In fact, after this week's unexpected camping tour, everybody's getting a little extra in their Christmas bonus. Don't tell the others that."

"That's nice of you."

"Along with bonuses, I'm bringing in a K-cup coffeemaker and better tea bags."

"Looking forward to those. What do you want to talk to Brian about?" Amelia asked. "Do you think there'll be a problem with the dead guy you found?"

"I hope not." Maile told Amelia how the police detective was allowing the kids to go home, and how he acted like it was no big deal. "The girls seem to have forgotten about it already."

"That's good."

"I just need Brian and you to be aware that the police are investigating, and somehow I've become their best witness. Not that I saw anything more than a dead body. But if a Detective Silva comes here looking for me, just have him call me."

"I remember Brock talking about how you were in and out of trouble with the police a few times. It was never your fault, but somehow you were always in the middle of it," Amelia said.

Brock was Brian's younger brother, someone Maile's age. They'd grown up in each other's orbit within the Hawaiian community on the island, and eventually started a romance. But as soon as that had started, Maile left for her service in the Army, with both of them making promises to wait for each other. They'd even progressed as far as planning a wedding to take place on her first leave.

It never came off, though. While Maile was away, Brock found someone that met his fancy better than having to wait for Maile. It wasn't long before she was pregnant, they were married, and were living in Las Vegas. Maile had long forgotten in what order that happened, but she was done with ever thinking about Brock again.

"Yep, me and good ol' Detective Ota. In some weird way, I played matchmaker for him and my Aunt Kelani. I guess that makes it all worthwhile."

"We got his daughter Susan out of the deal. She's our busiest guide, even busier than Christy," Amelia said. "Isn't there some weird story of how the two of you met?"

"Weird and best forgotten."

Amelia turned serious. "Maile, sorry about what happened with Brock."

"Don't worry about it. I was over that a long time ago."

"Just so you know, Brian got into Brock's face quite a few times about how he treated you."

"Well, water under the bridge, as they say. No reason to sweat the small stuff," Maile said as she left the office. "And Brock Turner is definitely small stuff."

Chapter Eight

Maile needed to leave the house early Thursday morning to join Christy and Daniel's tour of Waikiki. At least it was early in Maile's old pre-Army life. Anything before noon had been early back then. Now, a nine o'clock start time to her morning felt lazy.

She needed a substantial disguise because long-time guide Christy and her driver Daniel knew her well, and other people who might recognize her worked in Waikiki hotels. To hide in plain sight, she wore clothing that she wouldn't ordinarily wear, patted pale pink makeup on her cheeks to look more Caucasian, and used a curling iron in her hair to make it bushier than what it already was. Feeling like something was missing from her disguise, she got some chewing gum to chew, at least while checking in for the tour. She had no idea if Nebraskans chewed gum, but Gwen Wickerstrom was going to. Sunglasses completed the disguise.

She was a few minutes early arriving at the hotel where the other tour guests were staying. The only plan she had was to sit toward the back of the bus and mind her own business during the tour. She'd make a few notes of what she liked about Christy and Daniel, about the tour in general, and about how other guests were reacting along the way. The good thing about the tour was that she'd be able to visit a few places she hadn't seen in several years, a little homecoming gift for herself.

When Daniel pulled the van to a stop, Christy got out and greeted the group. Maile brought up the end of the line, getting on the bus last.

"Gwen Wickerstrom," she said, chewing the gum while she spoke.

"Oh, yes, you were just added to the tour late yesterday. You're all the way from Nebraska?"

"Yep."

"Well, that gets the long-distance award for today. Welcome to Hawaii, Miss Wickerstrom." Christy checked off the name on her clipboard and set it aside. "I've been to Nebraska. What city are you from?"

"Huh? Oh, it's just a little town." Maile had some quick thinking to do to dream up a name that sounded like a town that belonged in Nebraska. The problem was, she'd never been to Nebraska, and other than the state capitol she was forced to memorize as a schoolgirl, she couldn't think of a single city name there. "Pendergast Creek Falls."

"Sounds pretty. What part of the state is that?"

"Right in the middle."

"Isn't the middle too dry for creeks and waterfalls?" Christy asked.

Daniel closed the door, trapping Maile inside the van with Christy, who was intent on giving her the third degree. "Unless it rains. I have a bad knee. Mind if I sit down?"

"Of course. Please take a seat at the front, so we can talk."

Maile faked a limp for a few steps before she plunked down in her seat. Once Daniel had the bus going, Christy started her speech about Waikiki's famous sites. With that, Maile watched out at the ever-changing sights of Honolulu's most famous attractions, with an attentive ear turned toward the guide. It was the same tour that she'd given years before: Diamond Head, the main shopping and strolling boulevard of Kalakaua Avenue, Duke Kahanamoku's statue at Waikiki Beach, and a final stop at the mall for something to drink.

That afternoon's trickery and deceit would be easier for Maile, because Leah the guide and Ed the driver had met Maile only once and briefly. She still needed to do something to alter her appearance a little, and that meant a fedora and new sunglasses. Except for a few words she couldn't remember, she knew Canadians had accents similar to Americans, the role she was playing that afternoon. Mostly she kept quiet during the tour, exactly what she'd done that morning.

Most of the group were senior citizens, and had booked trips with the company for everyday that week. Maybe because of that, Leah had turned on the charm, and Ed drove like he was on a driver's license test. Both were pros, and she planned to tell Brian that he'd made a good choice in hiring them. But just like she predicted, she had a hard time not gossiping with strangers about people she didn't know.

Keeping clammed up tight gave her the chance to think about the dead man they'd found on the beach a couple of days earlier. While Honolulu had its fair share of petty crime like every big city, there wasn't so much violent crime or gangs. Organized crime concerned only big business and politics, not the everyday commerce and habits of the people who lived there. Oahu just wasn't the kind of place where people got whacked over the back of their heads for no reason.

Maile wondered about the .357 revolver that had been found beneath the man's body. Apparently, it had belonged to him, since it had his fingerprints on it, but why would someone wander around a campground in the middle of the night with a gun? Unless he was holding up other campers. But he'd come to their campsite, he only tried to frighten them, not hold them up. It had been bad enough for the kids to find a dead body; they never would've gone camping again if they'd been robbed at gunpoint in the middle of the night.

After the second tour was done and she'd been dropped off at the same hotel as the seniors she'd just spent the afternoon with, Maile went in to the hotel beachside café for something to drink. A walking path that fronted the beach was just on the other side of a low hedge, and she had a grand view of the ocean—in between joggers, surfers with boards under their arms, and families with umbrellas and picnic baskets passing by in every direction. Getting her over-priced glass of mango juice, she gave Detective Silva a call.

"Ms. Spencer, I came all the way into town to your office to see you and you weren't there. Imagine my disappointment."

Maile chuckled. "I've been busy today. I called to see if you have any updates on the case of the man we found at Bellows?"

"I do have a few things to talk to you about. Where are you right now?" he asked.

"Having something to drink at the beachside bar at the Grand Kalakaua Hotel."

"You know how to live a classy lifestyle, Ms. Spencer."

Maile chuckled. "This is a one-time event. Just checking out the kind of place our guests stay at."

"Drink slowly. I'll be there in about ten minutes."

Maile finished her mango juice and ordered iced tea while she waited. It was just being delivered when he showed up. He ordered the same for himself.

"I didn't mean to interrupt your day, Detective. You could've filled me in on the phone."

"This might take a little longer than a phone call. Considering I was already in town and rarely get the chance to have a cold one in a place like this, I figured I better take advantage of it when I can."

"Mostly what I'm curious about is if the gun that was found with the man actually belonged to him, and if he'd robbed other campers that night?" Maile asked. "I ask because I still get phone calls from parents of the kids looking for updates about the case."

"The gun did not legally belong to him, and there's some question of whose it was. His prints were all over it, but that isn't ownership. It only means he had it in his possession. Possession being nine-tenths of the law doesn't mean he legally owned it; that only means it was his at that moment as compared to being in someone else's possession. The courts are very specific about that."

"Was anybody robbed at the campground that night?" she asked.

"No, not that night nor any other night in years. I checked, and there's very little roughhousing at our beaches, and that's only between local punks, and rarely includes campers. Even still, patrol officers swing through campgrounds two or three times a shift, just to be a presence."

"So, you still have no idea why someone took a swing at him? You said the CSI techs found his wallet on him, so he wasn't mugged. Was he a camper there, and just got lost in the middle of the night while looking for the restrooms like I thought?" she asked.

"There's no reason to think he was camping. All tents and equipment have been accounted for. All we found was a car registered in his name in the parking lot. For some reason, he came to that campground in the middle of the night."

"Was he a pusher?"

"That was my next idea. No drugs on him or in his car, and he has nothing on his rap sheet related to drugs. He also didn't have a large amount of cash as though he were there to make a purchase."

"You know what I don't understand..." Maile stopped herself. "Sorry. I shouldn't be involving myself like this in your investigation."

"Dave Ota said you have a way of trying to be helpful, as he put it."

Maile looked at Silva through squinted eyes. "When did he tell you that?"

"I gave him a call this morning when I found out he's your uncle."

"He married my Aunt Kelani a few years ago, but it's not like we have a niece-uncle relationship."

"So I understand," Silva said. "While he was still working out of the downtown Honolulu station, your paths crossed a few times, and that's how he met your aunt. But that's a story for some other time. He did say you were never particularly intrusive, or at least not obstructive. It's just that you needed reminders every now and then that you were a witness or victim, and not an investigator."

"Except for the times that I helped with his investigations by being a part of an undercover team. There was a lot more risk in one or two of those adventures than either of us ever expected. Did he have anything else to say about me?" Maile asked.

"Only that you're quite possibly the last honest person in Hawaii, even to the point of being naïve about it."

"Maybe a few years ago, but I've suffered a few lessons along the way." Maile tried taking a drink of her iced tea but stopped when she felt a tremble in her hand. She was still discovering a few triggers that stirred her nerves the wrong way. "Can we get back to the Waimanalo case, please?"

Before he could continue, they were interrupted by someone that had come to their table. It wasn't the waitress, but a tall Asian woman with nearly blond hair.

Her clothes were simple but classy, expensive. To Maile's eye, she looked familiar.

The woman smiled politely to Maile and nodded before turning her attention on Silva. "Troy, what are you doing in my turf?"

"Hi, Caitlyn." Silva stood and waved to the waitress to bring another chair. "Have a seat. I was just talking with a witness about something. A second set of ears might come in handy."

"Thanks, but I'm meeting someone." She smiled at Maile again. "But again, why are you investigating in my part of town?"

"Oh, yes, some intros are in order. Maile, this is Detective Caitlyn Nakamura, the lead investigator for HPD in Waikiki. Caitlyn, this is Maile Spencer, a tour operator here in town. She had the misfortune to discover a body at the Bellows Airfield campground the other day."

"I've heard a little about that." The detective took another look at Maile, now with a note of curiosity in her expression. "Does that have something to do with me or Waikiki?"

"Hopefully not, no," Silva said. "I just happened to be in town when Ms. Spencer called, so we met here. Not taking any of your cases away, Caitlyn."

"Thanks. Keep it that way." When another woman was seated a few tables away that gave Nakamura a wave, she seemed to wrap up their little meeting. The detective gave Maile one last look. "What was your name again?"

"Maile."

"Yes, that's right, Maile." The woman detective looked at Silva one last time. "I'll give you a call later, Troy. Good luck with your case."

Maile watched as Detective Nakamura went to the other table to join the woman waiting for her there.

"Sorry about her," Silva said. "She comes on a little strong, but she's an excellent investigator."

"Hasn't changed much," Maile said.

"You know her? Why do you know so many HPD investigators?" he asked.

"I don't know her as a police officer. It's been over fifteen years since I've seen her, but other than hair color and carrying a gun, Caitlyn hasn't changed much."

"Fifteen years? I don't understand," he said.

"We went to high school together. In fact, we were on the same cheerleading squad."

"Nakamura was a cheerleader?" he asked.

"Very good one. She was the largest of the girls on the squad, and we had no guys. Since I was one of the smaller girls and the best tumbler, it was my job to get tossed to the top of the human pyramid."

"I've always wondered how you guys make that work," Silva said.

"It doesn't always. Believe me, those football fields are hard when landing in a heap."

"Sounds pretty athletic anyway."

"Cheerleaders usually are. I was a distance runner and ran on the boys' cross-country team, and Caitlyn was always taking up some sort of martial art. Judo, karate, whatever. Not many kids messed with her."

"They still don't," he said. Detective Silva checked his phone when he got a chime. "Hey, I got to go. If I learn anything about the Bellows case that you need to know, I'll give you a ring."

Maile waved him off from paying for their drinks. "Detective Silva?"

"Yes?"

"Let's keep that stuff about Caitlyn and me being cheerleaders under our hats, okay?"

Once he was gone, she gave Caitlyn's tablemate a long look to see it was someone she recognized. She looked a few years younger and dressed as though she was from the mainland. Figuring her break was done, Maile paid and left before she bought an over-priced meal.

***

When Friday rolled around, there was a lot more anxiety about her disguise. Lopaka was one of Maile's oldest friends, and had been her driver for the year she worked as a tour guide. He would surely spot her at a country mile if she wasn't careful.

Maile had met Susan under peculiar means. She was street savvy and cellblock hard, but once Maile scratched the surface, she found a mostly sweetly-natured teenager that was a lot more intelligent than she portrayed herself to be. Once they buried the hatchets they had for each other, Maile hired Susan to be the guide that replaced her. She never expected her to last a week, but she was still there after nine years, eighteen boyfriends, and a college degree later.

Maile somehow had to convince both of them that she was French, and figured the best way of doing that was to keep quiet as much as she could. That was going to be hard, especially when she needed to speak with a fake accent.

To prepare on the evening before, Maile watched *The English Patient*, with Juliette Binoche, practicing her accent and learning a few words. As far as she knew, neither Lopaka nor Susan knew any French at all.

Then there was the disguise. Wearing a form-fitting skirt and blouse, and leaving one button too many open, she used entirely too much makeup to hide her face. She wrapped her head with a silk scarf, and picked some of her wavy hair out here and there. With a large hat and

107

giant sunglasses to hide her face, and wearing a pair of heeled shoes to make her taller, her disguise was complete.

After getting to the hotel where the tour would start, she checked her disguise one last time. When she joined the group that was waiting, she minded her own business by hanging toward the back. The first problem Maile noticed was that they were ten minutes late in arriving with the van. She made a quick note about it.

It came to her turn to board. Susan looked at her expectantly, the list of tour guests in one hand. "Name?"

"Je suis Brigitte Lavigne. Pardon, my name is Brigitte Lavigne."

"Oh, yes, the Frenchie." Susan checked off the name. "Find a seat and take a load off. Snap it up because we're running late."

Maile sat, wondering if Susan was having an off day. Feeling generous right then, she didn't make any notes quite yet.

Lopaka seemed in a hurry as he drove to Diamond Head, their first stop on the tour. When he pulled into the parking area, he never opened the door, but quickly started backing around to leave again.

"Okay, that's Diamond Head," Susan said. "If you want pictures, get them now."

"Pardon, Mademoiselle," Maile said to catch Susan's attention. "We do not walk into zee cray-tor?"

"We're late, okay? We need to make up time. You want to see everything on the tour or not?"

This time, Maile made a note about talking to Susan about her tone of voice. No matter how bad a day she might be having, there was no excuse for that from one of her guides.

"Brah, how 'bout stoppin' for some grindz?" Susan said to Lopaka once they were out of the crater. That was something else Maile would talk to Susan about, using pidgin while on a tour. A little bit of it was cute to tourists' ears, reminding them they were far from home. But Hawaiian pidgin was almost a language unto itself, and a little went a long ways.

Instead of going back in the usual direction the tour followed, he drove down smaller residential streets. At one point, they got stuck going the wrong way, and he needed to reverse out. That required one of the passengers to get out and help him back the van out. While that went on, a couple other passengers started to gripe about the delays. Another complained about not feeling well, which was always a nightmare to the guide. Susan seemed to ignore it all, as she scolded Lopaka about getting stuck.

"Might be time for them to have a vacation," Maile mumbled as she made a few more notes.

Lopaka must've been starved, because he stopped at a fast food place and sent Susan in to get him a bag of food, which he ate while driving to the next stop. At one point, they were headed down Kalakaua Avenue toward Duke Kahanamoku's larger-than-life statue, one of the more popular stops on the tour. It was a place where they could get a group photo with everyone's camera, with women in bikinis and men with surfboards walking by. But as they approached, Lopaka wasn't slowing down to make the stop.

"That's the Duke out there," Susan said as they went past the statue. "He's like royalty or something."

"We're not stopping?" someone griped.

By then, Maile was ready to make refunds on all of their tours, and offer free replacements the next day with another guide.

"If you want to take his picture, you can walk back here from your hotel," Lopaka said while driving.

"Frankly, I've taken enough pictures of the guy to last me a lifetime."

"You can't talk to me like that! I'm a paying guest on this tour!" a man said.

"Look, brah. I'm tired to the bone of people like you coming on these tours. Clickety-click with your cameras, and then you cheapskates give us nothing in tips. Go to Disneyland next time, will you?"

"Will the two of you stop shouting?" a woman said. "All this anxiety is making my husband sick!"

Maile couldn't have been more embarrassed. Something had happened to Lopaka while she'd been away. Maybe it was time for him to find a new job driving for someone else, not just take a vacation. She gave up taking notes and put her pad and pencil away. It was going to be an endurance test to get through the remainder of the tour, and planned on skipping out as soon as they got to Ala Moana Mall.

Just as Lopaka was parking, the sick man started getting up too soon, leaving a moan in the air behind him. Before he could get off, he collapsed to the floor.

"Mike!" the wife shouted. "Oh my god!"

Susan bent over and gave his shoulder a shake. "Eh, brah, we're here. You can get off the van now."

Lopaka nudged the man with his toe. "Hey, you're blocking the aisle."

"Mike!" the wife said, crouching down next to him.

Maile was already leaving her seat to go to the man when she saw the wife feel for a pulse.

"He's dead! It's your fault!" the wife said, pointing at Lopaka. "Your bad driving!"

Maile tossed her hat aside and crouched down next to the man, ready to start CPR. When she felt for a pulse at the man's wrist, it was strong and bounding. When she peeled his eyes open, she got the surprise of a lifetime when he winked at her. Then he started to sit up with a smile on his face.

"What the heck?"

"When do we get the drink vouchers for the food court?" the man asked.

"I got them here," Susan said, handing them out.

"If you're sick, you need to go to the hospital, Sir," Maile said.

"He's okay, Mai," Lopaka said. When Maile looked at him, he was ginning ear to ear. So was Susan.

"What's going on?" Maile asked, stepping back to make way for the passengers to get off.

"Everything's okay, Maile," Susan said. "Just having some fun with you."

"You're pranking me? How'd you know it was me?"

Susan explained. "We've known since yesterday what you were up to. Christy spotted you right away. When we asked Amelia and Brian, they both denied knowing anything, but we could tell from the look on Amelia's face she knew something. She finally told us you were doing employee evaluations this week and would be on our tour."

"We decided to have some fun with you in return," Lopaka said.

Maile couldn't keep from laughing when she pointed his finger at him. "You are so fired. You too, Susan. But how did you get the guests to play along with your scheme?"

"They're just some of our friends that went along with it. The real guests were taken out by Christy and Daniel."

With that, Susan begged off for something she had to do. Maile and Lopaka went into the food court at Ala Moana Mall for something to drink.

"How've you been doing, Mai?" he asked once they were settled.

She tried flapping some air beneath her blouse, but it was too tight. "Still getting used to the humidity."

"I mean you, not the weather."

She looked over his shoulder past him. "Trying to get used to that, also."

"Used to what?"

"Nothing. Being a civilian again. Strange not living someone else's schedule."

"There's more going on than that," he said. He was playing with his soda more than drinking it. "I can see something in your eyes that wasn't there before."

"Something good or bad?"

"Something not right."

"Just tired. Time zones, you know?"

"You've been home for a week, and it's not like you to make lame excuses like that," he said.

She made eye contact again. "Lame?"

"You know what I mean."

"No, I don't, Lopaka. Explain it to me," she said, trying not to glare.

He waited for a couple of minutes before he said, "Are you still pissed about Brock?"

"Turner? Over him, brah. You and my mother are the ones keeping him alive. The more I think about him, the more I realize there was very little between us to begin with."

"What happened, then? You were so excited about going somewhere when you went on your trip a while back. It almost seemed as if you were going to meet someone. But since you've come home, you're sort of hollow." Lopaka took a drink of his soda. "We all see it, Maile."

"And you were elected spokesperson for the group?"

"No, just worried."

"Why do men always think it's got something to do with them when a woman isn't at the top of her game every moment of every day?" Maile set a personal record for keeping her molars clamped together before continuing. "It's not about Brock. At first, it was about some other chump, but I got over him pretty quick when I met his wife and kid. After that, I decided to keep going and see a few places I'd always heard about but never thought I'd see. That's it, okay?"

"It's deeper than that, Maile. Seriously, what's going on?"

Maile finished her drink. "Pretty sure you wouldn't understand."

"Try me."

She leaned forward so she was closer to him. "When I worked as an ER nurse at Honolulu Med, I thought I saw everything that could happen to a human being, and with them still surviving it. But when I had duty in some god-awful little first aid station in that damn desert, I had soldiers coming in that…"

"War's tough duty," he said quietly.

"Don't you dare try and placate me with some half-baked platitude." She stared him into silence. "Legs, arms, big chunks of their bodies were missing when they were brought in, and they were still alive. At least for a while. There were times when we had to choose who we'd try to keep alive, and who we had to let go. After a few weeks, I lost track of how many I had to walk away from, to let them die alone." Maile leaned closer. "That stuff doesn't go away very quickly, no matter how many therapists I talk to. Okay?"

"You're seeing a therapist now?" he asked quietly.

"Not anymore. I wanted time away, to be by myself, to just stop talking about it for a while. That's why I was away so long." She noticed the paper napkin she'd crushed in her hand and set it aside. "All I really wanted was some peace and quiet. It took a while, but I finally found it at a Japanese convent, of all places."

"Are you drinking?" he asked quietly.

"Too much of a cheapskate." She chuckled, but mirthlessly. "I worked on a farm that produced some of the best wine in the world, and I never did taste the difference between their high quality wine and the cheap stuff."

"Good for you."

Maile saw how much one hand was shaking and hid it in her lap. Something was close to the surface and she didn't want to bury it again. "They were peacekeeping troops. They were simply trying to keep others from killing each other."

"That was in Khashraq, right? Wasn't that where that Aziz guy was from?"

She nodded. "I thought I'd left it all behind. I thought he and his crappy little kingdom was disappearing in my rearview mirror, but then there he was, on his stupid honeymoon."

"Aziz? Where was that?"

"Maybe the place I wanted to see the most on my trip, and he messed it up for me. But ever since then, I can't get his ugly mug out of my mind. Going on tours, taking that hike with those girls, eating dinner with my brother, visiting my mom. That jerk's always there, along with visions of mangled bodies of men who were only trying to keep his pathetic little country safe from itself."

"That's a lot to haul around, Mai. What're you doing about it?"

"You know what I'd like to do? I'd like to hunt that jerk down, and…"

"Don't go there, for everyone's sake, Maile. Get that stuff out of your head."

"Yeah, I know." Maile heaved a sigh. "Is there anything going on with the company that I need to know about? Whenever I ask Brian or Amelia, they only tell me everything is great. No offense meant, but things can't be that good."

"I only pay attention to Susan and me," he said. It almost seemed as though he was being evasive about something.

"Things not going so well? Because I was surprised that Susan has stuck around this long. I figured after she got her college degree, she'd move on."

"Maybe she's moving on, but nobody is supposed to know about it."

"She's not working the street again, is she?"

"Not exactly that."

"Tell me, Lopaka. I need something else to worry about besides my own stuff."

"She's been making music videos."

"What, like pornos?"

"No, not exactly. Maybe risqué is a better word for them. Whenever a music video producer comes to town to make a video, she seems to know about it and gets hired. It's the kind of video they make at the beach, women in bikinis dancing to the music, weird looking people in zany costumes, all kinds of stuff going on. They're clean, just not exactly wholesome."

Maile swore under her breath. "Using her real name? Are our tour guests recognizing her?"

"She has some sort of stage name, but you wouldn't recognize her, unless you knew it was her dancing."

"You've seen them?"

"Don't worry about it, Mai. And don't let her go. She likes working for you."

"For me, or being a guide?"

"For you. She couldn't care less about being a guide, but she's good at it."

115

Maile looked in her empty drink cup. "How long has this been going on?"

"A couple of years. Sorry I didn't say anything sooner."

"Do I want to know her stage name?"

"Jenny Starr, with two Rs. She seems to be getting something of a following on social media."

Maile sighed again. "Anything else I should know?"

"We never had much of a welcome home party for you. I think I can speak for everyone else when I say you have no idea how proud we all are of you, and the work you did in the military. I'm so sorry it took its toll."

She got her things ready to go. "Not your problem, brah, but thanks. I wish my mom could get with that same program."

"We don't get her back again?" he asked.

"Get who back?" she asked.

"Good ol' Maile Spencer that everybody wants as a friend."

"That girl left some of her blood and a part of her soul on some crappy little sand dune a couple of years ago." Maile stood to leave. "If you can think of a way of returning lost blood, sweat, and tears to her, I'd like to hear about it."

Maile went home from there, half steamed about the mini-intervention, half glad that she's been able to unload a little of her burden.

When she got back to her parents' house, she started cleaning in preparation for her mother and dad getting home from Maui. Maybe with a few long talks and some home cooking, her sense of home would finally start to return.

Chapter Nine

Maile had broken into a sweat while cleaning the house. When she noticed an Uber car pull into the driveway, she knew it was her parents getting home from the airport. She hurried to put away the vacuum cleaner and took leis to the door to welcome them home.

"Maile girl! Not off on a junket?"

"No, Mom. You and Honolulu are stuck with me for a while." She put the welcome home lei over her mother's neck and kissed her cheek, getting a kiss in return. After doing the same with her stepdad, he went off to start a load of laundry before even settling in. Maile took the bag from her mother and rolled it into the bedroom. "How's Auntie?"

"Same thing, only different day. Why you so skinny, girl? You look like haole girls in the fashion magazines."

"Same weight as ever, almost. Haven't had any of your home cooking."

"Yes, that's right. Eating your own cooking. Same thing as being on a diet."

Already with the comments. "My cooking's not so bad."

"Pork lau-lau for dinner will put a little fat where it belongs," her mother said.

"I'm not eating meat right now. I haven't been in a few weeks, since I stayed in the convent."

"How was it being locked in the convent? They change you there?"

"They didn't lock me in," Maile said.

"You know what I mean."

"I found one or two things that need attention. Two weeks of silence did me more good than any therapist I've talked to." Maile noticed the size of her mother's muumuu, obviously smaller than usual. "You've lost weight, too."

"Doctor says one month, one pound. Gotta do what the doctor says, right?"

"I bet your blood pressure is perfect now. How's your blood sugar?"

"Ka'uhane checks both every day. Pressure is good, still got a crooked road to follow with the sugar."

"You look great, Mom. I'm so proud of you," Maile said.

Kealoha sat on the bed. "Short flight but a long day. Mind if I rest before we talk?"

"Before your interrogation of me? Of course. I have a call to make. If I go out, I'll bring something home for dinner."

"Who you calling for business?"

"Asher wants to talk to me about something. I get the idea Kenny's springing the question on her one of these days."

"He's been waiting for you to get home for that."

"Me? Why wait for me?"

"He wants your approval."

"He's marrying her, not me. Doesn't need my approval for that. He should talk to Dad about it, not me."

"Not even a date yet and the bride's already making plans. She'll exhaust me, that one," Kealoha said.

"Probably exhaust all of us. I'll be home early."

Maile pulled the blinds and closed the door for her mother. Her dad had gone to his little den, and with the way the door was closed, he was either dozing at his desk or writing a sermon that would never be given. Maile went out to the front porch to call Asher in private.

"Remember the girls you took on the campout?" Asher asked.

"How could I forget? It was just two days ago. Is there a problem?"

"You know what? Let's meet. I'm not busy this afternoon, so I have time to talk."

"At Koni's, across from Kahala Mall?" Maile asked.

"Let's meet outside the mall's food court. I need something to drink."

"It might be a little while before I get there. I'll have to take the bus."

"Just borrow your dad's car."

Maile cringed. "I don't like driving."

"It's easy. Push on the pedals at the right time and don't bump into stuff."

"It's the not bumping into things that's problematic," Maile said after she hung up. She knocked on her dad's door and peeked in. "Okay if I borrow the car for a couple hours?"

"Going for a drive?"

"Just to Kahala to see Asher about something. I'd spend half the afternoon going there and back if I took the bus."

"The tank should be full." He tossed her the keys. "Have fun."

"Yeah, fun. Easy for him to say," as she got the engine going. "He knows how to drive."

Maile drove like a little old lady all the way through town, while following the same bus route that would've taken her to Kahala.

It was another homecoming moment, seeing the familiar sights that she'd taken for granted in the past. Old buildings painted funky colors, diners that changed hands every couple of years, giant monkey pod trees shading open spaces, green mountains out one window and glimpses of the ocean out the other. They had all waited for her to return. It was all very reassuring, even if there was more traffic than ever.

119

At one point, a transit bus passed her. That's when she took Asher's advice and pressed her foot a little harder on the gas pedal. By the time she parked at the mall, she was exhausted, but at least the car still had all its paint.

Asher smiled when Maile found her at a table outside in the shade. "You got here!"

"I feel like I need one of your massages," Maile said. "I hate driving."

Asher sipped her drink through a straw. Even that simple act was cute somehow, another indication that Kenny's simple defenses against feminine charms were no match for Asher's wiles. "Don't book an appointment through the salon. I can give you a free rub at home just as easily."

"Thanks." All massages being equal, Maile would rather find a Roman gladiator masseur before going to Asher. "Okay, what's up with the girls that we needed to meet today?"

"First of all, they had a gas."

"Mainly because they got to look at a dead body. And I hate to say it, but the fun level went up when their scoutmaster abandoned us. The kids were great. They were all-in with the campout, while their leaders went home."

"That's how it was when I was in that troop," Asher said. She seemed preoccupied by the people that were going back and forth. "They paid more attention to their own stuff than to us."

"What's with Michelle, anyway?"

"Miss Jones? I don't know. She was there when I was a Girl Scout. No daughter, not really any leadership skills, or even motherly. I never did know why she was a Girl Scout leader."

"What does she do for work?" Maile asked.

"Grade school teacher."

"Yikes. I feel sorry for those kids. But what did you want to talk to me about?"

Asher took another seductive sip from her straw. "Nancy really took a shine to you. I heard from Uncle Steve, and...."

"Her father is your uncle? Nobody ever mentioned that," Maile said.

"Not exactly uncle. My mom and he are distant cousins, that kind of uncle. But all she's talked about since the campout is Maile this and Maile that. She's already planning a return camping trip."

"Yeah, and I got the impression that she has bigger ideas in her mind than camping."

"As in romance? She's been playing matchmaker for her father ever since her mom passed a couple years ago."

"He's a nice guy, but I'm not ready for the interisland dating scene." Maile watched as a group of teenaged Christmas carolers went into the mall. It was a reminder that she still had shopping to do if she was putting anything under the tree this year.

"They were here yesterday. Too many sopranos with voices that were changing." Apparently, Asher had never been in a choir as a kid. "There's more, and it's about Miss Jones, sorry, Michelle. I still can't get used to calling her by her first name."

"What about her?" Maile asked.

Asher sipped her drink. "She hasn't been seen since the campout. She was supposed to have a meeting at the hotel with the parents last evening like usual after a big activity, but never showed up. Did she mention anything to you about where she was going?"

"She left right after we spoke to a police detective about the dead body that was found. She said something about going to the campground restroom and never came

121

back. I had the impression she was heading back to the hotel."

"She never got there. Uncle Steve has been checking on the room every chance he gets, and she never answers the door. It's almost like she's a missing person. They're ready to call the police."

"Maybe they should?" Maile said. "The detective told both of us not to leave the island while he investigates the death."

"And she agreed?" Asher asked. She watched carefully as a woman went past them further into the mall.

"Sounded like it. That's when she stomped off to the restroom and apparently hasn't been seen since," Maile said. "The campout is done and the kids got back to their parents safe and sound. Michelle is a big Girl Scout. She can take care of herself. Why am I supposed to be concerned about her?"

"She has a few secrets."

At least Maile was getting some gossip. "What's Michelle's secret?"

Asher left the table for a moment to toss away her drink cup. "She's divorced now and that didn't exactly warm her up any, if you know what I mean."

"What exactly do you mean by not warm?" Maile asked.

"Exactly that. Doesn't date, and according to some of the girls in the troop that are also students at the school where she teaches, she has nothing to do with the men teachers at the school." Asher paused for a moment. "Reminds me a little of what I've heard about you."

"Me?" Maile wondered what kind of gossip was going around about her already, after being home for less than a week. "What about me?"

"You have the time, but you're not dating, from what I've heard. I was wondering why?"

"I've only been home a week." Maile wondered what attracted Kenny to Asher, since he didn't like pushy people. Right then, she felt like she was being crowded into a corner by Asher. "But again, whatever Michelle's problem is with men is her problem, not mine. I have enough trouble of my own with men lately to get too worked up about someone else's."

"There are a couple of nice guys that come for massages. I know they're single and I'm pretty sure they're straight. I could give them your number, if you like?"

"I thought we were talking about Michelle Jones? What are her problems with men?"

"The simplest question turns into a screaming match. There's even a rumor that she muscled one of the men out of the teacher's lounge a while back."

"She's a delight." Maile tended to believe that, from what she saw of Michelle during their campout. If she decided to dislike someone, they weren't allowed within her orbit. "I'm surprised the principal tolerates that."

"It's already got back to the principal about how she abandoned the group. He wants to talk to you about the situation. Mind if he gives you a call?"

"About?" Maile asked, wondering if this was one of the guys Asher was trying to set her up with.

"He needs concrete evidence that she's no longer fit to be a teacher."

"Forget it. I'm not getting involved in teacher politics on another island."

"It's a private school that she teaches at, and they hold their teachers to a very high level of conduct, in the classroom, and in their personal lives."

"I'm glad to know that."

"I'll have the principal give you a call."

"I haven't consented yet," Maile said.

Asher continued to watch the people going to and from the nearby exit. "What's wrong, then?"

"I need a little more reassurance that I won't get involved in some sort of lawsuit."

"There wouldn't be a lawsuit. He just wants a little more information about what happened on the campout."

"Okay, fine. Tell him he can call me tomorrow morning, but not on the weekend. I'm looking forward to a quiet Christmas holiday."

"Great. Thanks."

Asher and Maile smiled at each other. To Maile, it didn't feel entirely sincere.

"Anything else?" Maile asked.

"Sticking with that hairdo?"

Asher really knew how to work on a captive audience. All Maile needed was for it to get evened out a little, but Asher was trying to drum up business for Koni's salon. "Growing it out again."

"Need to lose the split ends for Christmas. A rolled perm or straightened into a little bob would look romantic for New Year's."

"You don't like asymmetric styles? Because the one I had was great." Maile dug out the Italian fashion magazine that was still in her bag and showed a picture to Asher. Somehow, Asher had a way of creating interest in something where there wasn't any originally.

"Yeah, that's nice, for Italy. We're in Hawaii and that's not popular here. Which means something with more sex appeal." Asher found a page in the magazine and tapped her finger on the model's image. "This."

"That?"

"Yes."

"Me?"

"Why not?"

"Forget it."

"Why?"

"Too high maintenance."

Maile was stuck at being indecisive. She liked keeping fashion simple, with inexpensive clothes from the mall, wore little jewelry, and the rare haircut from her mother was good enough. But she needed to look professional for her job interviews, and couldn't show up looking like she'd just got home from backpacking around the world, which she had only a few days before. She also wanted to start dating again, something high on her list of things to do in the coming New Year. Honolulu was as competitive as anywhere, and Maile wasn't getting any younger. With the looks of the women she'd seen at the mall that day, she knew she was lagging behind the competition.

Asher flipped to another page. "What about this?"

"I guess I could..." Maile's phone chimed with a text from her mother.

Getting hungry. Time for kau-kau.

That gave her a way out of the corner she'd been backed into.

"That's my mom. I told them I was bringing dinner home. I better get going."

"You're still moving in with us tomorrow?" Asher asked as they walked to the parking lot. "We're putting up the tree in the evening. If you get there in time, you're welcome to help."

"Planning to. I have a job interview at three, so probably after that." Maile gave an idea some thought. "I bet Koni's is busy right before the holiday?"

"Go ahead and give them a call. It might take several people to get all the work done, but I bet they could fit you in."

"It might take several people..." Maile said sarcastically, once she was inside the car.

Chapter Ten

When Maile got home with the large bag of take-out food, they put everything in serving bowls on the table and dug in. She got all the gossip from Maui that was fit to be heard while they ate. It sounded like every woman on Maui was either pregnant, trying to get pregnant, or busy weaning their babies.

Maile also heard about her Aunt Kelani's life being married to Dave Ota, a retired police detective Maile had met years before. He was Susan's father, and Maile's relationship with him had at times been as contentious as with Susan. But when he met Kelani through Maile, church bells rang.

"I have big news," Maile said, finishing her rice.

"Meet a man while camping?" her mother asked.

Maile thought of the dead body that had been found on the runway. She still hadn't mentioned anything about it to her parents. "In a way."

"Nice fellow?" Ka'uhane asked.

"Not real lively." She picked at the poi she'd brought home. "I have a job interview tomorrow to be a flight nurse. You know, the kind that transport emergency patients from another island to here because they can't be managed elsewhere."

"Sounds important," Ka'uhane said.

"Challenging," her mother said.

"It is. That's why I'm excited about it. I'd be working with a wide variety of critical care and emergency patients. I could put all my skills to good use with a job like that."

"Not gonna fall out of the helicopter, are you?"

"No, Mom. Most of the time they use airplanes and keep the doors closed, so I'm not going to fall out. I promise."

"That's what you said about the Army, that you wouldn't be in a war. Never have told me how you got those scars."

Maile absent-mindedly tugged her shirt down. "They're not a big deal."

"That's for me to decide. How'd you get those?"

"You won't like the answer. I can guarantee that right now," Maile said. Considering the status of her butt, she could risk a few more calories and took the last of the poi.

"I'll keep asking till you tell me."

Maile gave the abbreviated story that she'd developed for civilians, about how there had been an 'incident' with an MRAP, a military ground transport vehicle, during a trip across the Khashraq desert. There had been a 'brief encounter with hostile forces', and she'd been forced to use a gun in defense of their position. There had been a 'small explosion', and her 'minor injuries' needed little more than first aid at the time. What she didn't tell her mother was that she and two others had needed medical evacuation and emergency surgery, the long range result of which was still undetermined. Physically, she was back to normal, except that the possibility of ever having children was low. She was keeping that information to herself.

"So, you see? It's not a big deal, okay? Can we drop it, please?"

"You're going to big job interview looking like that?"

"I know how to dress for an interview, Mom."

"Talking about being too skinny."

"There's nothing wrong with my weight."

"You look tired, girl. Need to eat more meat and get more sleep. Take some lau-lau."

"I might be giving up meat, at least for a while. And I'm going to bed early tonight."

127

"Before midnight?" her mother asked.

"Probably. If you're done nagging me by then."

"Not nagging. Just worried."

"Nothing to worry about," Maile said.

"I thought Asher was fixing your hair today?"

"She's a massage therapist, not a stylist. At least for right now. She's hoping to get a chair in the salon one of these days." Maile took more potatoes. "She wanted to talk about something else, about me moving in with them."

"Still think you can't go to job interview looking like that. All grown up, looking for a grown-up job. You need to look like you deserve it."

Laughing, Ka'uhane excused himself to get the fruit cups they had for dessert.

"I have something I bought in Italy that should perk up my complexion a little. I was thinking you could even up my hair for me?" Maile asked.

"Me? Retired from being family barber."

"I just need you to make both sides the same length."

"Never was any good at it."

"Kenny and I turned out okay. Maybe Kenny not so great, but okay."

"Once I could afford to send him to a proper barber, off he went to Don. Never could get yours right."

"There wasn't much to my haircuts. Once a year, cut the ends off straight across. Nothing complicated about that. You always spent a lot of time on it."

"Straight across was the hard part. Make it crooked one way, then make it crooked the other way. Kept going until you started to whine. Never got it right, not even once."

"It was always crooked?" Maile asked. "I never noticed."

"Every time." Kealoha finished her fruit cup, and looked disappointed there wasn't more. "You're a grown up girl. Time for a grown up hairdo."

"You always took care of the leftovers. You never have told me what you did with the hair."

"No reason to risk kapu," her mother said.

"Yep. No reason to tempt the fates." Maile looked at a batch of her split ends before starting in on her fruit cup. "Maybe I'll go to Koni's tomorrow."

"Better places than there," her mother said.

"I thought she was one of the top salons in town?"

"Go to Don," her dad said. "He's inexpensive and doesn't waste too much time."

"I'm not going back to Don the barber. He's the nicest guy alive, but he knows more about men's hair than women's styles."

"Better than your mother working on you," he said.

"Are there any other Hawaiian shops in town?" Maile asked. "Someone named Domenico would be acceptable."

"Domenico?" her mother asked. "Is that your gladiator barber friend?"

"He wasn't a barber. He was a real hairdresser at a fancy place in Rome. I think I was the wrong type to be his friend. It was easy with him, though. I showed him the picture, he shrugged and said okay, and did it. What's so difficult about that?"

"Go to Don," her dad said. "What could go wrong?"

"A lot."

***

In the morning, a call from the principal of the school Michelle Jones taught at woke Maile. She didn't answer. Jones was someone else's problem, putting her at a low priority in Maile's life. Her entire focus that day was on her job interview, and somehow guiding her dad's new car through rush hour traffic, and eventually back home again, without removing too much paint from the fenders.

She felt under-prepared for her interview while she sat waiting for it to start. She had no references from the only civilian job she'd had, mainly because they'd fired her for another nurse's wrong-doing. That proceeded to courtroom hearings, and finally ended with a large settlement in her favor. She was offered her job back, but had already promised eight years of her life to the Army by then. With almost nothing to show the interviewer, she squirmed in her chair and sat up straight again.

"You can go in now, Ms. Spencer," the receptionist told her. "Good luck!"

Greetings went by in a blur, and when she sat down across from the man, she saw framed photos and a few commendations on the wall behind him. That's why he was so interested in Maile, that he had served in the Army also. He conducted the interview in a no-nonsense way, as was often done in the Army. He'd been able to pull her service records, and relied more on those than anything else. It almost sounded like she'd been hired before she even sat down.

"Can you do a fly-along next week?" he asked, finally slowing down.

"I'm free all week, Sir. Not a Girl Scout in sight."

"Girl Scouts? You liked the Army so well that you decided to become a Girl Scout?"

Maile chuckled. "It would seem so. I took a group on a three day campout earlier this week."

"How many?"

"Seven teenagers and a tweenie. Lucky me."

"Yes, I remember now. Where did that lucky situation take place?"

"We started and ended at Waimanalo Beach. Somehow, we all survived without anyone getting thrown to the sharks." She scolded herself for forgetting she was in a job interview. "Well, that was certainly an inappropriate thing to say."

"Not really. I'm sure it went well."

"How do you know there'll be a patient to transport while I'm there?" she asked, getting the interview back on track. "Can't really fabricate one, can we?"

"No, but you'll get to hang out with the crew in the barn while waiting for something to happen. Is that a problem?"

"Shouldn't be. Hurry up and wait, right?" she said.

"I like you more with each passing minute, Ms. Spencer." He shuffled papers. "When you're not busy transporting patients, there's a call center that's a part of the hospital. Patients call in with questions about their medications or symptoms, and nurses answer them. Is that something you can do?"

"I think so. I'd probably have to take a pharmacology book with me, though, just in case someone asks about a med I'm not familiar with."

"From what I've heard, it doesn't get complicated. Patients just need things explained to the in ordinary English rather than medicalese. I even called once after I had knee surgery. It was like talking to a friend that worked at the hospital. Keep it simple, answer their questions directly, and don't go off on tangents."

"Sounds good, Sir."

She got the contact info she needed, along with where she would meet the flight crew that day, and what she needed to bring. She almost felt as though she'd been dismissed by a superior officer when she left his office, but she was halfway to her dream job.

"Now I need to go move in with Kenny and Asher. Won't that be fun?" she said, guiding the car down the street like a little old lady from Pasadena.

**

131

Maile tasted something extra in the eggnog she'd been given by Asher at the cottage. She'd already helped decorate her parents' tree at their house before bringing three large bags of her clothing to move into the cottage. The last time she saw it at Christmas was days before she went into the Army. Brock Turner had just moved in after her mother had married Ka'uhane and moved into his house, with the intent on running the Manoa House next door. Kenny was still an underclassman in college then, completely detached from how much money Maile was spending to support his unemployed collegiate lifestyle.

Now, Brock was in Las Vegas with his family, her mother was living in retirement with Ka'uhane, and Kenny was a golf pro, with his beautiful girlfriend at his side. The way it was turning out, Maile was still in the same spot as years before, an unemployed nurse working as a tour guide—with no one keeping her company in bed at night.

She gulped her mug of eggnog and poured more, hoping for a numbing buzz to start.

Kenny must've remembered Maile's favorite ornaments, as those were the only ones left to hang on the tree. When it came time to mount the angel at the top, she got the same old one with the broken wing out of its box.

"That's okay, Maile," Asher said. "We bought a new angel,"

"But we've always had this one for the top."

"This one's better," Kenny said.

It was a gaudy thing, with too much glitter and not enough soul, obviously from a Christmas store.

Maile stood back to let them put it up together. Kenny held Asher's waist while she stood on a stepstool to reach the top of the tree. Once the tree was complete, Asher looked at the old angel.

"How'd this get broken?" she asked.

"Maile did that," Kenny said.

"Did not. You broke it when you were running through the house."

"You broke it when you took it away from me."

"Mom wanted it on the top of the tree."

Saving Asher from any further sibling bickering was a call on Maile's phone. Seeing the number for the school principal on Kauai, she slugged back her eggnog and took the call in her bedroom.

"First of all, thanks for sticking with the kids," he said. "Can you explain to me exactly what happened on the trip?"

"With Miss Jones?" She tried to remain impartial as she told the story, but the spiked eggnog had flavored her mind and loosened her tongue. "Once the detective was done with her, he said she could go but not to leave the island. That's the last I saw of her." Then she remembered how Silva had told her she wasn't supposed to leave the island either, but might have to for her new job. "By the way, he told me the same thing."

"She just left without checking on the girls? Just like that?"

"Unfortunately. But I got the idea there was something going on with her, more than what meets the eye. In fact...never mind."

"In fact what?" he asked.

"I should keep quiet."

"If you're concerned about something that might affect the kids in her classes, I'd like to know about it."

"I'm not sure how much it would affect the kids, but from what I've heard..."

"Heard from who?" he asked.

"Asher Kawika'kamaole. She was in Michelle's Girl Scout troop as a kid, and has just moved from Kauai to Honolulu."

"I'm familiar with Asher. She was a student here. How do you know her?"

"She's my brother's girlfriend. Or more like he's her boyfriend."

He laughed. "That's how it always was with her. The rest of us were always in an orbit around her."

"She does have a way of controlling things, however subtly. But she was telling me that Michelle has trouble with men, almost as if it were a deep-seated psychological thing with her."

"All of our staff and faculty need to undergo rigorous interviews and have a chat with a psychologist before the start of each school year, just to make sure they're healthy. I'll have to check on the results of hers. Anything else?" he asked.

"Not that I can think of right now." Maile bit her lip, wondering how much of an affect the eggnog was having on her curiosity. She lowered her voice. "Anything I need to know about Asher?"

"Like you said, she likes to be in charge wherever she goes, a real problem solver. Is she coming back to Kauai?"

"She seems to have carved out a niche in Honolulu for herself."

Chapter Eleven

When Maile went back out to the living room, her brother and Asher were making out on the couch. She backed up as quietly as the old wooden floor allowed and closed herself in her room.

"There's something I can't un-see." She got out some running clothes. "I need a place of my own."

A long run was overdue, and straight up the Manoa Valley was one of her favorites. The forest at the upper part was dark and gloomy, exactly what she needed. It had started to rain, even better. She could tire herself with some trail running, and if she scraped a knee or elbow by stumbling over something, all the better. There was nothing like a lonely run in the rain to set a girl's mind right.

Just as she was cinching the second shoelace, her phone rang with an unknown number.

"Ms. Spencer, this is Detective Silva. Are you available to meet with me?"

"I was just going out for a run, but I have a minute or two to talk."

"I'd like to meet in person, if at all possible?"

Maile checked the time. If she went to the police station downtown to meet Silva, she'd never get in the run she needed. The next two days, Christmas Eve and Christmas Day, would be busy. It was run today or wait until next week.

"Ms. Spencer?"

"What? Oh, yes. I'm trying to decide if I want to talk to a police detective or go for a run in the rain."

"That requires consideration before making a decision?" he asked.

"In fact, it does. Are you at the downtown station?"

"We could meet elsewhere, if you'd like?"

"I live in the Manoa Valley and don't have a car at my disposal. There's a coffee shop near where Manoa Road and Oahu Road meet. It's named Kiki's Diner."

"I can find it. How much time do you need to get there?"

"I'll be there before you are."

Maile took off at a sprint, with a downhill stretch in front of her. It was only a half-mile trek, but she was soaked through to the bone by the time she got there. Getting a couple of bar towels from Kiki, an old friend and co-conspirator in the game of gossip, she dried as best she could in the restroom. Looking in the mirror, she stroked her fingers through her hair to get some control and looked at her complexion. The hint of sunburn she'd gotten on the hiking trip had turned tan, bringing her color halfway back to its natural tone.

When she went back out, Detective Silva was at the counter looking at pastries.

"Am I allowed to buy an officer something to drink?" she asked. "I'm not sure if this is an official interview or not?"

"Half official and half friendly, and the answer is yes, you may. But this time, I insist on buying since I'm the one who called you." He scratched his head. "Since I'm the one who invited you. Not that this is a date."

"That means it's an official interview," she said. "I doubt you're allowed to conduct an interview while on a date."

"Not usually. This time around, it's less about the concept of the communication and more about the grammar."

Maile had lost track of what exactly they were talking about. "Does that mean I have to use good grammar while answering your questions?"

"Only if you feel beholden to."

Maile looked at the pastries in the case. "Beholden?"

"I don't know. The department is asking us to use correct grammar at all times when dealing with the public. The directive used the term beholden, and we're still trying to figure out what exactly that means."

"I think it means the department directive writers are still stuck in the Nineteenth Century."

"Could be."

"As if we, the public, know how to conjugate verbs properly. I think I've made up one or two new uses for a few verbs." Maile thought of what Kenny and Asher were doing on the couch. "In fact...never mind."

"In fact what?" he asked, when they went to the bar to order.

"The reason I went for a run was to get out of the house. You see, my brother and his girlfriend were conjugating one or two verbs on the couch, if you know what I mean."

Silva grinned. "I think I do. Did you slam the door to let them know you'd left?"

"No, I was as quiet as possible, just so they could wonder if I could hear them." It was Maile's turn to grin. "Was that wrong?"

"Devious, but not illegal."

Maile watched as Detective Silva went through an elaborate ordering process for his fancy coffee drink, with a blend of this, a dash of that, and a sprinkle of something else on top of the foam. When it came to her turn to order, she asked for a cup of coffee with cream.

"And one of those biscotti. Those are almond, right?"

"Sure are," Kiki said.

"Two of them, with one in a bag."

While Silva waited for his drink at the far end of the counter, watching closely as the barista performed a miracle of caffeination in a cup, Kiki waved Maile close.

"Who's this guy?"

"Just a detective wanting a little more information about me for his file."

"Information for his file?" Kiki asked.

"I don't know what that means. Just lyrics from a song my mother listens to."

Kiki looked down the length of the counter. "He's cute."

"In a law enforcement way. I've had enough of guys in uniforms to last the rest of my life."

"He's in plain clothes, not in a uniform."

"You know what I mean."

Kiki handed over the plate and small bag. "Open mind, Mai, open mind."

Silva took both of their drinks to a small table toward the front and sat facing the door.

"That's quite the drink you have there, Detective."

"I live it up on Fridays and holidays. I add so much fixin's that it becomes a meal."

"Fixin's?"

"People still say it."

"In nursing homes," she mumbled, taking a sip of her coffee. "What did you want to talk to me about?"

"Michelle Jones is missing."

"So I've heard."

He looked up at her over the mountain of foam on his drink. "How'd you know that? I just found out about that an hour ago."

"I have my sources, which will go unrevealed, at least for now. But please believe me, I have no idea where she might be."

"You don't know if she's still on Oahu or possibly gone home?" he asked.

"No clue. Why do you need to talk to her again? Personally, I've had enough of her."

"I don't have the option of walking away. There are some inconsistencies between the story you gave us, what she gave us, and what the evidence we've found on the body tells us."

"Well, my understanding is that hard evidence is always better than anecdotal," Maile said. "Is there something I can clarify about what I told you the other day?"

"We'll get back to that. What did your source tell you about Jones?" he asked.

"Two sources, actually, and one independently verified what the other told me. I don't know either one very well, but they both seem reliable."

"Okay, fine. For purposes of this conversation, you've qualified them as providers of anecdotal information. What's their impression of Jones?"

Maile took a bite of her crunchy biscotti and chewed. It was a good way of delaying while she thought of an answer. "Considering my impression and the impressions of both of them, my consensus is that she has no sense of kuleana."

"You mean the Hawaiian concept of responsibility toward the land?" he asked.

"Kuleana is more than that. Kuleana can be a sense of responsibility to anything, people, the land, the ocean, the sky, even a culture. But it's the sense of respect that drives someone's sense of responsibility."

"How does that relate to Jones?" he asked.

"I've been told she's a teacher at a private school for kids with Hawaiian ancestry. That means she has a legal and moral responsibility to see her students do as well as possible, not just in their schoolwork, but in life, right?"

"That's the impression I get of most teachers."

"But as a teacher to little kids, especially to Hawaiian kids that don't always get a fair break in life, she needs to

139

have an even greater sense of kuleana toward them. These islands were once a part of a kingdom, and not all that long ago. Those kids, no matter how dilute their Hawaiian heritage might be, are in many ways owed kuleana from the haoles who came here and took their sense of home away from them." She was feeling her ire right then, and couldn't hold onto it. "Still happening now, with ultra-wealthy buying every available piece of land they can find, leaving real estate priced beyond the reach of the ordinary working Joes and Janes. And if you know anything about ownership of Hawaiian lands, it just didn't work that way in the past. No one owned the land; they had the spirit-given privilege of living on it."

"You've given this a lot of thought, Ms. Spencer."

"Ever since I first started learning about my heritage, and with my mother, that was while I was still in my cradle."

Detective Silva blotted after taking a swig of this drink. "You just said the school she teaches at is private. I can't imagine the kids are suffering all that much."

"It's private, but not in the same way that some private schools operate. They go to school on a sliding scale tuition plan. The idea is that they get an education that shows their ancestry not just in a positive light, but still current. Hawaiians don't want to be relegated to the history books, Detective. Nor do we want to be labeled as a diaspora. We want to be viewed as being just as relevant as everyone else, the same as every other group of people." Maile started to take a drink of her coffee, but she was too wound up to hold the cup without spilling it. "Sorry I got on my soapbox there."

"No, that's alright. I grew up on the Big Island as fourth generation paniolo, you might say. I guess I've never really looked at kuleana from that point of view."

"If you ask me, Jones has lost all sense of kuleana, toward the kids, toward her profession, even toward herself."

"Herself?"

"She smokes like a chimney, eats junk food, and hates exercise with a passion. I've never seen anybody dislike themselves so much as she does herself."

"A lot of people smoke and eat junk. That doesn't mean they hate themselves."

"It just seemed like she had an attitude about it, that she was almost looking for ways to hurt herself passively. The girls have picked up on that, too. None of them like her, and a couple of the older ones are savvy enough to know why."

"You think she's suicidal?" he asked.

"I think if a speeding bus was bearing down on her, she wouldn't step out of the way. I also think it would be chalked up to being a horrific accident."

"I didn't get that impression talking to her a few days ago, nor from her rap sheet."

"She has a rap sheet?" Maile asked.

"There's not much on it. A couple of assaults on men. Charges were dropped in lieu of getting counseling."

"Yeah, that's something else I've heard about her. She doesn't like men at all."

"As in stay off her lawn?" he asked.

"As in stay off her planet, if at all possible."

He chuckled. "I need to get to know her a little better."

"Actually, you probably don't." Maile dropped the second half of her biscotti in the bag with the other one. "You know, we all go a little nutty sometimes, and maybe don't always treat ourselves as well as we should. Eventually we get over whatever it is that's bugging us and move on. We have to if we want to survive. But

141

Jones seems to have lost that sense of kuleana toward herself, and now it's affecting her relationships with everything."

"Everything like the ocean and the sky?" he asked. "I've never been able to wrap my head around that concept."

"Let me see if I can explain another way. Does your mother do any quilting?" Maile asked.

"She has one she's been working on for years. I think it's called a crazy quilt...You don't want to hear about the quilt, do you?"

"Not really. It's not just the tiny lines of stitches that make the quilt so special. It's the time, it's the gossip that's been shared, the friendships that have been forged while making the quilt. If they want to stay warm while they sleep, they could buy a blanket. But they want more than that. During all the time of making it, they develop a sense of kuleana, toward each other, toward that quilt, and to the activity of quilting. It becomes a very special moment in their lives, something that wouldn't have happened otherwise." Maile took a sip of her coffee, wondering if her lecture was making any sense. "Like soldiers that have trained together for months, even years, and then fight together in combat. They've forged a bond, and have an exceptionally deep sense of responsibility toward each other. They'll suffer any manner of wound or injury to rescue one of their own that's gone down."

"From what I've heard, you know a thing or two about that," he said.

"Maybe," she said quietly. "Anyway, Jones seems to have lost that sense of kuleana toward teaching and to her students that teachers need to survive in their professions. That's what makes teaching so important."

"Your mother deserves an award," Silva told her.

"Why?"

"For how she raised you to believe things like that."

Maile chuckled. "Detective, it took a village to raise this idiot. You said there was a second thing you wanted to talk to me about?"

"Yeah. I was going to beat around the bush and toss out a couple of compliments about how attractive I've always thought you were, but that seems a little lame right now."

"I'm sorry?" she asked.

"You don't remember, but we've met a couple of times before."

"We have?" Maile searched her memory for his face and name, but nothing came to her.

"I was a patrol officer when Detective Ota was still on HPD. He was the one who encouraged me to study for detective grade."

"How did we meet?"

"Maybe you remember the time when you were arrested in a restaurant while having dinner with some Middle Eastern prince, and I was one of the arresting officers?" he asked.

"How could I ever forget one of the most embarrassing moments of my life?"

"The other time was when you were arrested in a hotel lobby, Ota being the lead officer that day, also."

"And you were one of those officers?"

He nodded. "I was the one who put the hat on you so you wouldn't be recognized as we led you out. Brock Turner was the other officer."

"Yes, him. Why didn't you give me a call back then? I'm sure Ota would've given you my number. Unless it's against departmental rules?"

"Officially, I wasn't the arresting officer, so I could've called. But there was a department-wide unwritten and unofficial directive that went around about you being hands-off."

"Why me?" she asked.

"You belonged to Turner and no one else."

Maile cocked her head. "I belonged?"

"Once all the legal investigations concerning you were cleared, he'd be able to move in."

"Makes me feel like a gazelle on the African plains being stalked by a lion. Once I got tired, all the lion had to do was grab me for a tasty meal."

"Then you left town and threw all his best laid plans into chaos."

"He seems to have found a suitable replacement," Maile said. She thought of the time a few months before when she went to Las Vegas and watched him deal with his nagging, demanding wife. "He got what he deserves, anyway."

"What about now?" Silva asked, while fidgeting with his coffee cup.

"What about now what?"

"Are you involved?"

"I'm involved with people in a case concerning a dead body that you are investigating."

"But later?"

"I wouldn't want you to risk the integrity of your investigation by taking me off your list of witnesses too quickly. Or suspects, whatever I am."

"Later, once the investigation is complete?" he asked.

"We'll have to see. Whatever you do, don't take a lesson from Turner's playbook. That didn't work out so well for a lot of people."

Chapter Twelve

Maile had grown up in the little Manoa Valley cottage, and never before realized how thin the walls were until the morning of Christmas Eve. When she heard Kenny and Asher vowing their love for each other for the second time, Maile made a point of clearing her throat and walking heavily across the floor on the way to the bathroom. When she heard giggling, she slammed the bathroom door shut.

"Supposed to be my cottage," she muttered. She decided to extend her visit to the bathroom by locking the door and taking a long shower, and anything else she could think of to do while she was in there. When she was finally done and opened the door, Asher was there, wrapped in a bed sheet, smiling nervously.

"I thought you were never going to finish," she said, ducking past Maile to hurry in for her turn.

That brought a smile to Maile's face and somehow made the day a little brighter, despite the rain falling outside.

Getting to the coffeemaker first meant she was able to control how the coffee was made, and according to house rules, whoever made the coffee got the first cup. There was going to be order in the Spencer cottage, even if a stranger had invaded it.

When she heard them again, this time all the way from the kitchen, Maile finally figured it out. They were being deliberately loud, just to force her out.

Refilling her mug and turning off the coffeemaker, she went back to her room to pack her things.

"I can play that game, also," she muttered as she closed two suitcases and her backpack, all crammed with her clothes.

When she went back to the living room, she tried getting the desk drawer open again. It was still locked, even though her brother had promised to find the key for it.

"Kenny! If you have a minute, I still need the key for the desk!" She waited a moment for an answer. "Kenny? Did you hear me?"

It was five minutes before he came out, dressed in shorts and his T-shirt inside-out. "You need it right now?"

"I've been asking you for it for a week."

He yanked on the drawer, but it didn't budge. "What's so important in the desk that you need to get into it right now?"

"My keys."

"What've you been using for the cottage?" he asked.

"Mom's key, and I need to give it back to her."

Kenny yanked on the desk drawer again. "Where's the key for the drawer?"

"That's what I want from you. Where is it?"

"Probably locked in the drawer."

"Really?" Maile tisked. "You find that logical?"

"What's not logical is trying to get into a locked desk drawer so early in the morning. I still don't know why you need to get your old keys if you already have a key?"

"Because I'm using Mom's key and she wants it back."

Asher showed up, once again wrapped in the bed sheet. "Why are we getting up so early?"

"I couldn't sleep because of all the noise," Maile said.

"What noise?" Asher asked.

"I heard something that sounded like a cat in heat having its tail stepped on." Maile did her best not to snicker. "Kenny, do you know where the key is or not?"

He gave the drawer one last yank. "Probably locked inside the drawer. Where else would it be?"

"What do your keys look like, Maile?" Asher asked, when Kenny went to the kitchen for a butter knife.

"There are six or seven keys on a ring, with some sort of rainbow fob on it. Have you seen them?"

"I didn't know you're lesbian," Asher said.

When Kenny came back with the knife, he snickered as he sat in the chair. "She'd have better luck if she was."

"Shut up, Worm. What makes you think I'm lesbian?"

"The rainbow key ring fob thingie. Why else would you have it?"

"Oh, maybe because this is Hawaii and rainbows are popular here?"

"That means you're not lesbian?"

Maile sighed. "I might be a murderer if Kenny doesn't get the drawer open."

"Forget it. Hire a safecracker." He slapped the butter knife down on the desk. "What's so special about getting your keys?"

"There are keys to the Manoa House on my key ring that I need to use."

"You're going over there so early?" he asked.

"I'm moving over there, so you and Asher can have this place to yourselves."

"Find her keys, Kenny," Asher said as an imperative.

"Just give me your keys to the place," Maile told Kenny.

"Why didn't you say that to begin with?" he said, going back to the bedroom. He came back a moment later with two keys for her. "What do people say? Don't be a stranger?"

Maile noticed Asher watching closely as the keys to the old house next door were handed over.

"Thanks," Maile said, smiling. At least she'd won that battle. "When you have time to pull yourself away from everything else, try to find the key that goes to the desk, okay?"

Maile left her brother and Asher alone by taking her things to the Manoa House next door. She turned on a couple of lights to cheer the place up and inspected the refrigerator. Its emptiness seemed to echo back and forth when she looked inside. She made the plan to wait until both Kenny and Asher were out to raid the fridge at the cottage for the things she'd lugged home from the supermarket. The coffeemaker might come with everything else.

Later, she went to the tour office for a morning meeting, mostly to hand out the Christmas bonuses. Following that was last minute Christmas shopping at the mall. Other than the things she bought during her travels in the previous few months, it was the only shopping she was doing.

There was a children's Christmas chorale at the mall, singing carols almost continuously while she was there, more than a few of the young voices cracking into their preteen years. The massive tree was brightly decorated with all manners of ornamentation, this year's theme evidently being animals. After a second mug of peppermint mocha at a different coffee kiosk, and feeling like her heart was about to burst from all the caffeine she'd had that day, Maile went back to the giftwrap area and got the few things she'd bought.

It was her first Christmas at home since before serving in the Army, and she was trying to reach back in time and recapture the old magic that she'd felt in the past. But neither the colorful tree, the cheerful voices, the decorations, nor getting stoked on caffeine brought her the same jolly sense of tidings. The distance of foreign service and the horror of war had somehow taken a bite from the seat of the pants of holiday celebrations.

When she got home, she changed out of shopping clothes and took the gifts next door. The cottage was empty, Kenny's golf clubs were gone, and the bathroom smelled like perfume. That meant he was playing a round of golf somewhere, and Asher had gone to work. Maile had the place to herself.

The house hadn't been tidied and the breakfast dishes were soaking in the sink. Asher wasn't any better at keeping house than Kenny was. She wanted to peek into their room to see if the bed had been made, but somehow kept her hand off that doorknob. She turned on the lights of the tree and put their gifts below. Examining the others, she shook a few, listening for rattles or thumps. One thing that was missing was the small box that she and her mother were expecting Kenny to give to Asher the next day.

The last thing she did was try to break into the desk drawer. The butter knife had been bent out of shape, and no amount of persuasive tugging got it open. Maile found a paperclip and stuck that in, trying to pick the lock. After bending the tip in elaborate shapes, the end finally broke off inside the key hole. Looking closer, she could just see the broken end of the paperclip poking out.

"Well, that didn't help."

Feeling like a thief, Maile found Asher's eyebrow tweezers in the bathroom to use to pluck out the paperclip. She gave them a close look as she went back to the desk.

"Wow, these are fancy. Nothing but the best for her eyebrows, by golly."

Maile spent a few minutes trying to coerce out the piece of wire stuck in the lock. Once she got it free, she looked at the tips of the tweezers. The ends were bent and dingged, no longer useful as tweezers.

"Oops."

With one last attempt at the lock with the paperclip, she gave up. Instead of replacing the tweezers in the bathroom, she tucked them into a pocket, with the plan of replacing them with new ones later.

Maile retraced her steps by turning off the lights and the tree, and went back to the Manoa House next door. Taking a place on the couch with a book, she was unable to get the nap she wanted. Hoping the book might offer a distraction from her thoughts, she read half a page at a time until she gave up. There was still a little too much caffeine in her system to settle down.

The Manoa House hadn't been used as a residence for decades. It was more of a gathering place for Hawaiians, and served as a library and simple museum. The kitchen was bare necessities, used only when there was a function at the house, mainly monthly meetings, or the occasional wedding reception. The old bedrooms served as office space and display rooms, and the living room was the meeting hall.

Her mother had always had the chore of keeping the old house clean. She had no idea of who was doing that now, and wondered if Kenny had hired someone to come in occasionally. Getting out the old vacuum, she pushed that around the house until she was in a sweat. Then she tackled the bathroom, which seemed clean. She wiped down the counter and cleaned the mirror anyway.

Plunking down on the couch again, she focused on her book. She was almost asleep when Asher came home. Barely five minutes passed when there was a knock at the back door as Maile had expected. She'd already discovered the missing tweezers.

"Come in, Asher!"

"Sorry about this morning," the girl said, sitting down in a formal wing chair that faced the couch Maile was on. Her dark roots now hidden again, meaning Asher had spent time in a chair at Koni's salon having her hair done that day.

"Don't worry about it."

"Thin walls."

"Yep."

"We should've known to keep the noise down," Asher said.

"No way of knowing. I never knew sound went right through them so easily until, well, recently."

"We've heard you a couple of times."

"Me? I'm pretty sure I don't snore that loud," Maile said.

"No, crying."

"Oh. Sorry if it bothered you. Another benefit of me moving out is that you won't have to hear any more of it."

Maybe Asher hadn't discovered her tweezers were missing, and was there with something else on her mind.

"You don't have to move out, Maile."

"I'd forgotten how crowded it gets over there, especially in the morning."

"Yes, only one bathroom..." Asher stopped to look out the front window. "Somebody's here."

Maile looked and recognized the man behind the steering wheel. "Oh, him."

"He's kinda cute. Who is it?"

"Police detective investigating the death at Bellows the other day. Probably here with more questions."

The rain had stopped by then. Detective Silva took his time getting out of the car and going toward the cottage.

"They haven't found the guy that killed him?" Asher asked.

"There's not much evidence, except for what I've told him. He's looking for the two scout leaders to talk to.

Both of them have disappeared, which doesn't help his investigation."

They stopped watching as he got to the front porch of the cottage. Maile still got a surprise when he knocked on the door. Maile went to the front door of the house she was in and called him over to the right place.

"I'll leave you guys alone," Asher whispered before she went through the large house to leave through the back door.

Maile straightened her clothes and fluffed her hair before opening the door. "Detective Silva, what brings you to Manoa Valley two days in a row?"

"You do, Ms. Spencer. Do you have time to talk?"

"Of course. Come in."

He looked down at his feet, a signal that he didn't want to take his shoes off. "Maybe we should talk on the porch?"

"Okay with me."

There were two lawn chairs on one side of the porch, with holiday decorations around the door. When she went out, Maile plugged in the strands of lights that circled the windows and stretched across the front eave. He waited for her to sit before he did. That's when she realized her skills as a host had failed her by not offering something to drink. With nothing in her refrigerator, there was little to offer.

"How can I help you, Detective?"

"I expected to find you at the other house."

"Yes, well, it got a little crowded in the cottage, so I moved over here, at least until I can find a real place to live." She explained what the Manoa House was, and that it wasn't really set up to be used as a residence. "It'll be worth having to sleep on the couch, just so I can have the bathroom to myself."

"Bathrooms are very important to women," he said.

"Yep, sure are. But I doubt you came here to talk about bathrooms."

"Not really. Most of the evidence in the Bellows Airfield case has been collected. I have a positive ID on the victim. Are you familiar with a man named Leo Brown?"

Maile gave the name some thought. "I've never met many Browns. Your predecessor, Detective Ota, could tell you about one of his informants named Lefty Leo. It was something like that, anyway."

"I knew Lefty. The dead man wasn't him." He showed her a blow-up of a driver's license photo. "Does this fellow look familiar?"

In peculiar ways, it did. "I think that's the guy that tried frightening us the other night at the beach. Who is it?"

"The dead man." He found another photo, this one of mug shots, complete with identifying numbers below. "What about this fellow?"

Maile took the picture and gave it a close look. "Looks like the same guy."

"It is. Leo Brown wasn't a decent fellow, in a lot of ways. He left behind a four-page rap sheet listing every petty crime known to the justice system. Somehow, he spent very little time behind bars."

"So, what's that mean? He was an all-around jerk that liked scaring kids? Or did he have something else in mind that night?"

"He was a jerk, but he limited his abuse to muscling women. He seemed to have some limit. He'd go far enough to be mean, but not so far that he risked lengthy imprisonment."

"Okay, so he was a smart jerk. That doesn't answer how he found us at the campground that night."

"I have some ideas about that." Next, he got out three printed black and white security camera images that had been blown up to the point of being slightly blurry. The first was of a woman in a store looking at a display case. The second was of the same woman at a cash register, while the third was an exterior shot outside a store of someone leaving with a bag. "Does she look familiar?"

She looked closely at it before handing it back. "A little."

"It's you, isn't it?"

"Maybe."

"If I brought in an evidence collection team, would they find clothing in your possession that matches what's in those images?"

"Yes, but those are commonly worn, inexpensive running clothes."

He gave her another image. "Here's one of her face. It's grainy, but there's something a little unusual about her hair."

"Yeah, it's lopsided."

"Like yours."

Maile pushed her hair back from her face, but the longer stuff at one side seemed to mock her by falling forward again. She sighed. "Yes, like mine."

He took out something else for her to look at. "Courtesy of store management, I was able to pull all the credit card purchases made at the store within an hour in time of these images. I discovered you made a purchase there, including several items that would be used for camping. The time of purchase matches the time stamp on the video."

"Yeah, I made a purchase there. So what?"

"Remember the clerk?"

"I remember him well. Complete jerk...wait a minute." Men's faces flashed through her mind for a moment. "That clerk is the same as the dead man we found at the campground?"

"It appears so. When he never showed up for work for a couple of days, and was never seen at his apartment building, his boss finally filed a missing persons report. Because of the name, it came to my desk. When I went to his apartment, mail was piling up and old dishes were in the sink growing mold. To me, that means he hadn't been there in a while. As far as I'm concerned, the man that bullied you and the kids that night at the campsite is the same man that you bought camping gear from at that store, and is the same as the dead man that was found on the runway at Bellows with the dent at the back of his head. All three men have been positively ID'd as the same man."

Maile bit her lip, thinking. "And I'm a common denominator in all three. I met him at the store, during the night, and again saw him in the morning when we found his body. I know that sounds incriminating, but..."

"It's very incriminating," he said. "I have an eyewitness that has stated you chased the man, and have in evidence an object with damage on it that matches the injury on the back of the man's head, and that object, a flashlight collected from your tent, has your fingerprints on it. I can't think of anything more incriminating that that, Ms. Spencer."

"Except that I didn't kill him," Maile said. She sat back in her chair and folded her arms over her chest.

"I'm inclined to believe you, but I need some sort of reasonable explanation to keep me from not taking you in and the DA filing formal charges."

"I don't know what to tell you, Detective, other than your eyewitnesses are girls who were just a little more than histrionic at the time. Girls can be like that."

"To the DA, that would sound like passing the buck. Don't forget that Jones was the one who said you chased the man from the campsite. You are a runner, right?"

"Okay, what about the other flashlight we had at the campsite? The one that was left out all night for latrine use, but somehow disappeared by morning? Was that ever found?"

He used a single fingertip to scratch his head. "Not yet. I'm thinking of sending another team back to Bellows for a more comprehensive search."

"You're convinced the murder weapon was a flashlight? Not a tire iron, baseball bat, billy club, or any other of a hundred things that could be used to whack someone in the back of the head?" she asked.

"The dent in his head matches the rim on your flashlight perfectly, and considering there's damage to your flashlight, well…"

"Don't you need to collect blood or skin cells from the weapon to tie it to the victim? Because the other flashlight we had was just like mine. Different brand but same size and shape. Was there any blood on mine?" she asked, knowing full well there wasn't.

"None, but it could've been cleaned."

"There should be dirt or oxidation in the damaged part of mine. It's been like that for a long time. If I had cleaned it, the dirt would be gone, right?"

He scratched his head again. "We did find oxidation upon microscopic exam, but the crack in the lens looked new."

"Mind if I go back to the campground and look for the other flashlight? That's what you need, right?"

"That would be the worst thing you could do. If you happened to find it, there would be no chain of evidence. Just the fact that you showed up waving something around claiming it was the murder weapon would be dismissed as a fabrication."

"I suppose so. What can I do to convince you I didn't kill that man?"

"But you don't need to convince me of your innocence. It's my job to collect evidence of your guilt."

"You've decided I'm guilty?" she asked.

"Only more involved than I originally thought."

"Am I a suspect in his murder? What was his name again?"

"Leo Brown. Not a suspect quite yet. I can't very well ask you for an alibi, since there are multiple persons stating you were at the scene at and around the time of his death, including you."

"Those multiple persons also spent the night inside the tent with me. They're my alibi."

"Did any of them go with you as you followed Brown down the runway that night?" Silva asked.

"No. That was just two or three minutes, though. That's the only time during the night that at least a couple of the kids weren't with me."

"Those would be the most critical minutes, at least to the DA."

"What was my motive? Just because he bullied us a little in the middle of the night? That wasn't much more than a stupid prank. People don't kill each other over something like that."

"Not usually, no. Tell me, what did the two of you talk about at the store? There's no audio, but it looks as though there were thirty seconds of conversation about something?"

"He was making wisecracks about Girl Scouts camping outdoors, sexist stuff like that. Nothing worth killing him for."

"Did he know where you were bringing the girls?" Silva asked.

"I think I mentioned it at one point. Stupid me, letting a jerk like that know where we were camping. I've learned that lesson."

"That's all he needed. But I wouldn't think of it as your fault." He looked up at her from his notes. "Unless it is? Did you murder him, Ms. Spencer?"

"No. Sorry, you'll have to keep looking. What about Michelle Jones?" Maile asked. It was reaching, but she needed something to offer.

"What about her?"

"Why couldn't she have taken a swing at the back of his head? She had access to the other flashlight, apparently what you think was a potential weapon. She also had the opportunity."

Silva flipped back through his notes. "She stated that during your confrontation with Brown she started to come out of her tent but went back in again. Did you notice if that was true?"

"If I have the timeline right, I would've been following him then," Maile said.

"Could be, could be. That's one of the things I want to talk to her about."

"Is that enough to start investigating her as a potential culprit?" she asked.

"I already have been. She's getting more attention that you are, Ms. Spencer. The problem is that I can't seem to find her. I'd love to interview her, but I need to find her to do that."

"I wish I could help you, but I haven't a clue of where she might be. I specifically heard you tell both of us not to the leave the island. As you can see, I'm still here. Have you tried calling her?" Maile asked.

"I got her number from one of the parents, and other parents verified it as correct. Whenever I call, there's no answer and it doesn't go to message. Either her phone is turned off or she doesn't want to be bothered with answering calls. I've been to her hotel room a couple of times, and she doesn't answer her door. As far as I can tell, she hasn't rented a car, so there's no vehicle to watch for. Whatever she's up to, she's busy with it."

"Or she doesn't want to be found."

"You haven't heard from her?" he asked.

"Why would I? We're not friends. We'd never met each other before Monday morning. At this point, I'm a little sorry I ever met anyone from that group, or took them on that hike. The money my company made from it just hasn't been worth all this."

"I wouldn't guess so, but I've never been a small business owner."

"Like to buy mine?"

"I doubt I could afford it."

Maile took a deep breath and blew it out. "Are you taking me to the slammer?"

"Slammer?"

"That's what Nancy called it. She was the youngest one on the hike."

"The imaginative one?"

"Right."

They watched as Kenny parked in the driveway and went to the front porch of the cottage, his golf bag over his shoulder. He took one look at Detective Silva and kept going into the house before Maile could call him over to make introductions.

"My brother, the social butterfly," Maile said. "Is there anything else? Or am I free to go? Do you guys really say that? You're free to go?"

"We do when they are."

"Am I?"

"Are you what?"

"Free to go?"

"You're already here, aren't you?"

Maile gave the detective a long look. "Am I free to roam the city streets of Honolulu without being concerned about the police?"

"Just don't leave the island. And Ms. Spencer? Consider yourself lucky."

"Because I'm not in a jail cell?"

"As a veteran Army officer, you have something of a 'get out of jail free' card. But even luckier than that is the fact that the .357 magnum we found beneath the man was loaded."

"It was definitely his?" Maile asked.

"His prints were on it, and it was from the store stock. Like you said that day, that could've been a mess."

"The thing is, I never noticed him carrying it. It was dark, but I looked him up and down once or twice, shining my light over him. Seems I would've noticed something like that."

"We did find one stray latent print on the weapon, which complicates things a little for me."

"Well, it wasn't mine," Maile said.

"No, it wasn't. We compared it to yours and it's not even close."

"Is that my alibi?"

"Not one you can rely on, no," he said.

"But you have no idea who the print belongs to?"

"There's nothing in any of the most common print systems."

"But you have a guess, don't you?" Maile asked.

"No comment."

"You think the print belongs to Michelle Jones?"

"No comment."

"And you came here today to see if she was here?"

"I'd say no comment again, but it loses its impact after a while. I am hoping you might have something that belonged to her? Anything that she might've handled?"

Maile shook her head. "I can't think of anything. All the gear she used, the tent, sleeping bag, everything has already been returned to their proper owners."

"That was the local Girl Scout troop, right?"

"Yes, but I don't know which one. I'm sure some of the older girls would know."

He closed his notebooks and put away his pen. "Thank you very much. One last question. You haven't heard from either Jones or Mahoe?"

"My answer is still the same, which is no. Sorry. I'm not sure they ever got my personal phone number. If they wanted to contact me, they'd have gone through the tour office, and I haven't heard anything from either of them."

When he stood to leave, Maile stood with him.

"Big plans for tomorrow?" he asked.

"You just said you had only one more question. That's two."

"Does that mean if I ask if you're busy on New Year's Eve, I wouldn't get an answer?"

Maile smiled at him. "No comment."

Chapter Thirteen

When Christmas day finally rolled around, Maile, Kenny, and Asher had an early gift opening. They gave each other mostly meaningless gifts, until Kenny made a show of giving Asher a small box. Spotting that, Maile tried leaving them alone, but was pulled back onto the couch by Asher. The ribbon and paper on the box was carefully removed, and she gave a schoolgirl squeal when she slipped the diamond engagement ring on her finger, finally making the deal official.

What caught Maile's eye was the Mount Rushmore of diamond engagement rings on Asher's finger. With all the financial bailouts and seed money she'd donated to Kenny's bank account over the years, Maile figured she helped finance the ring—if not the entire relationship.

'Paying for the benefits of being engaged, but I'm the one sleeping alone at night,' she thought, as she looked at Asher's hand.

"Dang, little brother. You have good taste."

"I left him enough hints," Asher said.

After dressing at her house, Maile went back over to the cottage, ready to go to her parents' house with the others. Kenny was standing near the bathroom, looking apologetic while Asher rummaged around in kits and baskets for something. She was done dressing, her makeup on, and one section of her hair braided while the rest had been curled. She'd gone all-in with her image for the holiday, but Maile sensed a meltdown looming.

"Where are they?" Asher demanded as she dug into another kit.

"What's she looking for?" Maile asked Kenny.

"Some fancy tweezers."

"Oh." Maile figured it was a bad time for a confession. Even though she'd gone to a couple of drug stores looking for a matching type, she never was able to replace the fancy brand that she'd damaged on the desk. "I'll be waiting outside."

There were more gifts at their parent's house, again mostly meaningless. Asher showed off her new ring, followed by Ka'uhane playing Christmas tunes on his ukulele for a while. The best part of the day was the giant brunch their mother had made. Everybody's favorite was on the table, even Asher's. Somehow, Kealoha had been able to learn her soon-to-be daughter-in-law's favorite dish. When football was turned on one TV, and *It's a Wonderful Life* on another, Maile decided to escape to the guest bedroom.

She logged onto the computer, which had amazingly slow speed. She wasn't there just to surf, but to look for anything on the internet about Michelle Jones. There wasn't much, only a few mentions about teaching at the private school on Kauai. She found the social media site for the school, which looked carefully maintained to project a proper image. The site made no mention of her at all, or were there any pictures of her participating in school activities.

She found the troop of Girl Scouts that Michelle led, and again, there were no images of her or Mahoe, and not many of the girls. It turned out that the troop wasn't much bigger than the number of girls that went on the hike that week, which might've been why they took the underaged Nancy as a member.

"They stayed at the Kuhio Palms, wherever that is," she muttered, looking for the hotel's website. Maile thought she knew every hotel in Waikiki, at least what block it might be on. With that name, it must've been on Kuhio Avenue. "Oh, there it is. Mountain view facing the golf course."

163

It was a no-frills place, with no access to the beach, obstructed views of both the mountains and the ocean, no pool or tennis courts, not even a spa. It was twelve stories of rooms with beds, a rooftop patio, and not much else.

"Hey, I'm going out for a while," she told the others. They were all half-asleep in the living room, now watching a *Home Alone* marathon.

"Where are you going on Christmas?" her dad asked.

"Just to have a quick business meeting."

"Dressed like that?" her mother asked.

"What's wrong with how I'm dressed?"

"At least put on your new sweater."

It was the same thing every year, with being a contestant in the Ugly Christmas Sweater competition. Her mother insisted on giving Maile a sweater, even though they lived in the tropics and that day's temperature was close to eighty degrees. She pulled on her Rudolph sweater and fluffed her hair.

"Taking my car?" her dad asked.

"Planning on taking the bus."

He tossed her the keys. "Take the car."

"Yeah, Mai, take Dad's car," Kenny said, snickering.

"What's so funny?" Ka'uhane asked.

"Maile's not the best driver."

"I keep hearing that," Ka'uhane said. "So far, so good."

"I've been driving it lately," Maile said. "It still has all its paint."

The good thing about taking her dad's car was that she could take off the sweater and leave it locked inside while she went into the hotel.

If she wanted to get Michelle's room number from reception, she'd need a clever story to tell them, since personal information about guests was generally kept private. She decided to go with a version of the truth. For that, she needed to take the sweater with her into the hotel lobby, along with a plan that was still hatching as she walked toward the receptionist.

"Hi. My name's Maile Spencer. I'm the owner of Manoa Tours. You have a guest staying here named Michelle Jones that took a three-day camping tour with us earlier this week." She held up the sweater for display. "Unfortunately, she left behind an article of clothing that I need to return to her."

"Her room number?" the receptionist asked, clacking her glossy nails on her computer keyboard.

"That's what I'd like to know from you."

"I'm very sorry, but I can't give out information about our guests."

"Does that mean she's still a guest here?"

The receptionist clacked a few more times. "She extended her stay until tomorrow."

That was an inch closer and easier than she thought it would be.

"Oh, well, that's good for me that she hasn't gone home to Kauai yet. I can give the sweater to her in person today, rather than have to mail it to her." Maile made a show of carefully folding the sweater on the counter in front of the receptionist. "I'd really like to give this back to her, and tell her how much fun we all had."

"I'm sorry, but I can't…"

"You know how it is when you have a guest that you like so well you get a little attached to. You just hate to see them leave at the end of their stay."

"Yes, occasionally."

"Well, Ms. Jones is one of those kinds of guests for us at Manoa Tours."

When the receptionist began typing again, Maile hoped she was making headway. "She was here with a group."

"Right. Girl Scouts from Kauai. She's their merry leader. The whole thing was a ton of fun."

The receptionist looked more at her computer screen than she did at Maile. "I don't know…"

"Aunt Maile?" someone right behind Maile said.

Maile looked at who might be calling her that. "Nancy! You're still here?"

"Dad and I decided to stay a couple days extra and have Christmas here." The girl was dressed for the beach and had a towel and woven mat in her hands. "Why are you here?"

"I'm looking for Miss Jones." Maile tried hiding the sweater behind her back. The kid was too devious to let a Rudolph sweater pass by without making a comment. "I think she's here for another day or so, too."

"She's on our floor. What's the deal with the sweater?" Nancy asked, trying to see behind Maile's back where the sweater was being hidden from her.

Maile nudged the nosy kid away from the receptionist. "Where's your dad?"

"Gift shop. What're you doing with the sweater?"

"Nothing. What room is Miss Jones in? I need to see her about something."

"I'll tell you her room number if you tell me what you're doing with the sweater," Nancy said.

The kid drove a hard bargain. Maile took her further away from the receptionist. "It was a Christmas gift. I was wearing it, but it's too warm for a sweater today."

"Like, duh. It's the tropics."

"Hey! My mother gave me this."

"Put it on so I can see it."

"Tell me Miss Jones room number first."

"No, you put it on first. That's the deal," Nancy said.

"You can't change…If I put it on, you'll tell me her room number?"

"Okay."

"Promise me," Maile said.

"I promise."

Just as Maile pulled the sweater over her head, Nancy's father, Steve, walked up to them.

"Nice to see you again, Maile. What brings you here on Christmas?" he asked.

"Well, I wanted to see Miss Jones for a moment, but I don't have her room number." Maile shot Nancy a playful smirk. "Nancy was just going to tell me."

"Six-oh-five, just down the hall from us. I like the sweater."

"Thanks. I was just telling your daughter that my mother gave it to me."

"It's very pretty," Nancy said, now smiling.

"Too bad it's too big for you, or I'd give it to you, so you could wear it to the beach."

"Oh, it's much too nice to get sand into it. Would you like to come with us?" the girl asked.

"I should talk to Miss Jones first. Which beach are you going to?"

"Waikiki, like du..." Nancy stopped short when Maile shot her a glare. "Straight over there a few blocks."

"Maybe I'll drop by later. Don't forget to put on sunscreen and drink lots of water." Maile needed to get back at the girl somehow. "Oh, and Nancy? Be careful of the low-flying ducks at the beach. They're dangerous this time of year."

While Nancy looked at Maile with confusion in her face, her father shared a knowing look with Maile.

"Low flying ducks?" the girl asked.

"Yeah. They eat a lot of fiber." Maile smiled from ear to ear. "That's the dangerous part, so be sure to keep your hat on."

She watched as Steve and Nancy walked toward the exit, the girl going on about how there weren't ducks in

Waikiki, and asking what was the dangerous stuff she had to watch out for.

Now Maile had to get past the receptionist while wearing the sweater she had said belonged to Michelle. Hotels were protective of their guests, and often didn't like it when visitors went straight up to the room floors, so she had to sidestep the concierge and pretend she belonged in the passenger elevator. Once she was on her way up, she pulled the sweater off again.

"At least I wore this one for a few minutes."

She went down the hall to Room 605 and knocked. A *Do Not Disturb* sign hung from the doorknob, meaning Michelle was in. Or not. Not much made sense when it came to Michelle Jones, or her Girl Scouts.

Other guests passed her going one way or the other while Maile knocked and waited again. When she spotted a housekeeper down the hall, she decided to push her luck. The worst thing that could happen was that she'd get kicked out a hotel. If she were lucky, she might finally find the Girl Scout leader that was playing hide and seek with the Honolulu Police Department.

"Pardon me. I'm supposed to meet Miss Jones in six-oh-five, but she's not answering. Have you made up her room yet today?" she asked the housekeeper.

"Not while the sign is on the door, no."

"It's been there all day?"

"Since yesterday," the housekeeper said. She took a set of towels into a room and lowered her voice when she came back out. "Tell you the truth, I hate it when guests close themselves in like that. It's always a big mess to clean once they finally come out."

"Nobody's seen her since yesterday?" Maile asked.

The housekeeper pushed her cart to the next room. She went in to inventory the minibar and came back to get what needed to be replaced. "Not since Thursday, which is strange, because she extended her stay a day or two. Why stay in a Waikiki hotel if she's not going to see the sights?"

"Does anyone actually know if she's inside the room?"

"Where else would she be?"

Maile went to the next room with the housekeeper. "Maybe she went home?"

"Why would she extend her stay if she was going home? That doesn't make sense."

"Neither does hiding in a hotel room for several days, especially at Christmas time," Maile said.

They stopped outside Room 605. "I suppose you want me to let you in?"

"No. I want you to go in and make sure she's okay. I'm a little worried about her."

The housekeeper looked at her set of keycards for the doors. "I should get the manager."

"Why waste their time, when all you have to do is knock and announce yourself when going in. If she's there, just apologize, offer fresh towels, check the minibar, and come back out again."

"And if she's not there?"

"Change the towels and wipe off the bathroom counter like you normally would. Not so hard, right?" Maile asked.

"I should call the manager."

"You could be in and back out long before the manager ever got here."

"Still..."

"Do you really want to upset you manager on Christmas Day?"

"Well, no, but..."

"What if she's in there and, you know..." Maile suggested.

"That's what I was just thinking."

"You need to go check on her, to make sure she's okay," Maile prompted.

While the housekeeper got her minibar checklist ready, Maile got a ten-dollar bill from her coin purse. She put that in the jar of pens on the cart as a tip.

The housekeeper snatched it up. Using her master keycard, she opened Michelle's room door and went in. Maile tried seeing into the room from the hallway. What she didn't notice was the smell of cigarette smoke.

The housekeeper came back a moment later with towels and drinking glasses. "Not there."

"You looked in the bathroom?"

"Everywhere she could fit. No clothes, no bags, nothing personal at all. She's moved out."

"Moved out?" Maile asked.

"Yeah, packed her stuff and left. Now I have to make up the room every day, even if no one is in there."

"Sorry." Before Maile left, she had one last question. "She was here with some Girl Scouts. How many are still here?"

"The cute little one is still here with her dad, but the others have gone home." The housekeeper stacked fresh sheets for the room. "Funny thing, though. There was another scout leader lady with them, and she extended, also."

"Miss Mahoe?" Maile asked.

"Right."

"She came back early on Monday morning with a sprained ankle."

"She wasn't limping when I saw her," the housekeeper said. "Not all week."

"When was the last time you saw her?" Maile asked.

"Thursday, I guess. She also has a *Do Not Disturb* sign on her door."

"That's the same day Jones disappeared," Maile said.

"Think we should look in her room also?" the housekeeper asked.

"If you don't mind."

"These rooms don't fix themselves, you know."

Maile handed over another ten dollar bill. Mahoe's room was next to Jones's room, and the housekeeper went in. This time, Maile followed her.

"Nothing, just like with your other friend's room," the housekeeper said after she went around the room.

Maile detected something, though. There was the scent of perfume or body spray in the air, strong enough that whoever had been wearing it was recently there. The curtains were closed as if Mahoe had wanted complete privacy. She went to the sliding door to the balcony and held back the curtain to see the view.

She opened the sliding glass door for a better look. The balcony was small, just large enough for two people to sit together. Another building faced the hotel, probably a cheap condo with a lot of bikes, surfboards, and laundry on their balconies. Beyond that was the golf course, the city, and long narrow valleys that led up into the range of mountains that divided the island in half.

As she watched the clouds come over the mountains, she had the strange thought that maybe Oahu was no longer her home, that it was time to move on to a new and different place. Where that idea came from she had no idea, only that it floated in and out of her mind from time to time.

"Miss?" the housekeeper said from the gap in the sliding door. "I'd prefer it if you weren't out there."

Maile came back in, now returning to the world of questions about Mahoe, Jones, Girl Scouts, and a dead man. "Sorry."

Unsure why, she wiped off the door handle that she'd touched. That gave her an idea.

171

While the housekeeper stripped sheets off the bed, Maile quietly went into the bathroom. Nothing personal was there, but the drinking glass had obviously been used. Getting a wad of toilet paper, she wrapped the glass and tucked that into her sweater that was still under her arm. She thanked the housekeeper for her help and left the room. Going back to the cart, she collected the glass that she thought came from Jones's room and tucked that away before hurrying to the elevator. Just as the doors slid open, the housekeeper came out to her cart and Maile waved goodbye.

Chapter Fourteen

Maile wasn't exactly sure why she stole the water glasses from the hotel. She had been wondering if fingerprints had been left behind on them, and how many sets. But what would that mean? So what if Michelle had been a guest in Mahoe's room? Either glass could've been used by the other troop leader, or even any of the kids when they visited. What had made perfect sense a moment before seemed like pointless theft as she went to her car.

Forgetting it was Christmas afternoon, she called Detective Silva.

"Aren't you at a party?" he asked.

"Ate breakfast with my brother and his fiancé, went to church, opened a few gifts, and then ate brunch at my mother's house. That's about as festive as I feel this year. Anyway, to go to a party, I have to be invited to one. Am I interrupting something of yours?"

"I'm investigating a scene. Or at least that's what's going into my report. What's up?"

"Well, I broke a few rules and might've broken a law, but I couldn't help myself. This deal with Jones pulling a disappearing act right when I'm under the same police microscope as her is getting to me."

"First, please don't confess to me what laws you might've broken, because I'll be forced to investigate. Otherwise, what are you up to?"

"I've just come from the Kuhio Palms, the hotel where the troop stayed this week."

"Funny. I was there this morning. Why are you there?"

"I wanted to talk to Michelle Jones for a few minutes, just to see what she had to say about the death of the dead man. And yes, I know that could be confused with interfering with your investigation."

"More than confusing it, it would be considered interference. What did she have to say?" Silva asked.

"She wasn't in. In fact, it looked as though she's moved out."

"How do you know that? Because when I checked with reception, they told me she was booked into that room until tomorrow, just like I asked her to be."

"I had the housekeeper check the room," Maile said.

"How'd you accomplish that?" Silva said. "Without a warrant, she wouldn't let me in. I leaned on her for half an hour, and she never budged."

"Sneaky, I guess. But she'd packed her things and had left. There was nothing personal in the room at all. The same thing with Miss Mahoe, the other Girl Scout leader that came with the troop." Maile bit her lip for a moment. "I might've taken drinking glasses from their bathrooms."

He sighed audibly. "Why?"

"It seemed like a good idea at the time. Is there anything you can use them for?"

"Maybe. Right from the beginning of this investigation, there was something suspicious about those two going missing. You told me originally that Mahoe somehow sprained her ankle and didn't go on the hike, right?"

"Right," Maile said.

"When did she sprain it? On the hike? Because I can't imagine anyone spraining an ankle while walking across sand."

"She didn't get that far. In fact, she never made it to the tour office. I never even met her that day."

"You don't know what Mahoe looks like?" he asked.

"Not at all. I snooped through social media sites for the school and the Girl Scout troop, and there were no pictures of either her or Jones. They weren't even mentioned."

"That's what I found also, when I looked. It's almost as if they're hiding from social media. Are you sure they're actually scout leaders?" Silva asked.

"The girls treated Jones as though she was, and mentioned Mahoe a couple of times."

"There's something peculiar about Mahoe not showing up for the hike, and that limp."

"According to the housekeeper, she wasn't limping when she returned to the hotel that day. She also disappeared on Thursday, the same day that Jones disappeared. But they both extended their room stays until tomorrow. That's strange, right? That seems strange to me."

"To me, too. I'm wondering..." he said but quit.

"Wondering what?"

"If Jones and Mahoe are the same person."

"That certainly puts a twist in your case. But the housekeepers said they saw two different people in two rooms. Even the kids made it sound like there were two different leaders for the troop."

"Yeah, maybe. Where are the glasses now?" he asked.

"I have them. Where are you?"

"Back at Bellows Beach with a team looking for that other flashlight."

"You got CSI people out on Christmas?" she asked.

"I'm making one last sweep, this time with metal detectors and shovels. So far, we've found a rusty horseshoe and thirty-eight cents in pocket change, but we're only halfway done. I've also increased the size of the search field. Where I can't search is in the ocean. If someone had thrown the other flashlight in there, it'd be long gone by now."

"I hope you find something. What do you want me to do with the hotel water glasses?"

"Since you're doing nothing else today, can you bring them to me?"

She thought of the good luck she'd had with her dad's car so far, and wondered if she should push her fate with the car gods, even on a day with thin traffic. "All the way to Bellows?"

"You're taking the bus?"

"I've borrowed a car."

"So, just drive. I figure I'll be here for another two hours or so. I also have a bank robbery to look into. We've had a spate of them on Oahu this week."

"I saw that on TV. The newscasters said something about the thieves needing money for Christmas shopping."

"The perps must have big families. Considering the unusual number of banks and stores that have been hit lately, they've got away with just over a million dollars in cash. All they've wanted is cash. No checks, securities, no jewelry, no merchandise that would need to be fenced."

Maile thought about what he'd said. "Okay, I know nothing about police stuff, but wouldn't that mean they were new at being thieves? If all they wanted was cash, would that mean they didn't know what to do with checks or merchandise?"

"Very good, Ms. Spencer. It means to the police that they don't already have a network of fences to get rid of goods, which means they're rookie criminals. But we're getting sidetracked from Jones and Mahoe."

"I thought you dealt with violent crimes committed against people?" she asked.

"Normally, yes, but I'm lending a hand in running down a few leads in one or two bank holdups."

"Well, I'll be there in about an hour or so."

"Hour? There's no traffic. You could be here in half that time."

"Yeah, well, the faster I drive, the longer it takes me to get somewhere."

"I don't understand," Silva said.

"I'll explain when I get there." Maile chuckled. "If I get there."

Maile needed time to think, more about driving to another part of the island than the death of the sporting goods store clerk. Silva being at Bellows for a while was a reprieve from driving. To give herself time to mentally prepare for the drive, she went to the beach a few blocks away.

Waikiki Beach was busy that day, even if it was Christmas afternoon. It took a few minutes of meandering through the sunbathers before she found Nancy and her father. She stood to cast a shadow over Nancy.

"Oh, you found us! Maybe you should sit next to my dad," the girl offered.

Maile sat next to the girl. "It's you I came to see, Nancy. I'm interested in hearing about your scout leaders."

Nancy looked to her father for permission. "Oh, that Miss Jones has been a pickle. Nobody really likes her much, and she sure doesn't like us. When she came up with the idea to go on that campout, we all thought she was going to start being nice to us."

Maile glanced at Steve for confirmation, and got a nod.

"That's the impression I got also. What about Miss Mahoe?"

"She's okay, I guess."

"We haven't had much contact with her," Steve said.

Maile turned her attention on him. "They are two different people, right? Mahoe and Jones?"

"Oh, yeah. Sort of salt and pepper, you might say."

"Salt and pepper?"

"Jones has dark hair and light skin, and Mahoe has a complexion like yours and light hair."

That was good enough for Maile. "How long have you been a Girl Scout?" she asked Nancy.

"I just started a few weeks ago. The others say I'm way too young."

"Nancy is the right age to be a Brownie, but since we don't have any Brownie Scout troops near us, and the Girl Scout troop being so small, their little troop took her in," Steve said.

"It seems like you hold your own in the group," Maile said.

"When they try pushing me around, I just push back."

"Good for you. I'm more interested in hearing about Miss Mahoe. What's her role in the troop?"

"Not much," Steve said. "Like I said, she barely comes to any of their meetings. Honestly, I'm surprised she agreed to the camping trip."

"Does she have a specific role in the troop?"

"Fiancé officer, whatever that means," Nancy said.

"Fiancé?" Maile asked.

"I think it has something to do with the money."

"Finance," Steve said. "From the sounds of it, they've been running things on a very tight shoestring for quite a while. That's why they had to borrow so much equipment for the campout."

"And all the parents had to pay individually for the kids to come here? It didn't come out of some community coffer?" Maile asked.

"Right. We had to get group rates in a budget hotel to make it affordable. The parents took the offer just to get off Kauai for a few days while the kids camped. Mom and Dad in a hotel room without the kid around, if you know what I mean," Steve said.

"I think I do," Maile said.

"Even I know what that means," Nancy said, accompanying it with an exaggerated eye roll.

"So, the troop is on the ropes, financially speaking?" Maile asked Steve.

"Barely clinging to life. Parents kept shoveling in dues money each month, but there never seems to be any money for activities."

"I thought being a Girl Scout would be more fun," Nancy said.

"I bet it is a lot of fun. I had fun on the campout." Maile chuckled. "Except for finding that man."

"That was the best part of the whole thing," Nancy said, giggling.

"I bet if you guys found new leaders, ones with more experience in outdoorsy stuff, you'd have a better troop."

That brightened Nancy. "Will you be our new scout leader? Please Aunt Maile?"

"I'd think about it, but I live here on Oahu and you girls are on Kauai."

"Yeah, that's right."

Maile stood and brushed sand from the seat of her pants. "Well, I need to go somewhere. You and your dad have fun, okay?"

"As soon as the waves aren't so big, we're gonna try body surfing."

"You've never done that before?" Maile asked.

"Don't know how. Maybe kinda afraid of the water," the girl said.

"Take your dad with you then, and stick together."

"He's more afraid than I am."

Steve shrugged when he stood. "I'll walk you to the sidewalk."

"Be nice to her, Dad," Nancy said when they left her on the beach towel.

"Let me explain about the water," he said as they walked to the sidewalk.

"No need to explain. Some people aren't water people, although since we're on an island surrounded by warm water, that'd be a shame."

"It's a little more than that, a long story. Maybe we could meet for dinner?"

That came from out of left field. "Dinner?"

"This evening?" he asked. "Except that it's Christmas. You probably have plans."

"Mostly hiding from my brother and his fiancé making out on the living room couch." Maile blushed and laughed at herself. "Sorry. Too much information."

"There must be an interesting back story." He glanced back in the direction of where Nancy was on the beach. "Maybe this once you wouldn't mind skipping that and have dinner instead?"

"Anything would be better. I can come to the hotel and wait in the lobby. What time?"

"Seven?"

Somehow, Maile ended up with a date on Christmas after all, even it if was for dinner in a hotel dining room with a dad and his kid. But she still needed to pilot her father's car from Waikiki to Bellows Beach without getting in a wreck.

"No way I'm going over the Pali," she said, getting the car started. She took the older highway that followed the coastline, instead of taking a busy freeway with multiple lanes and tunnels to deal with. When she got to the parking lot at the beach campground, she parked and blew out a deep breath. "Add that to petty theft of drinking glasses: uninsured driver with an out of town license driving a borrowed car."

Maile put the two glasses in a plastic bag to take to Detective Silva. He was watching as CSI techs swept metal detectors over the beach, following a criss-crossing pattern.

"You got here," he said. "I was beginning to worry."

She gave him the glasses. "I had a chat with someone before I came. I learned a couple of interesting things about those troop leaders."

"Before we get started with that, let me ask you a question. What exactly did that second flashlight look like? The one that was left out for potty runs in the middle of the night."

"Well, it was long, four batteries, the same as mine. It was newer, silver metal with a red end cap. I never actually used it, since I had my own. When do I get mine back, by the way?"

"Pretty soon. Any identifying marks on the missing flashlight?"

"Like dents? I didn't really notice. I'm not even sure of who provided it. One of the girls, I guess, since Jones seemed underprepared for camping." Maile chuckled. "Or even surviving the wilds of windward Oahu."

"I heard that first day of the investigation it was hers that was left out for the latrine." Silva opened a box that contained several plastic evidence bags. He took out one bag in particular. "This is everything we've found today. Junk mostly, but this flashlight turned up in the bushes not far from the parking lot. Does it look familiar?"

"Could be the same one that we had. It has the red cap on the end."

"It doesn't seem to go with the rest of the flashlight, almost as if it was taken off another and stuck on." He clicked the *on/off* button several times. "As you can see, the batteries are fresh."

"If I had to guess, I'd say it was the same one. But like I said, I never used it. Are there fingerprints on it?"

"Wiped clean. Even the batteries were wiped, along with all the internal parts. The techs can check more thoroughly in the lab, but there's not a print on it."

"I guess that means you have no way of linking it to the injury on the guy's head? What was his name again?" she asked. "Unlucky Leo?"

"Leo Brown. There's something interesting about this flashlight that makes it a little different from yours, Ms. Spencer." He gave the bagged light a shake. "See how the lamp end rattles?"

"So? People don't take very good care of flashlights. Mine is a little banged up also, as you know."

"Yours doesn't shake like it's coming apart."

"Maybe the end needs to be screwed back on tighter?" she offered.

"Why are you defending this flashlight?" he asked. "You're as defensive of this one as you were with your own."

"I don't know why. I'm just trying to think of reasons why it's broken, that's all."

"I can give you a very good reason why. The end of it was damaged when it struck Leo Brown in the back of his head. That's why."

"That's the murder weapon?" she asked.

"Potentially. We found a smudge of blood on the edge of the lens rim. We even got a hair to go with it. Pretty lucky. Now all my team has to do is match the blood from the light to that of the victim, and I can call it the murder weapon. Matching the edge of the lens rim to the dent in Brown's head would be gravy, along with the hair we found on it."

"That's good, right? One step closer to finding the perp?"

He looked at her with a grin. "Yes, the perp. What I don't have are fingerprints or any other evidence linking it to the person yielding it at the time. That means all I'd have is the murder weapon, but still no lead to its user."

"I don't know what to tell you, Detective Silva."

"Are you sure you don't remember who provided the flashlight? You make it sound like it wasn't Jones's."

"There were too many flashlights and people going in and out of tents that night to remember who had what," she said. "Maybe one of the girls remembers?"

"I hate to call witnesses so long after the crime for one little piece of evidence, especially kids."

"The girl name Nancy is still on the island with her father. But does that mean someone was wearing gloves when the flashlight was used to hit the victim?" Maile asked. "It had been wiped cleaned before Brown got hit in the head, and the perp didn't bother wiping off the blood, right?"

"Very good. That leads me to believe that whoever used the flashlight knew ahead of time that they were going to use it as a weapon, not just as a source of light. They'd prepped it first by cleaning it, and then while wearing gloves as you just stated, waited to take a swing at Brown at the best opportunity."

"I had my own flashlight, and I never got up in the middle of the night. I'm almost certain none of the girls got up, either."

"Our estimated time of death hasn't changed since that first day, of not long after your confrontation with him," Silva said.

"Well, my only alibi that I didn't leave the tent again is staying in a room with her father on the sixth floor of the Kuhio Palms Hotel."

"Yes, Nancy Miller. I've already talked to her about that. She swears up and down that you never left the tent."

"She should know. She clung to me the entire night."

"That's the impression I got," he said.

The CSI techs wrapped up their metal detecting and passed by Detective Silva shaking their heads. He gave them the permission to leave, with the instructions to check everything they'd found thoroughly for blood and trace prints. Once they were gone, Maile and Silva were alone at the beach parking lot.

"Ms. Spencer, you look like you could use some caffeine. There's a place near here that serves a good cup of joe."

"Just joe, or one of those fancy, overly-wrought things that you like?"

"Joe for you, fancy for me." He gave her a ride to a small commercial area where a quiet coffee shop had a bored barista waiting for customers. Once they had their drinks, they went to a table in a corner. "What's the deal with the hotel glasses?"

"The more I think about it, the more they're just evidence that I'm a petty thief."

"You must've had a compelling reason to take them."

"One is from Mahoe's room, and the other is from Jones's room. I thought that maybe there were incriminating fingerprints on them, or whatever. I should take them back to the hotel."

"I doubt the hotel is going to miss them, considering all the towels and bathrobes that are accidently taken home by guests. Which one is from Mahoe's room? I don't have fingerprints for her, and she doesn't have a police record. As far as I can tell, she's never been printed by anyone."

"The one wrapped in paper."

"Paper?" he asked.

"I wrapped it in toilet paper. I figured that would protect the fingerprints. Honestly, I have no idea why I did that."

"Good thinking, I guess."

"If she'd been working at a private school, wouldn't she have been fingerprinted for that?" Maile asked. "I thought school teachers needed to be carefully vetted?"

"I called the principal of the school. Apparently she wasn't in a teaching role, or employed in a capacity that put her near the students. As an office drone, she didn't need to be printed to get her job."

"What is her job?" Maile asked.

"Their Chief Financial Officer. They hired her about three years ago and she's been trying to balance the books ever since. They even had a tuition hike and they still have a hard time making ends meet."

"That's strange. That's the same story I got about her and the Girl Scout troop. Mahoe is their finance manager, and they're having trouble, too."

"Who told you that?"

"My little source, Nancy Miller, and her father confirmed it. According to him, the troop is on its last legs, financially. I guess that's why they don't have many activities."

"Isn't that the point of Girl Scouts, is to do fun stuff together?" he asked.

"That's the idea I got from reading about them online. That, and to learn leadership skills. They're not getting that from Jones, though."

"You said earlier that you learned something them?" Silva asked.

"Oh, yeah. Mahoe might've been in her hotel room as recently as today."

"How could you tell that?"

"There was the unmistakable scent of body spray in the air. I don't know the name of it, but I've been picking it up from a lot of young women lately."

Detective Silva made a note about that. "If you happen to get the name, I'd like to know it."

Silva got a call, which went by too fast for Maile to guess what it was about.

He got up in a hurry. "Can you get back to your car? That was about a hold-up in Kahala and they're requesting available officers."

"Yeah, sure." She watched as he ran to his car and left in a hurry. It would be a while before he got to Kahala, even in light traffic, but she was left with the croissant he'd got but left behind untouched. "Who pulls a hold-up on Christmas Day?"

Chapter Fifteen

The dead man, Michelle Jones, Miss Mahoe, and their Girl Scouts were the furthest things from Maile's mind when she dressed for her almost-date with Steve that evening. She'd worn a new red and green plaid skirt a few weeks before on a failed date, but since it was Christmas and the colors were right for the holiday, she went back to it. That, along with a sleeveless red sweater, completed her outfit.

She was debating the value of makeup when someone came in the back door of the Manoa House.

"Hello?" she called out.

"Just me, Maile!" Asher said back. She came to the bathroom door. "I lost my good tweezers. Have you seen them around?"

"Tweezers? Do you have a splinter?"

"No. They're nice ones, gold plated and everything."

Maile decided a microscopic amount of perfume would be okay. "Sorry."

"You have a date?" Asher asked, checking out the bottle of perfume.

"Not really a date. Just meeting an acquaintance."

"A guy?"

"Yeah. And his daughter."

"Oh. Well, that's better than...never mind. You're wearing that?"

Maile looked down at her outfit. "It's Christmassy. What's wrong with it?"

"Sort of parochial, isn't it?"

Maile grabbed her comb and took a few swipes at her hair. "It is Christmas, after all."

"Want me to do your hair?"

"It's already done."

"Oh."

"There's a confidence buster," Maile said, tossing aside the comb.

"No, it looks good."

Maile squeezed past Asher to leave the bathroom. "It's good enough. This isn't a real date, anyway. Just dinner with a guy and his daughter. They don't live on Oahu, so it's not like it could lead to anything."

"Sure are going to a lot of effort for a non-date with a guy that's not available."

"I'm looking at it as a practice date," Maile said. "Been out of circulation for a while. The last time I tried getting back into circulation, I failed miserably. I figure if I practice on guys that are essentially unavailable, I might, I don't know..."

"Get your groove back?"

"Get something back." Maile tossed a few things in a small clutch. "These days, I'm more concerned about finding a job."

"Make an appointment at the salon so you can look professional for your interviews."

"Might be too little, too late. I have a long interview tomorrow that's supposed to last a couple of days." Maile explained about the flight nurse position, and how she was going to spend a couple of days with a crew that week. "It's a professional position, just not glamorous. I doubt anyone will care how I look. Is Kenny around?"

"Went to see a friend. Why?"

"He was supposed to give me a ride to Waikiki. Like always, he forgot."

"I can give you a lift," Asher offered. "I was thinking of going for a drive. Not much going on around here without Kenny. That's why I came over here to see if you needed anything."

Maile did her best not to take the comment the wrong way. She needed a ride and didn't want to take the bus.

Once they were on their way, Maile cleared her throat. Before she could bring up the subject of dressing in sheets and overuse of the couch, and about her possibly moving back into the cottage, Asher interrupted.

"What's new with that police stuff about the dead guy you found a while back? Was it, you know, a murder?"

"The police have known that right from the beginning. The last I heard was that they'd found the murder weapon. All they need to do is find the person that used it."

"Who was the guy? Do they know that?" Asher asked. She seemed to be taking the long way to get to Waikiki. Maile wondered if Asher was turning out to be as much of a gossip as she was.

"Some clerk in a sporting goods store. He was apparently also the same guy that harassed us that night at the campground. Just a professional jerk pushing his luck a little too far, and somehow it caught up with him." Maile wondered why they were going down Kalakaua Avenue. The Kuhio Palms was on the next street over, another one-way street that led in the opposite direction. "But it all implicates me, since I met him at the store the day before the campout, and stood up to him at the campground."

"Oh, no! That's why you've been so stressed lately?"

"I have?" Maile asked.

"With the way you and Kenny go at each other's throats, and how you moved out."

Maile smiled at Asher's cluelessness. "I didn't move out because of him. Plus, we always treat each other that way. We always have. We wouldn't recognize each other if we didn't take a poke at each other from time to time."

"You might be able to move back into the cottage pretty soon, anyway. Kenny's out looking at townhouses today."

"On Christmas Day?"

"No realtors to deal with. He's just peeking in windows and checking out neighborhoods," Asher said.

"He's seriously thinking of buying something? I didn't know he was doing that well with his golf."

"He's doing a lot better than he lets on. I have some money to invest, also."

"That's nice of you. Where's he looking?"

Asher made another turn, once again going in the opposite direction of where Maile needed to go. "There are some new townhouses at his home course."

"He's thinking of moving to Moanalua? That's pretty expensive for a first home," Maile said.

"It's a townhouse. Anyway, we can afford it."

"I suppose." So much for ever getting paid back all the money Maile had 'loaned' to Kenny over the years. A young golfer new on the pro circuit and a massage therapist just wouldn't have much money left over after making monthly mortgage payments on a Moanalua golf course townhouse. "You didn't want to go with him today?"

"I wanted to talk to you, get to know each other a little better." Asher made another pointless turn in Waikiki. "Where am I going, anyway?"

"Just drop me at the curb. I can walk from here," Maile said. "If you go straight ahead, you'll come to the McCully Bridge, which will take you back toward Manoa. You don't know your way around Waikiki yet?"

"Kenny does all the driving. All I do is drive back and forth to work," Asher said, stopping at the curb to let Maile out. "And hey. Your social life will get better. I'm sure of it."

"It'd be nice if there was a time and date I could mark on the calendar," Maile said to herself as she walked to the hotel. She went to the dining room that was open to the public. There was a line waiting to get in, always a sign the food was good. When she spotted Steve, his daughter wasn't with him.

There was no pretense of a peck on her cheek, just a quick handshake.

"Where's Nancy?" she asked.

"In the room with videos on the TV and room service on speed dial. I thought it might be more fun if we were on our own."

"Oh, well…" Maile thought of Asher's offer of doing something with her hair, and her lack of makeup. It was much more of a real date than she was expecting. "I was expecting three of us."

They were shown to a table next to a window that offered a view of the garden outside.

"I've already told my first lie of the evening," he said, after they ordered meals. "It was Nancy who convinced me to meet you alone."

"Not much of a lie."

"I didn't have anything planned to talk about. Nancy usually does all the talking when we go out."

"You date a lot at home?" Maile asked.

"Not really. I seem to date more here than at home."

"You come to Honolulu often?"

"Hardly at all. This is my first time in almost a year."

"I don't understand," Maile said as their meals were brought. "You just said you're busier here than on Kauai…oh, I get it."

They made some small talk about their meals, and about Maile's continued quest to remain vegetarian, something that was still new to her.

"What exactly do you do for work, Steve? All I know about you and Nancy is that you're from Nevada originally and you lost your wife a couple years ago."

"I was born here in Honolulu, but we moved to Nevada when I was still a kid. Eventually, I came back."

"That's an unusual combination. How did that happen?" Maile asked.

"I decided at an early age there was only one field of study for me to go into, and nothing else."

"Which was?"

"I spent every waking minute reading everything I could about it."

"You sound dedicated." Maile wondered what sort of career he could be in that would've started in Nevada and brought him back to Hawaii. "What did you go into?"

"It took a tremendous amount of study at a top university."

"Maybe to satisfy my curiosity, could you give me a hint?" she asked.

"I am, in fact, quite likely the only person you know in my profession."

Maile waited to take another bite of her meal. "You are employed, right?"

"Maile, you're looking at one of Kauai's highest paid hydrologists."

"You mean water flow and how it affects the surrounding environment?"

"Oh, you're familiar with hydrology?"

"Not really. You were right when you said you're the first one I've ever met. What I don't understand is how you got interested in water in a desert state?" she asked.

"Nevada has rivers. There's the Carson River, the Truckee River, the Walker River. All sorts of rivers. The problem is, they've all been surveyed to death for the last one hundred and fifty years, and they don't do many tricks these days."

"Rivers do tricks?" she asked.

"They're supposed to. Each spring during the snowmelt and runoff, rivers that drain the mountains flood. If there's enough floodwater, the natural river course will change. Rocks and boulders get pushed around, roads get washed out, and bridges get knocked around."

"That's the point of being a hydrologist, to use winter snow level predictive models to see if trouble is coming in the spring?" she asked.

"Wow. That's the first time anybody has ever guessed what I do. We also work with Fish and Game Departments to help assess the amount of water that will be in rivers during the summer and fall, so they can determine how many fish to plant and where. If there's not going to be much water, or the water will be too warm, they won't plant many fish."

"I didn't know Kauai had freshwater fish, other than little aquarium fish that people toss in streams when they get tired of having a tank in the house."

"There are a lot of tilapia in the streams there, along with trout in the Koke'e River. That's my focus, the amount of water in the Koke'e, and how many trout can be planted. It's a very interesting project."

Maile thought of her attempt to learn fly-fishing several months before. "People fish for trout on Kauai? I thought they liked cold water?"

"The water is cool enough for healthy survival, but never gets cold enough to force them to spawn. That's why they need to be planted every year."

"Personally, I'd rather spawn where it's warm…never mind," Maile said. She wondered if her cheeks were flashing red.

"That's where I come in. I'm something of a spawning expert. With fish, I mean. Since I worked on similar projects in Nevada, I was a natural for this project."

"You'll be staying on Kauai indefinitely?" she asked, changing the subject from spawning.

"As long as they keep tossing non-spawning trout into the Koke'e, they'll need me, so, yes."

He was well-employed and had an interesting job, but living on a different island was a strike against Steve. "I'd like to see your frigid trout someday."

"How do you like being a tour operator?" he asked.

"Oh, it's great. I have ten employees, an office full of desks and computers, and three vans. Salaries and bills get paid, and the vans are washed and maintained better than I am. Tourists are whisked from one end of the island to the other. Usually back again. After all that, last month I earned a grand total of fourteen dollars and seventy-seven cents of my own. If I didn't have nursing as a real career, I'd be living at the park." She took a sip of her water. "I almost do, anyway."

"You're a nurse? Nancy said something about you being handy with Band-Aids on blisters."

"Yep, that's me. The Band-Aid Princess of Khashraq City."

"Pardon?"

"Long story."

"I have time."

"You've heard of the civil war in Khashraq?" she asked.

"It's been in the news occasionally. What's that got to do with you?"

"I was in the middle of it." Maile laughed. "There were times that I felt like a crossing guard, with so many troops coming and going all the time."

"I still don't understand."

"I was in the Army Nurse Corps for eight years and served three tours in Khashraq. I just finished my commission a few months ago."

"An officer? Very nice," he said.

"Captain Spencer, at your service. Not anymore, though. Time to get a real job in the real world, as they say."

"Do you miss the military?"

"Oh, in some ways. The men and women I took care of earned their injuries doing some pretty hard work. I miss a lot of the camaraderie. Some of the stations I was posted at weren't exactly garden spots."

"Like a civil war?"

"Like a civil war." Maile noticed the slight tremble crop up in her hand. "Mind if we talk about something else?"

"Sure." When the waitress took away their plates, they ordered coffee as dessert. "You said something once about growing your business so it might include other islands. What ideas do you have?"

"I haven't a clue. I need to do some research on what visitors might want to do, what sorts of adventures they might want to go on, instead of the usual tours that I offer. Like beach camping last week."

"Except without the dead guy?" he asked, flashing a smile.

"Yeah, that was pretty unfortunate. Has Nancy been upset about that at all?"

Steve shook his head. "She's been a trooper. She really talked it out of her system the first couple of days, but I think Christmas got her thinking about other things. Speaking of which, I should get back to her."

"You guys go home tomorrow?" Maile asked, desperate to keep the date going. She wanted to keep him for herself for as long as she could.

"Noon flight. Would you like to come back to the room? Nancy's had two full hours. Who knows what sort of mischief she's gotten into?"

195

"I never took her to be mischievous," Maile said as they waited for an elevator.

"She's not, at least not in a destructive way. But I'm supposed to worry anyway. That's what all the parenting books tell me."

"That's more than I know. The only parenting I've ever done is with my brother, and I'm still trying to raise him."

When Steve unlocked the door with his keycard and opened it, the security chain was across. "Just me, Nan!"

He pulled the door closed again. That was enough for Maile to make a move. She had mere seconds before the kid got in the way of making her intentions clear. She wanted to leave him with the knowledge she wasn't done socializing with him. Pushing him back against the door, she leaned in to kiss him.

It was all fun and games until Maile heard the chain slide across its track and the door open. Their weight against it made them take a step in to keep their balance.

"Dad! What are you doing?" Nancy looked at Maile and smiled. "Hi, Aunt Maile." She gave her father a swat on his back. "Do you have to do that out in the hall? So embarrassing!"

Maile took a step back and waved goodbye to Steve as the door to her latest adventure into romance closed.

Chapter Sixteen

On Monday morning, Maile took everything she was supposed to take to the specified hangar at Honolulu International Airport, which wasn't much. She was going to meet the crew, have some long talks with them, get oriented to the aircraft, and if an emergency came along, go on the flight with them. It was forty-eight hour shift, which would allow her to meet two crews.

From what she learned from Dan Sink, the man she had the interview with, shifts were something like fire department schedules, with multi-day rotating shifts. During their downtime, they'd maintain equipment, review advanced care procedures, and study cases in other locations to learn how to adapt those situations into their practice. If there was enough time, the nurses would take calls in the call center, part of Honolulu Medical Center's 'customer care services'.

When she got to the hangar, there was a commotion.

"You're Spencer?" a woman shouted as she pulled on a flight jumpsuit.

"That's me." She heard the engines of the twin turboprop airplane start up outside. "What's going on?"

"Got here just in time. We have a call to go to Molokai. Traffic accident, multiple victims that need transport to Honolulu Med. Grab a jumpsuit!"

Not knowing what else to do, Maile tossed her knapsack on a bench and climbed into a spare jumpsuit that was hanging on a hook. She had to run to catch up and got in with the rest of the crew just before the door went up and the plane taxied away.

"Here's a headset. Put it on and plug in so we can talk," one of the nurses shouted.

Maile got it fitted to her head, adjusted the mike in front of her face, and plugged a coiled cable into a ceiling panel she was pointed to.

"Can you hear me?" one of them asked.

Maile gave her a thumb's-up. She could also hear the two pilots speaking to the tower, so she kept quiet.

"I'm Willie and this is Daphne. You can meet our pilots later," one of them said.

Maile nodded again.

"You can speak. You're channeled into talking only with us, but we can hear what the pilots are doing. Don't yell. Just speak in a regular voice."

"Copy that."

"What's your deal?" the one named Daphne asked. She seemed irritated that someone was going along with them.

"Just got out of the military where I served in triage, surgery, and ICU. Before that, I worked as an ER nurse at Honolulu Med."

Willie T'ed her hands as if she were calling for a time-out in a game. "We communicate by VHF, Spence. That means anybody with a long antenna and tuned to the right frequency can listen to everything we say. Because of that, we don't use real names for places, or ourselves. That place is known as the Mother Ship."

"Copy," Maile said. She was already making mistakes, and she'd been on the job for barely five minutes.

"Got all the right certifications?" Daphne asked.

They were already airborne by then, Maile barely noticing. There was one bump as they climbed smoothly before leveling out.

"I showed everything to Mister...the boss last week. After the interview, he had me take a couple of exams. I brought certs and licenses with me today, but left them back in the hangar. It looked like we were in a little bit of a hurry, so I tossed everything else aside."

Daphne gave a slight nod before looking out the window.

"That's the right idea, Spence," Willie said. "Looks like you're going to be known as Spence, since we don't have any others. Everybody knows me as Willie. We heard all about you from Dan. Ever serve as a flight nurse in the Army?"

"Been on a few of their flights, but not dedicated to a team. Got a lot of patients off their flights, though, if that counts for anything."

"We'll see how you hold up," Willie said as the plane made a turn in the sky. They were already descending toward the Molokai airport. She watched out the window as they prepared for landing. "Not everybody can handle it."

"You can see the wreck below us," the pilot said over the onboard comms system. "Looks like two cars and three pickup trucks. I just got word that Junior League is taking most of the victims, and we'll get two."

"Junior League?" Maile asked, unable to decipher which hospital that could be.

Willie slipped off her headphones and held them aside when she yelled the answer. "West Maui Medical Center. Second busiest trauma center for three thousand miles in every direction. Good place. Just don't tell them our little nickname for them!"

"Spence," Daphne said to get her attention. "We're a courier service. It's all about continuity of care for us. We take over from where someone else leaves off, and deliver the patients in the same condition got 'em. That means don't be stupid and don't be heroic."

"I understand."

"Good. You want to be a hero, go back to the military," Daphne said, before looking out her window again.

"Spence, I hope you didn't eat a big breakfast today?" the pilot asked over the comms.

"Not much, why?"

"Two pilots and five passengers maxes out our capacity."

"I hope you take me back on the return run. I don't feel like swimming," Maile said.

There was a masculine chuckle, followed by, "I like you, Spence. Looking forward to flying with you again."

One ambulance was already waiting at the airstrip when they landed. Both pilots waited inside the plane, while the two experienced nurses took control of the victim. Maile helped move him onto their transport stretcher, and got him loaded into the plane. When the second ambulance arrived, Maile went into action by taking over his care, getting a report from the paramedics. Willie took over with squeezing air from the Ambu-bag through the tube in the patient's throat to feed his lungs the oxygen they needed. Once they had patients secured in place inside the airplane, the plane taxied and lifted off on their way back to Honolulu's airport.

While Willie continued to squeeze the Ambu-bag, Maile quickly checked vital sign monitors and dressings, before checking the status of a tourniquet that been applied to the leg of her patient. He was strapped and taped down to the backboard, with full spine precautions. She hit the silence button on the EKG monitor to quiet it for a moment.

"He's got an arrhythmia. Should I medicate him for it?"

"I see that," Willie said. "Nice catch. Maybe you should call the Mother Ship."

"How do I do that?"

"I'll switch you," the pilot said. "Hono Med, this is Alpha Airlift, inbound from Molokai. Patching through the nurse. Over."

There was a moment of delay and some crackling, before, "Go ahead, Alpha Airlift."

"Hono Med, I have a forty-four year old male on spine precautions, seatbelt marks on his abdomen, and contusions on his left anterior chest. I suspect multiple broken ribs and fractures in the extremities. He's developing an arrhythmia similar to what I've seen in cardiac tamponade. How should I medicate? Over."

The moment came and went so fast that Maile never noticed that she was in action again after a long layoff.

Whoever was at the hospital wasn't coming in clear. All Maile heard was a request for vital signs.

"Eighty over palp and descending. Rate is one-thirty and climbing." Maile tapped her finger on the EKG monitor, hoping what she was seeing was artifact. She stuck on another lead in a slightly different location, but that didn't help. "I'm about to lose normal sinus rhythm. Over."

"ETA?"

"Seven minutes until we're on the deck at Hono International," the pilot answered. Maile heard a thrust in the engines at the same time.

The communication back was still scratchy. "Elevate feet for shock...start another IV...Lactated Ringer's...wide open."

"I'm having a tough time getting air into his lungs, Spence," Willie said, using two hands to force air through the tube.

"Hono Med, I think we have a hemothorax," Maile said, wondering if anyone was still listening. "Unable to ventilate by hand, over."

Maile heard something about a needle. Looking at the other two nurses for confirmation, Daphne was busy with her patient and Willie only shrugged.

She couldn't wait for clarification. The patient's blood pressure was nose diving faster than the airplane was descending, and the EKG was erratic at best. Finding the largest bore IV needle they had, she wiped the man's chest wall with an alcohol wipe and shoved the needle between two ribs. She needed to move back when blood flooded out. Tossing a towel on the deck collected it.

She and Willie watched the monitors for an improvement, anything that might suggest the patient might survive his trip from the airport to the hospital. When his blood pressure numbers started to stabilize and blood stopped coming from the small catheter she'd jabbed into his chest, and Willie was able to force more air into lungs desperate for oxygen, Maile took a breath of her own. It was then that she felt the airplane touch down onto tarmac.

"Nice job, Spence," Willie said, once they were all back in the hangar. Maile had gone with them and had been returned by the ambulance crew that was also stationed at the airport.

"Thanks. I probably broke all sorts of rules, though."

"He's alive, and that's what matters."

Daphne was stowing some gear. When she looked at Maile, even she smiled for a moment.

"Welcome to the team, Spence," one of the pilots said, giving her a pat on the back. He gave then her a bottle of hydrogen peroxide and some towels. "Now, if you don't mind, clean up the mess you made in my plane."

***

Maile was tired from her two-day orientation stint as a flight nurse when she got home Wednesday morning. They'd had five flights altogether, including two pregnant women with complicated deliveries that needed to be taken to the women and children's hospital in Honolulu. Those were the hard ones for her, since most of her nursing experience had been with adults and not in obstetrics.

On the way home, she stopped at the university bookstore for texts on advanced OB nursing and the Care of Complex Obstetric Patients for a personal refresher course.

She was woken from a long nap by her phone.

"Ms. Spencer, this is Dan Sink from Airlift. Do you have time to talk?"

"Hi, Dan. Yes, I have time."

"I checked those exams you took last week. Some of the highest scores I've ever seen. Are you sure you didn't have the correction key?"

"I've been studying a lot lately. How did my orientation go?"

"You tell me. Did you feel like you were up to the work?"

"I thought it went okay. I'm pretty rusty on OB, but I bought a couple of texts to study. Did Daphne or Willie have anything to say?"

"First, Daphne doesn't like anyone, but she's one heck of a nurse, so we're all glad when she's on a flight. Willie had some glowing things to say, though."

"What's that mean? Should I go on a few more flights with other crews?" she asked.

"I'm ready to hire you. How do you like the sound of working that weekend shift that we talked about?"

"That sounds good. Is the other weekend nurse OB-trained?"

"You're in luck, Ms. Spencer. The other weekend nurse is Daphne. She's our best OB nurse."

Maile and Daphne hadn't seen eye to eye on some things during their flights. "Daphne?"

"She was filling in for someone that's been on vacation. Back to normal this weekend. I'd like you to come in tomorrow to fill out more forms and get an ID tag to wear. I also need to do a police background check. I doubt that'll be a problem, though."

Maile worried about that one. "So, I'm hired?"

"Sure are. What are you going to do to celebrate?"

"Oh, something really exciting like read a textbook about complex OB patients."

Chapter Seventeen

When Maile finished with paperwork at the medical airlift office on Thursday morning, her phone rang as soon as she got to a bus stop. She had two days before her holiday weekend stint as flight nurse started, and still needed to go to the tour office before getting some overdue sleep. She was on something of a mental high over the good news that her career was still heading forward, and she didn't feel like taking the call from a police officer.

"Detective Silva, I'm a little busy. In five minutes or less, is there something I can do for you?"

"I'd like to talk to you about Jones and Mahoe, and at the downtown police station. Where are you?"

Maile thought she felt her shoulders sag. "What about them?"

"New information that I need to talk to you about. Once again, where are you?"

"Not far from the station. I could walk there before you could come get me."

"I'll give you ten minutes, then I'll send a patrol car out looking for you. Understand?"

"Understand what?" she muttered as she walked to the station. "Maybe he found them and just needs me to pick them out of a line up."

Silva was waiting in the small police station lobby when she went in. She needed to sign in and get a *Visitor* tag to wear before he took her back to a desk in the detective's squad room. It was a place she knew well, from her dealings several years before with Detective Ota. It didn't seem the same without him there.

"Okay, I'm here," Maile said, crossing her legs. "I really do have other places to be today, as in a business to run. Will this take long?"

"It'll take as long as it needs to take. I hear you left the island earlier this week?"

"Oh, yeah, I forgot to tell you about that. It was my first couple of days with a new job as a flight nurse. We went to Molokai twice, the Big Island twice, and Maui once. Is that important?"

"I asked you not to leave the island."

"I came right back. Barely gone for two hours each time."

"Give me a head's up next time, okay?" He handed over a black and white photograph for her to see. "She look familiar?"

"That looks like Michelle Jones. It also looks like a morgue photo."

"Right, on both counts. She was found dead early this morning, floating face down in the Ala Wai Marina. Imagine their surprise when a group of tourists discovered someone wedged between two charter fishing boats."

"I don't understand. She was supposed to be a passenger on a charter?"

"No. They found her at dawn while boarding. They fished her out of the water, no pun intended, and when they figured out she was dead, they called us."

"How'd she die?" Maile asked.

"Took a whack to the back of her head. Sound familiar?"

"A little. What's that got to do with me?"

"Where were you between four AM and seven AM this morning, Ms. Spencer?"

"In bed until six, and then on a run until eight o'clock. And before you ask, no, I don't have anyone that can verify. I doubt either my brother or his fiancé saw me leave, and they were both gone when I got home again."

"Yes, that's right. You live next door to them now. How's that working out?"

"Better than before, although sleeping in a bed would be nice."

"Bed?"

"The Manoa House doesn't have beds, so I sleep on the couch. Is that why I'm here? Do my sleeping habits have something to do with Michelle Jones?"

"Maybe. You ran for two hours?" he asked.

"Yes. So?"

"That seems like a lot of miles. You got an entire week's worth of miles in one day?"

"I try to run every day. Why is that important?"

"It's not. I'm just trying to verify your whereabouts for the time that Jones was killed and her body dumped."

Maile told him the route she followed through the city that morning. "Maybe she wasn't killed at all? Maybe she was down there to meet someone, and slipped and fell, hitting her head on something?"

"That would likely be her forehead, not the back of her head. It was also a single dent, much like what Leo Brown suffered at the beach a while back. In fact, the coroner said it came from the same angle as his, and had an identical depth to his injury." Silva shifted a few papers to find something. "What's it called? Depressed skull fracture?"

"That would be the clinical terminology, yes. I still don't see what this has to do with me?" she asked.

"Something the coroner does in forensic investigation is determine the general height and build of a perpetrator of a crime like this. He determined that with Brown, the perpetrator was likely five-two to five-six and needed moderate strength to cause the fracture."

Maile knew right off what he was getting at, but wasn't going to make it easy. She also knew there was nothing she could say as an alibi. "I still don't see what that has to do with me?"

"How tall are you?"

"Five-five."

"You look athletic. You've had athletic training, and physical training in the Army, right? Would you say you had moderate strength?"

"For a woman. I run much more than I go to a gym. Mostly just pushups and situps."

"And running, of course."

"Of course." Maile made a show of checking the time on her watch. "Still have places to go, people to see, Detective. Am I here because you think I took a swing at Jones with a flashlight at the marina?"

"No, it would've been a tire iron. We found one in the water just below where she was floating. I figure it was the murder weapon since it hadn't been in the water for long, and it fits the injury on Jones's head."

"What's the weight difference between the flashlight and the tire iron? That might make a difference in how hard each murder weapon was swung," she said. She hoped she was on to something with her idea. "It would take more strength to swing the heavier tire iron than the flashlight, right? But the flashlight would have to be swung harder to cause the same injury as the tire iron."

Silva scratched his head while giving that some thought. "That only confuses things, Ms. Spencer, not clarifies them."

"Did you happen to find any fingerprints on the tire iron?"

"None. Even though it had been in the water, something should've shown up. Again, just like the flashlight, it looked like it had been wiped clean."

"There goes my alibi."

"Maybe not yet. What sort of car do you drive?"

"I don't. I've driven my dad's car a few times lately, but I don't have one of my own. If you like, check his trunk for his tire iron. That's the only one that I'd have access to," she said.

"I already have, earlier this morning. It's there, along with everything else for changing a tire. Very nice man, by the way."

"I'm lucky to have him as a step-father."

"I also checked your brother's car. He seemed a little put out."

"He's a little put out about everything lately. He just got engaged and hasn't smiled since."

"I wanted to check her car, but she'd already left for the day. I'll try to catch up with her later."

Maile recrossed her legs and bounced a foot. "Have you entertained the thought that maybe Mahoe might've knocked off Jones?"

"Knocked off? Yes, I thought of that. She's still at the top of my list of suspects, for a lot of crimes. If only I could find her."

"You mean both murders, of Brown and Jones?"

"Along with bank heists and some convenience store holdups."

"Bank heists?" Maile asked.

"Two Waikiki branch banks, two in Kahala, and one downtown, along with three convenience stores, and a gas station have been hit since your campout with the Girl Scouts a while back, Ms. Spencer. We've collected Jones's fingerprints from every site, plus a few others that are unidentifiable."

"Jones has been robbing banks? Our Miss Jones from the Girl Scout troop?" she asked.

"Not much of a Girl Scout value, is it?"

"She wasn't particularly likeable, but I never pegged her as a thief."

"Fingerprints don't lie," he said.

"You said once that the robberies you were investigating were being done by amateurs. I guess a school teacher and finance officer aren't exactly born criminals."

"Not exactly Girl Scouts, either," he said.

"Maybe those other prints are Mahoe's?" she suggested.

"That's my hope. Something interesting showed up, though. The latent print that was collected from the .357 revolver found beneath Brown's body matches one of the unidentified prints we've collected from the bank heists."

"I have no idea what that means, other than throwing another twist into your investigation. I can see why you might feel stymied over not having Mahoe's fingerprints. But once again, what does that have to do with me?" Maile asked.

"Too many deaths associated with that campout last week. Of the four adults involved, two are dead and one is missing, leaving only you."

Maile leaned forward to make certain eye contact. "I didn't kill either one of them."

"I'm sure you didn't. But I do need to ask you once again if you've had any contact with Mahoe?"

Maile sighed as she sat back in her chair. "Not at all. We never met, I don't know her contact numbers, and have no idea of what she looks like. Okay?"

"Sure, fine. Relax a little, okay? Refresh my memory of what you do know about her."

"Mahoe was the financial officer for the private school those girls attend, and the person responsible for the troop's finances. Both of those are failing. She may or may not have sprained her ankle on the morning of the campout. That's about it. I do know I'm getting tired of hearing about her."

"So am I. But she's the missing link in so many investigations, from convenience store holdups, to bank jobs, to the possible murder of two people. What I can't figure is if that latent print on the gun belongs to Mahoe, and she and Jones were pulling bank jobs together, why would she kill her partner?"

"Or kill Brown?" Maile asked. "You think they came here to rip off a few banks and convenience stores while the girls were on the campout?"

"It's beginning to look like Mahoe was the ringleader of the crime spree, and not the girls' troop leader."

"Is that why Mahoe pretended to sprain her ankle, so she could go case a few banks?"

"Could be, but prints from two perps have been found at every site. I'm checking on recent Kauai robberies, to see what prints might've been collected from those crimes."

"Have you built any kind of timeline for all the robberies?" Maile asked. "How many of those holdups or whatever took place while we were camping out?"

"Excellent question." He shuffled papers to find a hand-scrawled timeline. "That's why I keep asking you about all the activities during the campground, and whether Jones participated in them. From what I've pieced together from what you and the girls told me, two of the convenience stores were held up during the time of the campout. Those two holdups just happened to be while Jones was MIA from the rest of the group." He tapped his pencil on the timeline a few times. "They were also not far from the campground at Bellows Airfield."

"It sounds like you have your perpetrators of those crimes."

"Except Jones is dead and Mahoe is still missing." Silva slapped down his pencil. "I could arrest and charge them both for every crime except the two murders."

Maile got a text message chime on her phone. She barely hid her smile when she saw the number. There were only a few words, as usual, but she didn't reply.

"Okay, why would either of them want to kill Leo Brown, and why should Mahoe want to kill Jones? That's the part that doesn't make sense to me," she said.

"Not to me, either. Once I find Mahoe, I might have a chance to find out."

Maile crossed her arms and bounced her foot even more vigorously. "Well, I don't have her."

"Nor have they been to your house. Once I was done with your brother's car, I sent a team to your house in Manoa Valley. I asked for you at the door, but you weren't home. Your brother was kind enough to let my team collect prints from both houses."

"I'll have a talk with him about that. What did you find?" she asked.

"A toilet that needed to be plunged."

"You can teach Asher how to do that."

"I took care of it."

"You plunged their pot?"

"It wasn't difficult. Moving on, we found none of Jones's anywhere in your house. None of Leo Brown's, either."

"That's not a surprise to me, Detective Silva."

"Nor did we find any that matched the latent print from the gun found beneath Brown's body, which I am currently considering to be one of Mahoe's."

"To my ears, that sounds like good news, but somehow it must incriminate me for something," Maile said.

"Hopefully it doesn't, no. But the problem was that my team was unable to find any prints at all in the smaller house. It was almost as if someone had expected us and gone through and sanitized every surface in the place of potential evidence. Do you have a professional cleaner come by?"

"Not that Kenny has ever mentioned. I sure haven't cleaned the cottage since moving into the main house next door. It's not like Kenny would ever lift a finger to do housework. I guess Asher must've gone on a cleaning binge. Sorry."

"We collected hairs from the living room furniture and each bed. Once we have those figured out who they belong to, I'll be happy. We did find two blond hairs on the couch."

"Asher's. She and my brother..." She made eye contact for a moment. "That's one of their hangouts."

"She's blond? You brother told me her family name is Kawika'kamaole."

"Blond, courtesy of L'Oreal, or whoever. It looks good. Has my brother fooled."

Silva made a few more notes. "She's from Kauai also, right?"

"Yes. So?"

"How long has she been here on Oahu?"

"A few months, I think. However long she and Kenny have been dating, which hasn't been long. I'm not sure of the exact timeline. She grew up on Kauai and went to the mainland for a while before coming back. She said Kauai seemed too small, so she came to Honolulu. But you can't seriously think she had something to do with Jones and Mahoe, do you?"

"Kind of a coincidence that she's your roommate, and that she's from Kauai just like Jones and Mahoe."

"Not my roommate. I live next door, remember?"

He jotted something on a timeline. "Thanks for clarifying that."

"Here's a little more coincidence for you. She also went to the same school where Jones teaches...taught, and Mahoe works, and was in the same Girl Scout troop as a kid."

Detective Silva wrote furiously for a moment, before slapping down his pen. "I have a sporting goods store salesman murdered after he picked on Girl Scouts from Kauai on a campout, one of the troop leaders is now dead, and both troop leaders were robbing banks and stores of cash on a mini-crime spree. As far as I can tell, you're the only common denominator, and now I discover your roommate is from Kauai, and not only was a student at the same school, but a girl in the troop in the past."

"Ten years ago," Maile said. "You didn't know that before?"

"I would've been nice if you'd told me about her earlier. As far as I can tell, your two sources are a nine-year-old Girl Scout and a massage therapist?"

"I'm not really in the business of investigating crime, Detective."

Maile got another text chime on her phone from a number that looked familiar but she couldn't quite place it.

"Need to answer that?" he asked.

"Not yet. Are we almost done?" she asked.

"Pretty soon. There was one thing that my CSI team noticed. Your floors were exceptionally clean."

Maile chuckled. "Vacuuming was my job at the cottage, but it's been a week since I ran one. Maybe Asher did that when she cleaned the rest of the house?"

"What chores does your brother do at home?"

"Not much. May I go? Because I'd really like to have a meeting with my office manager before he goes home for the day."

"As long as you don't leave the island." He looked at her. "Except for brief round-trip flights."

When Maile was outside, she decided to walk off the steam that had built during her interview with Detective Silva. She got out her phone and read the first message again. She decided to call.

"Gunny! You kept your word!"

"I did?"

"You told me during your invasion a while back that you'd give me a call, and you have! What's up?"

"Well, I have some leave and was wondering if you have time to spend with me?"

Gunnery Sergeant Gustafson wasn't the brightest bulb in the chandelier, but he was built solid and knew what to do in a woman's bed. They spent parts of two deployments to Khashraq, spending more time and effort hiding their trysts from prying eyes than on 'fraternizing'. But that was the past.

"I don't have to be at work until Saturday morning. What did you have in mind? Because I have this evening and all day tomorrow."

"I can't get off base until Friday afternoon."

"That's okay. I'm available then."

"Friday evening is New Year's Eve, and you have to work first thing in the morning?" he asked.

"Morning muster, oh-seven hundred at the airport, bright and cheerful."

"You have a car?"

"Not really. Can you get from Kaneohe to town? I can get us a room in Waikiki," she said. "Not at the Hale Koa, but someplace nobody will know us."

"Don't have to hide now, Maile. The room sounds good. Have a meal, hang out, reconnect, you know?"

"Yeah, reconnecting sounds good. Overdue, actually. Let me reserve the room and I'll text you the info on it."

215

"Not going to have Girl Scouts there, right?"

"Ha! No, no Girl Scouts. Not even a nurse acting like one, buddy."

Here was an unusual dilemma: two men interested in her at the same time. True affection was just beginning to sprout with one, while it never really existed with the other. If she spent the night with a Marine, would she be two-timing the hydrologist?

Once Maile was off that call, she looked at the other message. It was from David Melendez, a lawyer that did some work for her in the past, now the governor. It was heady experience, getting a text message from the governor, and she reminded herself not to let it go to her head. All the text said was to call him at her earliest convenience. She kept walking to her office when she called.

"Governor Melendez, this is Maile Spencer. You sent me a text message earlier to contact you?"

"Yes, thank you for calling back so promptly. Do you have a minute to discuss something?"

"If you have the time, so do I," she said.

"Good. I'm calling as your lawyer, not as a politician, so keep that in mind as we talk."

"Sure."

"What do you know about the Manoa House? Isn't that something you're involved in?" he asked.

"The Manoa House is one of the oldest buildings in the Manoa Valley, an old missionary house that's used as a meeting place for people of Hawaiian descent. There're membership dues, but it isn't much. It's listed officially as a non-profit. The money we collect goes into the minimal amount of maintenance on the place, pay a few bills, and the rest is divvied up into scholarship money for college kids. Why? Is there an issue with its non-profit status?"

"Not that I'm aware of. My concern today is that someone is trying to buy it."

"The Manoa House? I don't see how they can."

"Who exactly owns it?" he asked. "The actual building and lot of land it sits on?"

"I'm not real sure. Never really gave that any thought. The organization, I suppose. How did you hear about that?"

"You might not like the explanation. One division of the firm handles real estate law. Whenever scuttlebutt comes through the internet about property or business concerns of one of our clients, it's routed to the proper division. Then they take a look and decide what to do about it. This time around, it was about the Manoa House."

"And since the Spencer family is responsible for its upkeep, and my residence is listed as the same address as the Manoa House, I'm involved?"

"Right. But when realty division checked for ownership, there's no clear indication of who exactly owns it."

"Does that mean that anybody can come along and buy it?" she asked.

"Maybe. The problem is that someone ostensibly needs to own it for someone else to buy it. Do you suppose the missionary family that originally lived in the house might still own it?"

"I...wow. I hope not. I'd hate to lose the house in that way. We have weekly, sometimes only monthly meetings, but it's a nice way for us to stay connected with people we don't see very often. If we lose that, we'd lose just a little more of our identity. Don't get me wrong. I'm in no way one of those people who are constantly protesting at the Iolani Palace, demanding the Kingdom get restored. But I do like having a place where we can

217

meet, something that we can consider ours, and not let others make up the rules."

"I can see that," he said.

"Any idea who is trying to buy it?"

"No idea. Bids have been made as though it's on some sort of hidden online auction."

"Auction?" Now she was getting steamed, that the place she'd always considered home was up for auction, even when no one knew who the real owner was.

"Is there any way you can look into the matter? You know, ask around but quietly?" he asked.

"Yeah, I know a few people I can talk to. Not sure if they'll be much help, though."

"Well, you're much more tuned into who might know something than my office could ever be. Take a few days and send me a report."

"Sure."

"Thanks, Maile! Happy New Year!"

Maile put away her phone.

"Great. Someone is trying to buy my home, and I don't even know who owns it."

Chapter Eighteen

Instead of stopping for something to drink, Maile hurried to get to her office. The excitement of being hired for the job as weekend flight nurse was over-shadowed by the on-going investigation into Brown's death, and now Jones. That's when she realized she would likely have to leave the island again during the weekend to transport patients, but she wasn't going to tell Silva that, or the others at the airlift barn.

Now there was the matter of her home possibly being stolen out from under her. That meant she had research to do in the Manoa House library, searching for the original owner and occupants of the Manoa House, and who owned it now.

Along with work and doing her research, she also had a date with Gus to prepare for. A plaid skirt just wouldn't do for that. She was just getting to the office when her plans for the next few days were congealing into a mess in her mind.

"Brian! You have no idea how good it is to see a sane person. Is Amelia home with the kids?"

"Yep, her turn today. She has them on Tuesdays and Thursdays, and her parents have them the other days. What did you want to meet about?"

"I was hoping there would be a few more of us here. Has anyone come up with any big ideas of how we can grow the business without turning it into a chore?" she asked.

"It might be doing that all by itself." He handed her a sheet of paper with a few notes about a possible tour. The amount he circled at the bottom looked good to her. "You mentioned a while back about wanting to branch out to other islands. Well, these guys are chocoholics, apparently. They take their vacations to different cacao growing regions around the world, go on tours of the farms, and taste-test the products."

"When did Hawaii become chocolate central?"

"It's not yet, but the Big Island has a small and growing chocolate industry, with about a dozen farms and several tasting rooms and gift shops."

"That's a tasting room I could spend the day at."

"That's what Amelia said. I never knew there was so much chocolate there until they told me about it. If it keeps growing, it'll become the third largest crop after coffee and macadamia nuts."

"Why did they contact us?" she asked. "Why not just go with a tour company on the Big Island?"

"I asked about that. They said none of them were equipped to do what they need."

"What, drive them around to tasting rooms and gift shops? Anybody can do that."

"They want to stay at inexpensive but authentic lodging, like bed and breakfasts and old hotels, historic stuff. Then go see cacao farms and end each day at a tasting room owned by the same people who own the farm they toured."

"Okay, they're cheapskates. That's still something a local tour company can do for them. They have vans there to drive these guys around, and we don't. I still don't see why they're calling us."

"I got the impression nobody on the Big Island wanted to deal with them because they're cheapskates."

Maile tapped her finger on the total amount that Brian had circled on the booking sheet. "They agreed to pay this?"

"Right. I factored in the approximate amount for the van that we'd need to rent for the three days they'd be there. It would be a nice job, but I need someone to go there. All of our guides and drivers are booked up for the week."

"What about you?" Maile asked.

"My sight is good enough to get a driver's license, but there's no way I could drive on roads I'm not familiar with. Anyway, Amelia needs help with the kids. She's determined to be the best mother ever, but she needs help. That leaves you, Mai."

"Me?"

"Unless you have a driver in your back pocket, yes, you."

"I'm not familiar with Big Island roads. It's been ten years since I've been there."

"Nothing changes much over there. A few more cars here and there, Kona gets a little bigger with each passing year, but that's about all."

"But me, driving a van?"

"What is it with you and insisting on not driving places?" he asked.

Maile sat back in her chair. "I'm not exactly the best driver."

"What's that mean? You get a lot of tickets?"

"Tickets would be an improvement. I have a tendency to remove paint from fenders and give the bumpers a run for their money. The only car I've ever owned barely last five years and needed to be towed away at the end."

"There's less traffic on the Big Island. Would that help?"

"Maybe." She read the booking sheet again. "How many are in the group?"

"Three men, two women. That would require an ordinary van with windows so they could see out. You did that Girl Scout campout a while back. This can't be any harder, right?"

"Dead guy that time, remember?" she said.

"You got tour trouble out of your system. What can go wrong with driving a few chocoholics around the Big Island?"

"I don't know, but I bet I could find it." Maile rubbed her face, thinking about Gus. "Why are you trying to talk me into this? Who's the owner of this dog and pony show, anyway?"

Brian smiled. "She abandoned us a few years ago to see the world."

"Smart girl. The group wants to do this two weeks from now?"

"Right. Maybe Lopaka could give you a few lessons before then?"

"I'd never hear the end of it." Maile tossed down the booking sheet. The money was too good to pass up for such a simple trip. "Okay, book it. But I want it paid in full ahead of time. I guess you better reserve a van for me also."

Maile waited for Lopaka and Susan to return from their last tour of the day. Before he could get away, she cornered him in his van.

"Hey, brah. Got a big favor to ask."

He smiled that same smile she'd always liked. "Whatever you need, Sistah Hokuhoku'ikalani."

"I need some lessons."

"On?"

"Making one of these things go up and down the road without bumping into stuff."

"You want to be a tour van driver? Mai, stick to guiding. You were good at that. In fact, stick to nursing. That's what's in your soul."

"Not much choice. We've booked a trip to the Big Island and it looks like I'm going to be the driver. It won't have to be a full-sized van like yours, but a minivan. Maybe if I learn on something bigger, driving a smaller one will be easier."

"You want to drive Manoa One? My Manoa One?"

"Yes, I know. You're as dedicated to this van as much as you are to your kids. But brah, I need to know what I'm doing before I take a tour group on roads I don't know in a vehicle with gigantic fenders."

Lopaka laughed. "Okay, time for your first lesson."

"What? Now?"

"I'm not busy."

"It's rush hour! I have places to go."

"No better time, and you can drive yourself to wherever you need to go." He forced her into the driver's seat and sat in the same seat she'd used in the past. "I'm assuming you know the rules of the road?"

"I pass the written test with flying colors. It's making these things go where they're supposed to that's the problem."

"We'll figure it out as we go." Once Maile had the van out in traffic, Lopaka began to shift in his seat. "We can go faster, Mai."

"We can?"

"That's what all the honking is about."

"How fast am I going?"

"Twelve miles per hour. Rush hour, remember? Twelve isn't rushing."

Keeping a firm grip on the steering wheel, she pushed on the gas pedal a little. "Where am I going, anyway?"

"Kahala Mall. We can drive around the parking lot for a while."

"Okay. How do I get there?"

"Mai, relax a little. Take a breath. Go the same way as the bus goes."

"Oh, yeah." She had to think about the direction. Basically, it was straight in front of her. She'd driven her dad's car there recently, but that had been on a Sunday, not during rush hour with cars and buses moving back

223

and forth, honking horns, and weaving between her and the vehicles in front. She needed something to distract her mind, and nerves, from the traffic. "Hey, why would two women come here from Kauai with a group of Girl Scouts, and then rob banks and grocery stores?"

"For the money. Be careful of the motorcycle."

"Tell him that. I can see the money, but why would one of them kill a man who played a prank on the girls?"

"Being protective of them. Let the bus merge, Mai."

"He can merge with this."

"Can't make gestures like that."

"It was just a mental gesture. This time. Why would one of them kill the other?"

"Someone else died?" Lopaka asked. He stomped on the imaginary gas pedal below his foot.

"Remember Miss Jones from the Girl Scout campout? She was found floating in the Ala Wai Marina this morning. Somebody had taken a homerun swing at the back of her head with a tire iron."

"That's why you were at the station this afternoon? The police think you know something about it?"

"How'd you know I was there?"

"We saw you walking in while taking a tour group to the Iolani Palace." Maile stomped on the brakes, then the gas to dodge something that didn't happen in front of her. "For some reason, this Silva guy is more suspicious of me than Ota ever was."

"I don't know why one would kill the other. I have two suggestions for you, though."

"I'm open to anything right now."

"Stay away from that investigation. Don't get involved with any of it."

"Easier said than done, brah. What's your other suggestion?"

"Better make this next turn or you're going to miss the mall completely."

After twenty minutes of driving around the mall parking lot, parking in small spaces and making tight turns, she guided the bus back toward downtown. Rush hour was going full blast, but she got to where she needed to go in time.

"Thanks, brah. I think. Did I do okay?"

He took his place at the steering wheel. "Didn't wreck Manoa One. That's all that counts."

Dashing across the street flooded her mind with a memory from ten years before. That moment had been tough, but she'd survived, which was all that mattered. When she stretched one leg to reach the curb, she waved to the proprietor of the business she was headed to.

"Maile Spencer!" he said, holding the door open for her. "Back from the war, safe and sound?"

"Hi, Don. Safe, but I'm not always sure about sound. I know it's close to closing time, but I just need a few minutes."

"I see the haircut I gave you back then didn't hold up so well. Is that why you're here?"

Maile pushed the longer side of hair back from her face. "I have something else I want to talk to you about. How familiar are you with the Manoa House?"

"Been a member since I was old enough to afford the dues. Why?"

"Someone is apparently trying to buy the place."

"That's a problem. I thought membership was still okay? Why are we selling it?" he asked.

"We're not. Someone else is." She explained what David had told her about the purported online auction, and that bids were being made anonymously. "You've been a member for longer than I've been alive. Any idea of who might own the actual building and lot?"

"No idea. I can ask some of the old timers, if you like?" Don asked.

"Yeah, but keep it quiet. See if anyone has heard about the auction."

"You bet. I hope it's all some giant mistake, that the bidders have it all wrong."

"Me, too." Maile noticed when Don seemed to take a long look at her hair. "Yeah, I know, it's a mess."

"Want me to square things up a little? I have time."

Maile was stuck for a reply. She needed to be diplomatic. "You see, I have a big date tomorrow, and…"

He smiled. "Yes, New Year's Eve was when you came that other time. This time around you're looking for a little more style than that?"

"What you did was great, but somehow I need to find a style that works with my new job." She explained about her job, and the gear that she needed to wear. "Something low maintenance, but looks great. I'm thinking I should find a new stylist, so when they screw it up, I can get mad at someone I don't know."

"Nicely played," he said, smiling again. "Very diplomatic. Have you given Koni in Kahala a call?"

"She's booked up for weeks in advanced, and I'd like something before tomorrow evening."

"For your date. I understand." He went to a drawer for a business card. "There's a young woman named Kaia that just opened a small shop. She's looking for customers."

"Hawaiian?" Maile asked, looking at the card.

"Of course. I've been telling the men that come in here about her, for their wives to go to. She's young, but I haven't heard anything bad."

"Thanks. I'll give her a call." She gave the business card back after memorizing the phone number. "Sorry you're losing a customer."

He got the door for her. "Yes, that once every ten years customer that I can't live without."

Chapter Nineteen

Maile decided to eat dinner with her parents Thursday to share the good news about her new job.

"Mom, do you know any families on Kauai named Mahoe?"

"Mahoe?" Kealoha gave it some thought. "Mahoe…Mahoe…not on Kauai, no. Not many of them around. A couple of them on Maui, and a few here. Kauai? No. What about them?"

"Oh, one of the Girl Scout leaders a while back was named Mahoe."

"She's the same one that's been causing the trouble lately?"

"Maybe trouble, maybe not. The detective that's investigating needs to talk to her, but can't find her."

"Talk to her about what?" Ka'uhane asked.

Maile wasn't going to let on about the bank robberies Mahoe had been tied to. "I'm not exactly sure of what, but basically everything about the case. You're sure we don't know anybody named Mahoe on Kauai?"

"Don't know everybody," her mother said. "What are you doing for New Year's Eve?"

Maile sat up straight, knowing she had some good news to share. "I have a date."

"Oh? With who? Anybody we know?"

"No. He's someone I knew in the service. In Khashraq."

"Turn into something this time?"

"Mom, don't start. I'm just glad I have a date. That's good enough."

"Where's he taking you?" Ka'uhane asked. It was his subtle way of preventing an argument.

Maile wanted to answer with 'to bed', but thought better of saying that to a retired minister. "Just to dinner. I have to be at the airport early the next morning for work."

"Well, have fun anyway," Ka'uhane said, as he took the dishes to the kitchen.

That left Maile and her mother alone at the table. They stared each other down for a moment until her mother broke first.

"This boy treat you good?"

"He's a nice guy. He works hard at the job he has."

"Soldier boys move around. He's staying here for a while?"

"He was just assigned to Kaneohe. I think his deployment days are done."

"He called you, or you called him?" her mother asked.

"He called me. I think he's getting out of the military soon and might be thinking about settling down here."

"Bring him home for dinner sometime."

"It's just a date for the evening, not for the rest of my life. Changing the subject, do you know who owns the Manoa House?" Maile asked.

"We do."

"I know the Hawaiians on the island feel a sense of ownership and entitlement to the place, but who actually owns the building and lot?"

"We do, I said."

"What do you mean, we do?" Maile asked.

"The Spencers. Me, you, and Keneka."

"We're caretakers, not the owners," Maile said.

"Maile girl, you're not listening. We own it."

"You mean the cottage?"

"The whole thing. The lot, the house, the cottage, dirt, flowers, trees. All of it."

Maile sat back. "I thought we got free rent in exchange for housekeeping and landscaping? How did we ever end up owning it?"

"Long story. My great great grandparents were servants in the house when the missionaries lived in it. Those missionaries stayed in it all their lives, but the kids left home for New England. Just before they died, they gave the house to our kupuna Kalama."

"Queen Kalama?"

"Right. But Kealalawe and his wife, Esther, the house servants back then, returned to Kona where they came from originally. They had a child, who was adopted by Kalama. Before Kalama died, she signed the house over to the oldest son of that child. A few generations later, his descendant married a man named Spencer, and you were born a year later. Keneka came along a few years later. You don't know these things, girl?"

"I knew we were descendants of people from Kona that included an adoption by Queen Kalama, but I've never heard about the house being handed around like that, or that we'd been servants in a missionary house. Why are we considered royalty?" Maile asked.

"I'm not. Neither is Keneka. Only you are."

"Just me? Why am I stuck with it?" Maile asked.

"Because you're the older. I'm, well, you know..."

"Yes, kahuna. We're not supposed to talk about it."

"Because of that, I couldn't take the title of princess. When you were born, you inherited the title from your grandmother."

Maile rubbed her forehead. "Okay, am I royalty through blood or was it bestowed upon someone who handed it off to the rest of us?"

"Both. Kealalawe was an ali'i of Kona when Kauikeaouli reigned."

"Kauikeaouli was Kamehameha the Third, right?" Maile asked.

"Time for more study, girl, if you can't remember that. But Kamehameha bestowed a royal title upon Kealalawe and Esther's child before he was adopted by Queen Kalama. Both titles have been passed down and reside within your soul," her mother said. "Take good care of them."

"Is any of that written down? Or is there a deed for the house? That's the important part."

Kealoha gathered the dinner plates. "There's all kinds of things in those cabinets in the house. You'll have to look."

"Mom, these are some of the most important documents for Hawaiians today, and we don't know where they're at?"

"They're over there. Just look."

***

"Yeah, in my spare time, when I'm not flying patients between islands or taking visitors on tours of candy stores, I'll take good care of the Kingdom of Hawaii," Maile said as she walked home that evening.

When she got there, she went straight to the archive room and logged onto the computer. It had been updated since the last time she used it, and now had a flat screen monitor. She spent two hours reading about Queen Kalama and King Kamehameha III, and searched for information about their descendants—her ancestors. All she got, though, was a refresher course in early modern Hawaiian history. That meant she would need to dig through cabinet drawers one at a time, sifting through old documents in a quest to find something that indicated the Spencers might indeed own the Manoa House.

She spent another two hours searching through old, time-stained documents written in fading ink, looking at tiny notations with a magnifying glass. She made a few notes about what she saw, before starting an outline for a report for David Melendez. Seeing it was well after midnight, she put everything away, and locked up for the night.

After a quick shower, she settled onto the couch with a romance novel. She was quickly distracted by her little research project.

"Okay, why would a governor care so much about the Manoa House?"

She went back to the book and tried replacing the college football quarterback in the story with Gus. It didn't work. Instead of him, Steve crept into her mind.

"I was almost making out with one guy a couple days ago, and now I have a date with another tomorrow night. This close to making out with him, until Nancy caught us." She reached up to turn off the lamp. "Talk about a prison guard."

***

In the morning, Maile went back to the archive room to keep searching for anything about the original family that built and lived in the Manoa House. As far as she could tell, it had always been known as that, even back to the missionary days.

Then she made a discovery about the Manoa House.

Heiaus are sacred structures built by the ancient Hawaiians. Most were large platforms of rocks, with some having structures built from wood poles and palm fronds for shade. They were used in ceremonial rites, places to leave specific offerings, to treat the ill, and even for sacrificial use.

Missionaries were primarily the ones that brought the beliefs and practices of the Hawaiians to an end in the early 19th Century, dismantling the old heiau and using the stones for foundations for their homes and towns. Churches were often built directly on top of heiau, a show of power and dominance of one religion over another. The idea was that if the native Hawaiians wanted a place to worship, they'd have to do it in a church that had replaced their old heiau.

That led to the discovery that Maile made that morning. She found letters written back and forth between missionary families in the Manoa Valley and where they came from originally in New England, telling the story of how small heiau had been appropriated, the flat stone platforms being useful as foundations for homes, businesses, and churches. One of those places was the Manoa House, which had been built upon a place used by kahuna to heal the sick and injured.

"Not much different from what they've been doing in the Holy Land and Europe for centuries. When a new religion comes to town and takes over, they simply knock down the old statues and icons and put up their own, erasing the old ways and beliefs. Voilà! New religion for the people to practice."

She made some notes and scanned some of the letters to send to David Melendez later. What she never did find was anything that mentioned her family name of Spencer as being the rightful owners of the house.

So, she tried Kupule, her mother's maiden name. That was the 25% of Maile's Hawaiian heritage, also the portion that housed her royal genes. But after an hour of scanning letters and documents, she'd found nothing that indicated the Kupules owned the Manoa House.

Checking the time, she still had plenty of time before her date with Gus that evening.

Grabbing a book, she flopped down on the couch and read a few chapters about high-risk obstetrics in preparation for her weekend shift. At least until she slammed the textbook closed.

"What am I doing? It's New Year's Eve, and I'm sitting around reading about placenta previa, whatever that is." She grabbed her phone and started to dial a number. "That's Daphne's forte. She can take care of that stuff while I stand around looking officious."

When her call was answered, there was some noise in the background. "Kaia's salon. May I help you?"

"Yes, I hope so. I know it's a holiday weekend, but I was wondering if you have appointment time available today?"

"Not like I have a long line waiting. I was just vacuuming. When do you want to come in?"

"I need enough time for hair and a facial. You wouldn't happen to have any Roman gladiators working there, would you?"

"Pardon me?"

"Sorry, dumb joke."

"Be here at noon, and you can have the entire afternoon. Once I'm done with you, I'll probably close for the day."

Kaia's salon would be easy to get to, just off a major bus line near the university. It wasn't far from the old boarding house Maile had lived in for a year, and she was curious to see how the neighborhood had held up. She laughed at the memory of some of the characters that had lived in the place.

"What was that hooker's name again? Coincidence? Something like that."

She laughed again.

"And Mrs. Taniguchi! Eighty-five pounds dripping wet, and she had an iron grip on the building. For as forgetful as she was, she sure was able to meddle in other peoples' lives."

When Maile left that day, she took everything she needed for her overnight date with Gus, plus what she would need for the weekend of work. She even found a way of stuffing her textbooks into her overnight bag.

She got off the bus one stop early, just so she could walk past her old residence. The building had gotten a fresh coat of paint in the years since, but the characters hanging around the entrance and the street corner outside hadn't changed much. Instead of a woman working the corner, it was a man. When he acted disinterested in Maile as a customer, she realized the people had changed more than the color of the walls. She almost wanted to cancel her appointment, just so she could sit in the coffee shop across the street and watch the comings and goings at the old boarding house.

When she got to Kaia's place, she was a few minutes early. The hairdresser was just finishing with a client, putting the finishing touches on her hair.

"You're Maile?"

"That's me."

"I'm Kaia. Have a seat. I'll be done here in a few minutes. Cut and facial, right?"

"That's the plan."

Kaia gave Maile a longer direct look, not from the mirror. "Looks like you're running away from home."

"Been there, done that, as they say. This time, it's just for the weekend."

The client in the chair laughed and gave Maile a thumbs-up.

Maile watched the stylist work for a moment. She was dressed in clothes that fashion magazines called 'contemporary chic', but found in local Honolulu stores rather than expensive clothing 'galleries'. Kaia's blond mane reminded Maile of Asher's color, and she wondered if braided blond was the coming trend for twenty-something year olds. She also noticed she wore no wedding ring on her hand, but did wear other rings. One thing was for sure, that if she ever wanted to break up Kenny's relationship with Asher, all Maile would have to do was send him in to Kaia for a haircut.

When the other client finally left, Kaia pushed her little broom around the floor to clean up the mess. "Would you like the cut or facial first?"

"However it works best. Actually, I'm splurging a little for New Year's."

"Good for you. I'll do your hair first." Kaia took Maile to the chair and pulled the bobby pins out to let hair fall forward. She began fluffing the waves, stretching them out considerably. "Asymmetrical. Who did it for you?"

"That Roman gladiator I mentioned on the phone earlier." Maile explained how she'd been traveling in Italy several months before and had it done there. "There's something about a man built like gladiator running his fingers through you hair. He could've talked me into almost anything."

"Honey, if I had a Roman gladiator around here, he could talk me into all kinds of stuff."

"Yep. I might have to go back to Italy someday," Maile said dreamily. Before straying a little too far into a fantasy of a vineyard tryst, her mind raced back to the here and now of the moment. "Today, I just need you to do something about the split ends and even up the two sides."

"You're done with the asymmetrical?"

Maile gave the style one last consideration. "Yep. It was fun looking fashionable for a while, but that's not who I am. Back to real life."

"Deep down inside, who are you?" Kaia asked. She quickly began snipping off the longer hair at one side. "Personally, I think your hair rocks asym."

"Italy was the first time a Spencer ever rocked something fashionable," Maile said. She sighed internally as the old style fell away and a simpler hairdo slowly emerged. "For me, it's all about comfortable clothes, low maintenance hair, and sneakers on my feet."

"You said Spencer. You're Maile Spencer?"

"One and the same. Why?"

"I know you. I mean, I don't know you personally, but I've heard about you," Kaia said. Her eyes roamed over Maile's face and hair as she spoke, gathering information in the same way that Maile examined a patient.

Maile knew what was coming, and wanted to avoid it. "Whatever you've heard is all lies."

"You're responsible for the Manoa House, right?"

"It seems I was elected president in absentia, but yes, I have something to do with it."

"And you're also..." Kaia paused again.

'Please don't say it...please don't say it...' Maile thought.

"A princess. Our princess."

Rats. "That's more of a hollow title than anything real. We're a hundred years beyond those days."

Kaia started working on the other side. "Ohmagawd! I'm doing the hair of a real live princess!"

"Yes, well, this princess is an ordinary girl with split ends and a date she needs to go on later tonight."

"A date on New Year's! We need to do something special," the hairdresser said.

Maile decided to plead her case one last time. "I just want both sides evened up. Same length all the way around, you know?"

Kaia looked closely at a lock of hair. "Maybe at least some color?"

If there was one driving lesson she'd learned from Lopaka, it was to squeeze the brake pedal with her foot, not stomp on it. Maile needed to press her foot on the brake pedal right then, and stomping wasn't out of consideration. "I...well...better not."

"Next time." Kaia looked disappointed. "We're definitely doing something new next time."

"I like what you've done already. Maybe this is enough for today?"

Kaia stopped and stood back with her hands on her hips. "You're a nurse, right?"

"Yes."

"Do you let your patients tell you what to do, or do you already know how to take care of them?"

"Well, I listen of course, but I know what's best from experience."

"And they trust you, right? Even though they've never met you, they let you do all sorts of things to them, right?"

Maile knew she'd been outwitted. "Yes."

"Just trust me in the same way patients trust you, okay?" Kaia put away her things and eased the chair back. "I can do more later. Time for the facial."

Maile closed her eyes and let her mind calm down. She had no idea what Kaia was doing to her skin, but at least it was relaxing. She was close to dozing off when the girl started talking again.

"I cleaned your pores, and this mask will soften your skin." Kaia began smearing something thick on Maile's face.

Just as her natural darker skin tone was returning, it was being moved again. "Where did you train?"

"Everybody asks that because I'm so young, that I must not have much experience. As soon as I graduated from high school, I went to the best cosmo school on the west coast. They worked us to death, too. For two years, it was hair, skin, makeup, tattooing for permanent makeup, piercings, you name it. We even had a week of working with a mortician. There's something I never want to do again."

"Hair and makeup on a body?" Maile asked. "I wouldn't want to either."

"Something creepy about it." The smearing stopped and eyebrow plucking started. "Once I finished that program, I got into a real apprenticeship in LA. Spent a year in Hollywood, in fact."

"That sounds like fun. Meet anybody famous?"

"Actually, yeah. The place I worked at catered to TV actors. The more famous ones went to established stylists, but the bit players came to me, along with regular clients. They had me focus on hair. Anything and everything that can be done with hair, I've done it."

"So, you really are well-trained then?" Maile asked.

"It sounds like I'm tooting my own horn, but yes. Much more so than those ones at Koni's."

"You don't like Koni's?"

"There're better places in town than there," Kaia said.

"If Koni offered you a job with a clientele of your own, would you take it?" Maile asked.

"No way."

"You know, your story sounds very familiar, about going to the mainland for training before coming back here. I know a gal from Kauai who works at Koni's that..."

"I'm from Kauai. What's her name?"

"Asher Kawika'kamaole."

"Asher...Asher...Asher...no, doesn't sound familiar. What school did she go to?"

"The private school for Hawaiian kids. I can't think of the name of the place."

"I was a public school kid. What cosmo program did she go to on the mainland?" Kaia asked.

"I don't know if she's ever mentioned. West coast, maybe?"

Kaia took Maile to a sink to wash her hair. "How do you know her?"

"She's dating my brother. Actually, they're engaged now."

"Where's she working?" Kaia asked.

"She's just doing massage at Koni's until a chair opens up for her."

"Hmm, that's strange. Koni usually only hires from her own beauty school downtown. That way she knows they can do the three most popular styles. Unfortunately, those have become so popular, everybody looks alike."

"Koni has such a good reputation," Maile said. "I don't see how they can stay in business if their styles are boring."

"It's not that they're boring. They just don't have much to offer. You walk into Koni's looking for something new, and you walk out with style A, style B, or style C."

"Sounds like a Chinese restaurant. You get a choice of the combination A or combination B plate," Maile said.

"That's exactly what it is."

"Okay, for the big question of the day, which style did you give me?" Maile asked. "A, B, or C?"

"Your own." Kaia sat up Maile and took her back to the chair. "Now to finish it up."

"There's still more to do?" Maile asked.

Kaia stood with her hands on her hips. "You have somewhere to go?"

"Yes, a date." Maile crossed her legs and bounced a foot. She was enjoying the chitchat, but felt like she was being forced into a corner. "Like I said earlier, it needs to be low maintenance for when I'm at work. I don't mind glamming things up a little for special events, but in my approach to life, the simpler, the better."

"You do understand that glam is the opposite of low maintenance, right?" Kaia asked.

"I know. All I really want is to get everything the same length so I can grow it out again."

"You've mentioned that once or twice already." Kaia set a reassuring hand on Maile's shoulder. "I'm not going to do anything too wild, Maile."

Maile wanted to put on her best face for Gus later that evening. Along with feeling emboldened by Kaia's enthusiasm, that was good enough to make her consent to a little more work.

Kaia started working again. "Maybe we should talk about something else so you don't stress out too much?"

"Good idea." Maile picked up Kaia's scent. It was the same as what she'd smelled in Mahoe's hotel room a few days before. "What's that scent? It's nice."

"A body spray called Send Me. It supposedly has pheromones that attract men."

"You have a date this evening, too?" Maile asked.

"Not yet. I'm going to a party later, so there's always hope. The stuff is expensive, though." Kaia shifted her position to the other side of Maile's face, where the scissors started breaking a few of Kaia's promises. "It's meant more for young adults."

"I see." That homily was becoming a recurring theme lately. Maybe that's why Maile had liked the gladiator stylist in Rome. He'd told her believable lies about how young she looked. "You never mentioned your last name."

"Mahoe. Kaia Mahoe. I was trying to decide if I wanted to call my shop Kaia's Salon or Mahoe's Hair. I might change it. I have all kinds of plans. I just have the two chairs out here, but I have a ton of space in the back to open private rooms for massage, tattooing and piercings, and more chairs if I get busy enough. I'll give you some business cards to hand out to your friends."

"Sure. Your family name is Mahoe?" Maile asked. "M-A-H-O-E?"

"Even if I get married someday, I'll keep Mahoe. I like my name. It's different."

"Sure is. You said you're from Kauai?"

"Lihue. I have some cuzzes in Koloa, and some other cuzzes in Hanalei, but we're the Lihue Mahoes. There's another Mahoe family on the island, but as far as anybody can tell, we're not closely related to each other. Why?"

"I heard about a Mahoe that works at the private school in Lihue as some sort of finance manager. Is she part of your family?"

"What's her first name?"

"I don't think I ever heard it. I never have met her. Do you know anybody that works at that school? What's the name of it, anyway?"

"Lihue Preparatory Academy. I know a couple, but they're not Mahoes. Not even close."

"Okay. Know any Girl Scout leaders named Mahoe?"

"Girl Scouts? I never got involved in them. I was always involved in schoolwork and dance classes after school. We're big-time quilters in my family. If we have nothing else to do, we start stitching pieces of fabric together."

"Maybe that's why you're so good with your hands."

"Funny things to talk about, finance managers and Girl Scouts. How did you think of those?" Kaia asked. She was working in the back where Maile couldn't see.

Maile gave the crib notes story of the campout from a couple of weeks before, along with some of the problems that resulted in police investigations.

"You were a part of that? I read something about that in the online news a while back. This Miss Mahoe that works at Lihue Prep is somehow a suspect in the murders?" Kaia asked.

"She's a person of interest, or whatever it's called. Did you know Michelle Jones at all? She was the other Girl Scout leader, and was a teacher at Lihue Prep," Maile asked.

"Michelle Jones? I had a teacher with that name in junior high."

"Describe her."

Kaia stopped working for a moment. "Kinda chubby, brown hair, uptight, smoked a lot." She snipped once or twice and stopped again. "That was almost ten years ago, so I don't remember so well now."

"Any idea why she was so uptight?" Maile asked.

"I think because she was going through a divorce. She didn't get along with the other teachers so good, and with the kids even less."

This was leading to something. "Happen to remember her husband's name?"

Kaia shook her head. "Sorry. For as little as Lihue is, you'd think we'd all know each other."

"Been a long time since I've been to Kauai." Maile wondered if she should bring up one other name. "Ever meet a guy named Steve Miller? He has a daughter named Nancy, about nine years old?"

"The only Steve Miller I know is that old-timey singer."

"Yeah, my mom listens to his music sometimes," Maile said.

Kaia set down her utensils and began using the curling iron. "Who's the guy you're spending the weekend with?"

"Oh, somebody I knew in the military. It's not the whole weekend, just tonight. I have to be at work in the morning."

"Can't even sleep in together?" Kaia asked.

"Unfortunately. And I need to get some sleep if I want to be functional tomorrow."

"Is he someone special?"

"In bed he is."

"Well, that's important."

"I let it slip to my mother that I have a date this evening and she already wants to meet him."

"Honey, if it was my mom, she'd already be knitting little baby booties," Kaia said with a laugh.

Someone called to make an appointment, and Kaia assured her she could come in as soon as she wanted. Kaia toiled for a few minutes before stepping back. "Okay, done."

"Oh, wow." It was shorter than what Maile had wanted, but even all the way around like she'd asked. Rome had fallen, her gladiator now only a memory. "Just what I wanted."

Kaia worked with some gel to hold things in place. "I already have big ideas for next time you come in."

"Big ideas?"

"You'll see. Is there going to be a next time?"

"Yeah, I survived this, which means I'll be back. Not so sure about trying something new, though." Maile got her bag. Digging down for her coin purse, she found Asher's fancy set of tweezers that still needed to be replaced. "Are you familiar with this brand?"

Kaia looked at them. "Fancy Gal Cosmetics. How'd they get buggered up?"

"Not on my brows. I just need to replace them."

"You can find all that expensive stuff at the cosmetics store at Ala Moana Mall. They sell Send Me body spray, also. Not cheap, though."

"Thanks." Maile noticed the mess on the floor. "Um, the thing is, I'm a little superstitious."

"Black cats and Friday the Thirteenth type of superstition? Or something else?"

243

"Maybe traditionally but somewhat irrationally old-fashioned Hawaiian in some of my beliefs."

"Oh, I get it. You're concerned about your mana, and you need something to offer to Kuka'ilimoku and Lono?" Kaia asked quietly.

"Kuka'ilimoku has enough of my blood. I'm more concerned about Lono these days." Maile felt her cheeks turn pink when she handed over two small envelopes to Kaia. "Maybe a little worried about more kapu coming into my life. Do you mind?"

"I'm glad to." Kaia put locks of Maile's hair into the envelopes and handed them back. "It's nice to know some of us still take these things seriously."

Maile tucked the envelopes away, safe and sound. "About the rest…"

"Maybe I'm as old-fashioned as you. I take care and put it where no one could ever find it."

"Thanks," Maile said. "I guess it's a little silly, but…"

"Not worth the risk, right? What about when you went to that gladiator in Italy?"

"Oh yeah, him." Maile felt her cheeks flash red again. "When he was done, I had him collect it in a bag and I took it with me. You should've seen the looks I got when I left. The strange American chick taking her hair home with her."

"He sure has a great story to tell, though," Kaia said, chuckling. "What did you do with it?"

"I guess it's safe to mention so far away. I worked on a farm with a vineyard and winery. Early one morning when no one else was around, I buried it beneath an old oak tree where no one will find it. It seemed like a good thing to do."

Kaia's appointment came in, and she sent her to the chair.

"I'd love to hear about your adventures in Italy someday, but I have work to do," Kaia said. She leaned in close. "You really are coming back?"

"Already a dedicated client, Kaia." Maile gave her answer some thought. "Unless I find a gladiator named Domenico instead."

Chapter Twenty

It was a sunny afternoon without rainclouds in sight, so Maile decided to walk to Waikiki. She took tentative glances in shop windows as she went, and felt the skin on her face a few times. She knew she looked great, or at least a few years younger. That put a little extra energy in her pace, and she got to the hotel in no time at all.

After getting into her room, she still had an hour before she could expect Gus to arrive. The outfit she'd put on that morning made her feel underdressed for the hotel, and for the date. Grabbing her wallet, she went to the shops on the lobby floor of the hotel.

"What size are you looking for Ma'am?" a clerk asked.

"Probably a four, maybe a five? I was always able to crowd myself into a size small until a few years ago. Medium now, I guess."

"That happens to all of us," the clerk said, flipping through dresses on hangers. "For a party tonight?"

Maile looked at one in a flowery design. "Just a date."

"Maybe a little black dress?"

"Not really my color."

The clerk took out another. "Red?"

Maile looked at it. "Kinda low cut, isn't it?"

"New Year's Eve is only once a year."

"That's true." Maile looked at the price tag. In New York, London, or Milan, it would be considered affordable. She was in a classy hotel on Honolulu's Kalakaua Avenue, after all, the Pacific's answer to global fashion. When she tried it on, it fit perfectly, another reason not to ignore it.

Maybe this once she could make a hasty fashion choice, so she left the dress on and took her old outfit to the clerk. She found a tiny sheer silk scarf to go with it, one of her few fashion accessories.

"Can you do me a favor and take the tags off?" Maile asked when she paid.

"Not able to return it once the tags have been removed."

"I'm calling this my year-end bonus to myself."

"You might want to stand while you wait for him to show up," the clerk suggested, as she snipped the tags off. "Don't want to wrinkle it."

"I'm not sure of where I'm going to put my dinner while wearing this."

The smile on the clerk's face was more of a knowing wink. "Wherever you put it, I'm sure it'll have the effect you're hoping for."

Maile knew her face was as red as her dress as she left the shop. Tossing her things in the room, she had just enough time to get to the dining room. She sent Gus a text message to meet her there. Before rushing back out, she tied the handkerchief-sized scarf around her neck and let the ends do what they wanted.

It wasn't unusual for Gus to have been late for 'personal time' together in the past, as both of them had to come up with excuses for who they were meeting. With Gus as an enlisted man and Maile an officer, 'meeting' was tricky and considered 'fraternizing', forbidden in the military. That was no longer the case, though, and she wondered where he was as she waited near the seating hostess.

"Ma'am? Maybe you should take your table?" the hostess offered. "I'll watch for your date."

Maile was seated in the middle of the dining room at a cozy table meant for two. A candle flickered in a goblet, and gold tableware rested on red napkins. It couldn't have been more elegant. The only problem was that other

247

diners were at the tables around her, making Maile reconsider how flirtatious she wanted to be.

When a few more minutes passed and she had to send away the waiter for the third time, Maile sent another text to Gus.

Where are you?

She fired off another when he didn't answer.

Waiting in the dining room.

Finally, forty-five minutes late, her phone rang. "Where are you?" she hissed.

"Illinois," Gus said.

"What? What the heck are you doing there?"

"Deployed. Waiting for an onward flight."

"Deployed? To where?"

"On the QT."

"I don't understand. We have a date for this evening," Maile moaned. "When did you go to Illinois?"

"A couple days ago. Sorry. Kinda forgot to call you," Gus said. "I should go. Need to prep and load."

"You're at Scott Air Force Base?" Maile asked. She'd been to the same giant base a few times, a major staging area for military flights to the Middle East. "Prepped for what? All you have to do is stuff your gear in a duffle and load into a transport."

"Sea bag."

"Yeah, you know what?" Maile said. She could almost feel the steam come off her, she was so embarrassed. Or insulted, she wasn't sure which. She'd gone to the trouble of reserving a nice room and a table in a classy restaurant, and she'd been stood up. "Why don't you stuff your sea bag into your duffle and take a hike."

When the waiter brought the ticket for the glass of wine that Maile had guzzled, he asked if she was sure she didn't want a meal.

"Never mind. What time does the dining room open for breakfast?"

"Six AM. Want me to reserve a table?"

"No, thanks. I'll be gone before then."

"I could have room service bring something?" the waiter offered.

"Sounds good. Two orders of waffles, two fruit cups, and a pot of coffee, along with a four AM wake up call."

The waiter smiled. "Enough for two. Your friend will join you later?"

"No, that's all for me. And have a chef salad brought to my room in about an hour." Maile stood from the chair. "I'll be done crying by then."

***

Maile left the room service salad alone and drank a beer instead. She'd already changed into a running outfit and had her hair secured back from her face with a band made from a bandana. Finishing the beer, she set it aside and left the room. She was barely out the door before she was running.

"Stupid jerk."

Kalakaua Avenue was still busy for so late in the evening, and she figured they were all visitors wanting to ring in the New Year with a stroll along Honolulu's most famous street. She wasn't feeling the same excitement, and weaved her way down the flagstone sidewalk, dodging kissing couples and avoiding groups of young adults looking for fun.

"All he had to do was show up."

Maile got to the road that went past Diamond Head on the beach side. With less foot traffic, she picked up her speed. The humidity was heavy that evening, the sky threatening rain. A drop hit her cheek, and she wasn't sure if it was a raindrop or a tear. She wiped it away.

"He couldn't call? Nice room, new dress, hair, perfume, and I'm spending the night alone."

The route was clear of pedestrians in front of her and she kicked up the pace even more.

"Just a call so I could cancel reservations. But no. He leaves me sitting there like some dope in the middle of the restaurant on New Year's Eve. Talk about insulting."

It began to rain in earnest, but Maile kept running away from the hotel.

"That's it. No more guys that speak in short choppy sentences."

She leapt a puddle like a steeplechase runner.

"Date anybody I want…"

A car drove slowly down the street and she tried keeping up with it for a moment.

"Work any job I want…"

She was beyond Diamond Head now, still following the route for the Honolulu marathon, something she'd done once and still wanted to do again.

"Live anywhere I want…"

Lights were on in the houses she passed, and the places that were holding New Year's parties overflowed with cars and music.

"Wear skanky red dresses for no reason at all…"

A dog barked and chased her from behind. She tried to out-sprint it, and when it got up next to her, she glanced down at it several times.

"Not the right day to mess with me. Go bark at someone else."

The dog seemed to understand and eased off. She barely slowed, enjoying the pain of the hard run. Rainwater and sweat were falling heavily from her face, along with another hot tear or two.

"I can do anything I want…"

She came to a busy intersection. Instead of waiting for the light to change, she ran through the little traffic that was there. Getting honked at only provoked a mental middle finger.

"I pity the poor jerk that tries to get in my way. I've worked too hard to start settling for second rate…"

She laughed as she ran.

"…or guys that don't bother calling."

Finding herself in a residential neighborhood, she eased to a walk. The streets were quiet, nearly empty, making her feel alone. It was exactly what she wanted. Firecrackers were being lit somewhere, a Honolulu tradition in every neighborhood. With the first few cracks, she shuddered as they sounded too much like gunfire.

"Where the heck am I?" She looked at the street sign but didn't recognize the names of the streets. Rain pounded her body, and rolled down her face in waves as if she were taking a shower. "Oh, forget it. I can figure out where I am later."

Following a meandering route for another half hour, she found Kahala Mall. From there, she'd need to run for half an hour to get back to her hotel, but she still wanted, still craved more exercise. She pulled her tank top off exposing her bikini top, and blotted her face and head. The heavy rain brought up the scent of the shampoo Kaia had used.

"And if I want to be a princess, I'll be a princess. If anybody doesn't like that idea, I'll smack them upside their head with my royal scepter!"

She ran through another neighborhood that would ordinarily be quiet that late at night. Being New Year's, families were lighting fireworks, flashing in the low-hanging clouds. Each time she heard a boom in the distance, Maile wondered if someone lost a finger.

When the noise came to a fevered pitch, she figured midnight was passing and a new year was beginning. She stopped to watch one family light a dozen fireworks fountains at once, along with several long strands of firecrackers. Once the festivities died down, she finished her long run back to the hotel, her personal New Year's celebration complete.

Chapter Twenty-One

Maile was exhausted by the time she got home from her weekend duty as flight nurse. They'd had four runs to three different islands, two of which were complex obstetric cases. By the end, she felt like she'd had a grand tour of the islands.

She barely had the energy to shower before stretching out on the couch. Just as her world was turning to grayscale, her phone rang with a call from Detective Silva.

"Wrong time and wrong day to call, Detective Silva. I hope it's worth it."

He laughed. "And if it's not?"

"I have access to sharp things, and a license to use them."

"I think you'll want to hear this. First, I have a question to ask. It's been a few days since we've talked. Learn anything about Mahoe's where-abouts?"

"No, sorry." Maile wondered if she wanted to tell him about Kaia Mahoe, the hairdresser. Even if she was innocent in every way, being investigated and scrutinized by the police could cause her a lot of trouble. But Maile felt deep down inside that Kaia, or at least her family, was somehow involved in the deaths of Jones and the man at the beach. "I wish I could be more helpful."

"Well, there's good news and bad news about the case. The good is that one of the fingerprints on the drinking glass you took from Mahoe's hotel room matches the latent print on the .357 that was found beneath the dead man, Brown."

"That sounds like a little more incriminating evidence against someone. Mahoe, I guess."

"That's how I see it. The bad news is that you collected it and not a police investigator. I can't really use it for anything."

"Would you have collected the glasses anyway?"

"Probably. Drinking glasses are excellent for providing fingerprints."

"There you go, then," she said. "At least you have something that helps guide your investigation."

"Not substantially," he said. "The problem is that by the time I got a warrant to search their hotel rooms, they'd been cleaned and new guests had moved in. The only evidence I have from those rooms was from you."

"Am I supposed to apologize?" she asked.

"No. At least I have that much. I have another question for you, Ms. Spencer, and you're not going to like it."

Maile sighed with exasperation. "No, I didn't kill either Michelle Jones or Leo Brown, or whatever his name was."

"Thanks for confirming that, but that's not my question. Are you the highly sought after Miss Mahoe?"

"Ha! No, sorry. Good idea, though. I never saw that coming."

"I never did take your prints."

"They're in the system."

"Maile Spencer's, pardon me, Hokuhoku'ikalani Spencer's prints are in the system. I don't actually know if that's you, or if you're Mahoe trying to pass yourself off as Spencer."

"Only one way to know for sure, and that's to come get my prints. But I'm making you come to me. I just don't have the energy to go back downtown to the police station."

"You're at home?"

"In the Manoa House. Just come to the front door. But don't take too long, because the longer I have to wait, the crankier I'm going to be."

She was just relaxing into the soft cushions of the couch when a CSI van parked at the curb in front of the house. The two techs waited for Silva to show up, and they came up to the porch together. This time, Maile went out to greet them.

"Am I supposed to wash my hands?" she asked. "I just showered a couple of hours ago, so they should be clean."

"It doesn't make much difference. It's a digital scan," one of the techs said.

"How was your New Year's?" Silva asked as he watched the tech press Maile's left hand on the face of the electronic tablet.

"Different from what I expected, but good enough."

"Sometimes good enough is all it needs to be."

"Yep, if we're sitting up and taking nourishment on our own, it's a good day. How was yours? A busy weekend for the police department?" she asked.

"I spent most of it working on the Bellows case."

"Personally, I was done with that a week ago." She let the tech press her other hand on the tablet to collect those prints. "How long does it take to prove I'm me?"

"A couple of minutes. You look tired," Silva told her.

"Thanks a lot," she said with as much sarcasm as she could.

"No, you look good. You look like you were up all night."

"I was. I think I told you I have a new job working as a flight nurse? That started this weekend. I just got home from a forty-eight hour shift."

"And we're keeping you up, just to see if you're you?"

255

"I'm so tired right now, I'm not sure who I am." She nodded at the tablet that was still searching for results. "I'll stick with whatever your little machine says."

Like magic, up popped the results.

"Oh, look. I really am me. Can I go to bed now?"

Silva sent the CSI team on its way. "What time will you be awake?"

"Middle of the afternoon. Is there something else you wanted to talk about? Because I'd rather get it out of the way, instead of having it hang over my head. I have somewhere to go this afternoon, anyway."

"Where do you have to go? Another job for the workaholic?"

"I need to go to the tour office, and then I have a therapy appointment. You're partly to blame of that, by the way."

"Me? What did I do that drove you to a therapist?" Silva asked.

"I need to explore why I stole two drinking glasses from a hotel. There must be some deeper meaning to it than just fingerprints."

"Have fun with that. Let's have a seat." He sent a text to someone and put his phone away again. Once they were seated, he started flipping through pages on notepads and sheets of paper. "You were my last hope, Ms. Spencer, for finding Mahoe."

"In a way, I wish I was her, just so you could close your case. But what do you mean by last hope?"

"The murders are being back-burnered for more pressing cases."

"More pressing than a double homicide?" she asked.

"It's being looked at as two separate crimes by the DA. He's the one that wants to set it aside so other investigations can get more attention."

"So, that's it then? Two people have been killed and since you don't have enough clues to arrest someone, they're relegated to the dustbin?"

"Not relegated, and they're not going to be cold cases. I'll keep working on the case, and I'm even going to bring in the Kauai Police Department. I'm hoping that maybe they'll be able to provide some insight on the case. If nothing else, they can at least cruise by Mahoe's residence every now and then to see if she ever shows up there. So far as they know, she hasn't yet."

A red luxury sedan stopped at the curb. A tall woman with sunglasses got out and scanned the neighborhood on both sides of the street. Once she was done with that, she tossed her sunglasses inside the car and closed the door. Maile immediately recognized her.

"What's she doing here?"

"Detective Nakamura is investigating several bank heists in Waikiki. I think I mentioned when you met her the other day that she's the investigator for everything that happens in Waikiki?"

Maile watched as the woman detective walked to the porch. "Yes, I remember. But neither of the murders happened in Waikiki."

"Not exactly true, Ms. Spencer," Detective Nakamura said when she got to the porch. "My district covers the Ala Wai Marina, where Michelle Jones's body was found."

Maile stood to shake hands. "Please have a seat."

Nakamura stepped back and leaned against a porch post. "I'm fine here, thanks."

"I wasn't expecting so many visitors or I would've made tea," Maile said, doing her best to keep sarcasm from her voice this time.

"Not here for the tea service," Nakamura said. She looked at Detective Silva. "I've got it from here, Troy."

257

Silva said goodbye and left at a gallop.

Maile and Nakamura locked eyes for a moment, until Maile invited her guest to sit down. Again she refused, which meant Maile wasn't sitting either. She took a position leaning against the front door frame and gave her old friend from the high school cheerleading squad a long look.

Caitlyn had turned out as beautiful as everyone had predicted, with a tall, slender build, soft cheeks and level Japanese eyes. Her complexion was professionally attended and Maile was jealous of her nearly blond hair. Her sleeveless blouse and long trousers would be considered 'business casual'. Maile saw the telltale bulge beneath her blouse that had to be her sidearm. She held nothing in her hands, no tablet or pad of paper, just a few rings scattered over her fingers and a narrow gold bracelet.

"Hokuhoku'ikalani Spencer, AKA Maile," Nakamura said, pronouncing it correctly. She watched a car drive down the street. "Captain in the Army Nurse Corps until only recently, Registered Nurse, graduate of the university school of nursing..." Nakamura looked back at Maile. "...and graduate of Central Honolulu High School. Divorced after three years..."

"Yes, you've done your homework. Let's drop the pretense and call each other by our first names, okay?"

"We both know a few things about each other, don't we?" Nakamura said.

"Your secrets have always been safe with me, Caitlyn."

"As are yours with me."

"At least until we need to use them," Maile said.

Caitlyn's mouth started to crack into a smile. "For the betterment of all mankind?"

"Isn't that what we used to say? Why are you here? Get to the point, because I'm short a day or two of sleep."

"No kids of your own but you took a troop of Girl Scouts on a three day hike and campout?"

Maile sighed, half from fatigue, half from giving up. "I'm sure Detective Silva has filled you in on that, but here's my story, and I'm sticking with it."

Maile spent several minutes telling the detective what had happened on the campout, trying to remember as many of the details about Leo Brown shaking their tents that night, and then finding his body the next morning.

"I really don't care about him," Nakamura said. "Tell me what you know about Michelle Jones."

Maile told that story, of how she came and went a couple of times during the campout, and how Silva was considering the possibility of how she and Mahoe had waged a crime spree while they were on Oahu.

"Waging, as in still active, Maile. There was supermarket holdup on Saturday on Kuhio Avenue, and a bank was hit this morning, also in Waikiki."

"I have alibis," Maile quickly said. "I was at work all day Saturday, and I just got home a couple of hours ago. What time was the supermarket robbed?"

"Mid-afternoon."

"I was transporting a patient from Maui to here then. There are flight logs, and…"

"Yes, you're a flight nurse now. Still over-achieving, aren't you?"

"Achieving what I can, just like you, Caitlyn."

"I'm not concerned about you being a part of the holdups, but I think you might know something about who's behind them, and Jones's murder."

"I might know something that can help you."

"You have Mahoe tucked away in a secret hotel room?"

"No, but first, what's Mahoe's first name? I never have heard."

259

"Betty. Elizabeth, I presume. You've heard from her?"

"No, but I know of a Mahoe from Kauai originally, now here on Oahu, someone Detective Silva was never able to find. Her name's not Betty, and I seriously doubt she knows anything."

Detective Nakamura went to the porch railing and scanned the neighborhood again. "Who is she?"

"First, I want an assurance that you won't go leaning on her as soon as you leave here."

"I don't lean on anybody unless I need to. Who is it?"

"Kaia Mahoe. She has a hair salon near King Street and University Avenue."

"A friend of yours?"

"Just met her Friday afternoon when I went to her salon. Before then, I never knew she existed."

"She's Hawaiian?" the detective asked.

"Some part of her is. Always glad to support Hawaiian-owned businesses."

"Yes, the Hawaiians stick together."

"So do the Japanese on the island."

"What's special about her that makes you think she can be helpful to me?" Nakamura asked.

"Like I said, she's originally from Kauai."

"Why didn't you tell Detective Silva about her earlier? He was just here a few minutes ago. You could've said something then."

"I doubt she's involved. She didn't seem to know much about the private school Jones taught at, nor did she know any Mahoes that work at the school."

"You almost got away with your evasive answer, Maile. Did Kaia know Jones previous to her death?"

"She told me that Jones had been a teacher at her junior high. Before you ask, I have no idea how or when she went from public school to the private school."

"I wasn't going to ask." Caitlyn turned around to face Maile again. "Still running?"

"Life is getting busy again, but I try to run every day. Still going to the dojo?"

"Spend more time at the shooting range."

"I suppose so." Maile wondered if she should bring it up. "I heard about what happened with your husband a while back. That's rather heartbreaking."

"Ex-husband, and it couldn't be avoided. But thanks. Something else that should be consigned to the secrets bin."

Maile chuckled. "I have a few ex-husband secrets, also."

"I know you're needing some sleep, but I need to take you somewhere."

"Where?"

"I want to have a chat with Kaia Mahoe, and I want you there with me at the time."

"For?" Maile asked.

"Do you like it when police investigators just show up and start asking questions?"

"Not really, no. You want me there as a liaison?"

"For lack of a better word, yes. You'd be helping her out more than you would me."

Maile gave it some thought and derived a little plan of her own. "Fine. Give me a minute to change my clothes. And you're buying coffee on the way."

When she went through the house, Maile grabbed her phone from the end table next to the couch. Going into the room where she kept her clothes, she closed the door and windows, just in case Caitlyn might be eavesdropping.

Maile called Kaia.

"How was your date the other night?" Kaia asked.

"Didn't happen."

"Sorry. How's the new style working out?"

"It's great. I called because I might've burned you a little."

"What do you mean?"

Maile sniffed a blouse before pulling it over her head. "There's a police officer here at the house, a detective investigating Michelle Jones's death. Somehow, your name came up and now the detective wants to talk to you."

"When? Because I have an appointment later."

"We'd be there in a few minutes."

"You're coming too?" Kaia asked.

"Kinda feel like I need to, since I was the one who implicated you by handing over your name."

"I had nothing to do with any of that, you know that."

"I know. I'm just giving you a heads-up call to let you know we're coming. But if you take off, that'll only make you look guilty to them."

"I'm not going anywhere. I have clients coming in later."

"Hey, she's yelling at me to hurry up. We'll be there in a few."

They stopped at Kiki's Diner, the same place Maile had Silva stop at one day. Maile got her usual coffee with cream, while Nakamura got something more elaborate. Kiki looked desperate for why Maile was there with yet another detective, or maybe just for some gossip. All Maile could do was whisper a promise she'd call later.

The detective noticed Maile looking at her cup as she drove. "What?"

"Do all police detectives get fancy coffee drinks?"

"Don't laugh. All those empty calories will probably end up being my lunch. I have to say something."

Maile hated comments like that. They were always followed by a criticism. "About?"

"I was surprised when I heard you were serving in the Army. You were about the last person I'd expect to serve in the military."

"Nobody was more surprised than me. But that part of my life is done. At least the public part."

"I've heard some stuff went wrong once?"

"That's one way of putting it." Maile pointed to the building they were going to. "Mind if we drop it?"

"Sure. If you ever need someone to talk to, give me a call."

As they walked to Kaia's salon, Maile wondered if Caitlyn might be the right person to talk to. Everyone else she'd ever confided in about her time in the military had never aimed a weapon at another human being, let alone pull the trigger.

When they went in, Kaia was sweeping the floor, even though no client was there. Maile did the introductions and they all sat in the waiting area to talk.

"Detective, you gotta believe me when I say I haven't seen Michelle Jones since I was in junior high. That was almost ten years ago," Kaia said.

"Okay, enough about her," Nakamura said. "I'm more interested in knowing about Elizabeth Mahoe. You're a Mahoe from Kauai, and so is she. How long have you been on Oahu? I'd appreciate an exact date."

"November 17th. A few days later, I signed the lease on this shop. That was the day before Thanksgiving and I opened for business on the Monday after. Hasn't exactly been a stampede of clients."

"How long is your lease for?"

"Two years, which will kill me if business doesn't pick up pretty soon."

"Two? I thought one year on places like this was normal?" Nakamura asked.

"Yeah, but I got a great rate, way cheaper than what I would've been paying for a one-year lease."

"Good business sense," Nakamura said. She checked out the walls and décor. "Might want to get more cheerful paint and some fashion posters on the walls."

"Which costs money. Considering I'm sleeping in the back room on a bed made from a pile of flattened cardboard boxes, I'm doing pretty good."

When Maile heard that, she discovered how important that business card was that Kaia had given her a few days before. While Nakamura asked about services, Maile dreamt up plans of how she might be able to help.

"You live here?" Nakamura asked.

"The landlord doesn't know that, but according to city zoning laws, it's legal. I'd probably be charged more rent if the landlord knew I lived here."

"City zoning laws are someone else's problem," Nakamura said.

She took a lap around the small salon, looking at the things Kaia had laid out on a counter, and pulled open a few drawers. After that, she went down the dark hall to the back rooms. While she was gone, Maile gave Kaia's hand a supportive squeeze. A moment later, Nakamura came back.

"Along with Jones's murder, I'm investigating several bank robberies and supermarket holdups in Waikiki that have occurred in the last few weeks." Nakamura open the manila envelope she'd brought. "These are video captures of the culprit from several of those jobs. To me, and according to our facial recognition expert, there is an eighty percent likelihood that these are all the same person. Take a close look and tell me what you think."

She handed black and white photos to both Maile and Kaia. In the pictures that Maile saw, the person was obviously a woman, with long light-colored hair and a dark complexion. She wore a surgical mask and sunglasses to hide her face, a short-sleeved T-shirt and jeans, but did little else to change her appearance. Maile knew what was coming.

"I see what you're getting at, but that's not me," Kaia said, handing back the pictures.

"I hear that a lot, and it's surprising how often it turns out not to be true."

Kaia's hands trembled slightly. "Maybe, just maybe this one time it is."

"How much do you weigh and how tall are you, Kaia?"

"Five-six, one hundred thirty five pounds."

Nakamura went to the cash register and pulled the framed beautician's license off the wall. "This license is dated September, and you have dark hair in the picture. How long have you been blond?"

"I moved in on Thanksgiving when no one else was around to see me. I guess I got bored. I opened a bottle of wine and gave myself a new color."

"On Thanksgiving? You didn't have a date?"

"I don't really know anybody here on Oahu, except the ones I've met since then. I can't afford to fly home to Kauai, just to see my parents. Maybe I should've, anyway."

To Maile, there was something admirable about how Kaia was approaching her new business, especially at such a young age. She kept to a tight budget and was sacrificing a lot to make a go of it. She also wondered what Caitlyn thought of Kaia, if her detective mind only saw what could be construed as deceit.

"My lab techs have run several body habitus programs on these images. Those are computer programs that use 3-D modeling to determine quite accurately a person's height and weight, just from still images. They can also determine a person's age by how they move and walk, and previous injuries they might've had."

"Okay," Kaia said nervously.

"They've been able to determine the person in each of these pictures is the same, a woman from her late teens to late twenties, and has never suffered a serious injury. She's five foot six inches tall and weighs one hundred and thirty two pounds. Kaia, does that sound familiar?"

"Yes, but I didn't rob any banks or grocery stores. Please believe me."

Maile took all the images to look more closely. It was less at the image of the woman pulling the holdup, and more at the time stamps in the corner of each photo.

She handed one over to Nakamura. "Detective, this one can't be her."

"Why not?"

"Look at the time stamp."

"One thirty-eight PM on Friday December 31st. There have been two more holdups since then. What about it?"

"I was right here in this salon having my hair done by Kaia at that exact time and day."

Kaia nodded when Nakamura looked at her.

"Fortunate alibi that doesn't carry much weight."

Maile got out her phone and scrolled through her pictures back in time to that date. She'd taken an after selfie, and she'd included Kaia.

Nakamura took the phone for a closer look. Maile watched closely as the detective tapped her thumb quickly on the screen. She found the display page for time and date, before going back to look at the pictures. The times for those matched what Maile told Caitlyn.

Maile dug through her coin purse. "If that's not enough, here's the credit card receipt for that day."

Nakamura looked closely. "Almost two hours after the commission of the crime."

"I had a lot done." Maile shrugged. "We're gossips. No crime against that, is there?"

"Fortunately not, or we'd all be behind bars." The detective gave back the receipt. "From what I've heard, someone has to be pretty tech savvy to change the time and date imprints on most phones, without them reverting back automatically." Nakamura kept scrolling and looking at pictures, even the ones Maile had taken over the weekend during her long shift as flight nurse. "This is you at work, Maile?"

"Victims before and during transport for documentation. You really shouldn't be looking at those."

Nakamura gave the phone back. "Okay, you have one solid alibi. Any others?"

Kaia got out her phone and brought up pictures of satisfied customers at the end of their services. "Can you compare the times and dates on these against the other crimes?"

Caitlyn took the phone. "I can, if you act as my scribe."

Maile stifled three yawns while Kaia jotted down the time stamps that Caitlyn read off the phone's pictures. They then compared those to the times marked on the pictures from banks Caitlyn had brought with her.

"Well, I have two things to say," Nakamura said when she finished looking at images on the phone. "First, you have solid alibis that you were in fact here in the salon at the exact same moment as four of the crimes. Since my techs have already determined it's the same woman in every picture, that leaves you off the hook for all of them."

"Thank goodness!" Kaia said.

Maile gave Kaia a supportive pat on the back. "You said there were two things?"

"Yes. You're one heck of a hairdresser."

"Thanks."

"Now, I want to get back to Elizabeth Mahoe," Nakamura said. "Kaia, is she related to you in any way?"

"Unfortunately, yes. Betty is some sort of distant blood cousin that we'd love to forget about. I never knew her very well, maybe meeting her once or twice a long time ago. She's sort of the black sheep in the family."

"How'd she get stuck with that designation?"

"Kinda weird."

"Weird how?" Nakamura asked.

"Oh, I don't know how to explain. She was sort of a dick. There was one time they came to our house for Christmas and she broke a tree ornament and blamed someone else. Then she let the dog into the house and everybody knew the dog had to stay out because it jumped all over the place. When it knocked the tree over, it was all the dog's fault, according to her. That was the last time they were invited over to the house."

"To mine, also. We've looked for arrests, but nothing turns up for her Do you remember anything like that for her?"

"You know, I think she was too smart to get arrested. It was like she was always one level of sophistication above whatever trouble she was getting into."

"Those are the most successful types of criminals. They only commit crimes they know they can walk away from." Caitlyn hung the framed license on the wall where it belonged again, careful to make sure it was level. "Do you happen to have any pictures of your cousin Betty?"

"Sorry. I haven't seen her since I was a kid. My mom might have an old picture of everybody together, though."

"Never mind." Caitlyn gave Kaia one of her business cards. "If you think of anything about Betty Mahoe that might help in finding her, please give me a call."

"I will. Thanks for believing me." Kaia handed Caitlyn one of her business cards. "I'd appreciate it if you didn't let on that I'm using the back room as…"

"Storage?"

Maile saw Kaia blush. "Yes, storage."

"Give me a few more of your cards," Caitlyn said. "Some of the fellows at the downtown station are in dire need of some help."

Kaia smiled when she glanced at Maile. "If you know any Roman gladiators, send them in."

"Roman what?"

"Inside joke, Detective," Maile said.

Chapter Twenty-Two

Maile had Caitlyn drop her off in downtown rather than at home since her therapy appointment was coming up later.

"You're convinced about Kaia, right?" Maile asked. "That she's not holding up banks?"

"Oh, yeah. I'm also convinced she's not Jones's murderer."

"Why?"

"She doesn't have a dishonest bone in her body. Plus, we know who killed Jones. We're not sure why she was killed, but we have a little time to figure that out."

"Who killed her?" Maile asked.

"Betty Mahoe."

"Why would she kill her own partner?"

"It happens. They have a disagreement over how to split the money, one wants to walk away, a circular cycle of distrust starts. It could be anything. Once the killing starts, it gets too easy, and they turn their sights on each other."

"Criminals killing criminals. Something kind of pathetic about that," Maile said quietly. "Is there evidence Mahoe killed Jones?"

"Just like all the security cameras at the banks, the marina has cameras outdoors aimed at each row of docks, and also near the entrance. There's video feed of two women that match the descriptions and earlier images of Jones and Mahoe coming into the marina and going down one of the wharfs. The video isn't clear of what happened at the far end of the wharf, but there was some pushing and shoving between them before one is pushed into the water. The other then leaves alone, and is an excellent match to the images we already have of Betty Mahoe."

"And the dock where their fought was where Jones was found floating the next morning?" Maile asked.

"Exactly. What I don't have is video of the vehicle they arrived in, or she left in. For whatever reason, the security video system for the parking lot was turned off that night."

"That seems suspicious," Maile said.

"To Silva and me, also."

"Why don't you think Kaia killed Jones?" Maile asked.

"No motive. Plus, it was in the middle of the night. Kaia would've been in her little salon at that time. I'm going to check the security cameras for that neighborhood if she shows up on any of them, but I just don't see Kaia killing anyone."

"Either do I," Maile said.

"What we, or I should say Troy Silva, doesn't know is who killed the man you found at the beach. Anyone's best guess is that it was Jones."

"Michelle Jones killed Leo Brown, just because he pranked us in the middle of the night?" Maile asked.

"There's something you don't know about Jones and Brown that Detective Silva just uncovered last night. They were married in the past, and had an ugly divorce. It was so bad, they both had restraining orders against each other, which rarely happens. It wasn't long before Brown moved here to Oahu, just so they could keep the ocean between them as a buffer zone."

"Well, that explains a lot," Maile said.

"Such as?"

"Why Jones started getting out of her tent and went right back in again when I was confronting Brown. She must've recognized him, and didn't want to deal with him in the middle of the night."

"More like she went back into her tent looking for a weapon. I heard something about a flashlight that was left out all night, and that became the murder weapon?" Nakamura asked.

"Yeah. Detective Silva found it in the bushes near the restrooms a couple of days later. He wasn't able to link it to anyone, though."

"News on that front," Nakamura said. "Two partial prints were found on the recovered flashlight, and they're good matches for Jones's right hand."

"I thought the whole thing had been wiped down?" Maile asked.

"Not well enough. When they checked it for latents in the lab, they found the two partials. That would've been good enough to get her in an interrogation room, followed by a holding cell. The DA is sure he would've brought charges against Jones for the murder of her ex-husband Brown."

Maile wanted to laugh at the irony. "Brown scared us, Jones killed Brown, and Mahoe killed Jones. I wonder who's next?"

"Hopefully not you or Kaia."

"Yeah, she's kind of a sitting duck in there, if someone wanted to harm her." Maile bit her lip for a moment, wondering how, or even if, she should proceed with an idea. "Caitlyn, I have some ideas about Betty Mahoe, but before I can talk to you or Detective Silva, I need to get them straight in my head first. Otherwise, I'll sound like a crackpot."

"Are you safe in the mean time?"

"Nobody wants to kill me," Maile said.

"That we know of."

Maile swore under her breath, forgetting she was with someone.

"What's wrong?" Caitlyn asked.

"That just really pisses me off."

Caitlyn pulled into the drive-thru at a fast food restaurant. When she paused at the ordering station, she asked for two iced teas. Once she got them at the drive-thru window, she pulled around and parked in a back corner of the parking lot. She turned down the volume on her police scanner so they could talk.

"What pisses you off?" she asked Maile.

"Michelle Jones got away with murder."

"A lot of criminals get away with their crimes, including murderers. But considering the outcome of her being murdered only a few days later, she didn't get away with much."

"It still isn't right. She needed to face justice."

"If being killed by a whack to the back of her head wasn't justice, which wasn't much different from execution, what would be?" Caitlyn asked.

"I don't know. She never had to answer for her crimes. I hate the idea that she got away with murder, and right in front of the girls she was responsible for." Maile tried to sip from the straw, but her hand was shaking too much. "How in the world does that get explained to them?"

Caitlyn took the drink from Maile's hand and put it in the cup holder. "If you could be her judge, jury, and executioner, what would you do to Jones?" she asked quietly.

Maile continued to stare straight ahead at the fence in front of them. "I don't know."

"If you could do anything, what would it be?"

Maile rubbed her hands back and forth on her thighs, thinking.

"She's dead, Maile. You can't get in trouble for threatening a dead woman."

Maile slowly shook her head. "Bring her to me right now. I'd like to slap that nasty smirk off her face. Just let her have it once, right across the chops."

"For killing her ex?"

"For being such a god awful leader to a bunch of girls that tried their best to look up to her as a role model. For letting them down the way she did."

Caitlyn gave Maile a napkin to blot a tear. "That war really did a number on you, didn't it?"

"War?" Maile asked, coming back to the here and now of the car.

"Khashraq, or whatever it's called. Did somebody let you down there? Is that how you got injured?"

"I was injured by being stupid."

"What happened then that makes Jones's so important to you now?" Caitlyn asked. "Who let you down?"

"Nobody," Maile said. "I let them down."

"Who? The military? They were lucky to have you, Maile."

Maile continued to stare straight ahead while another tear rolled down her cheek. "The soldiers. Grunts dying alone, while I was elsewhere."

A call came through the scanner, which Caitlyn listened to for a moment before turning it down again.

"Maile, I have to roll on that call." Caitlyn started the car. "But girl, you need to talk about these things. The only way you're going to get back to normal is to talk them out."

"What am I supposed to get back to? My old self? Because she's gone forever."

"I don't know what your normal is right now," Caitlyn said as she got back out into traffic. "But I'm going to make sure it's better than this."

***

Maile squirmed in her chair as she was stared at by the therapist, Tess. She had no idea of how to answer the question, and had been thinking about it for so long, she wasn't even sure what the question was.

"What's inside the two glasses you stole, Maile?" Tess asked again.

"Blood in one, water in the other."

"Okay, good. What else about the glasses?"

"One's half full, the other is half empty."

"Which is half full, and which is half empty?" Tess asked.

"That's the part I can't figure out. I never have known what that means, about glasses being half full or empty."

"An optimistic person sees the glass as half full."

"That's the part that doesn't make sense to me at all."

"Why not?"

"Both glasses have the same amount of fluid in them. It doesn't matter if something has been put in or removed. All that matters is the amount, that half the volume of the glass is fluid and half is air. Both glasses can be filled with more fluid, and both can be emptied of the fluid that's already in them."

"You might be overthinking it a little, Maile."

"I just want to know why I stole two glasses from a hotel, if there's a secondary meaning to it."

Tess checked her watch. "I'd like to know why there's blood in one and water in the other, but we're done for the day. Are you coming back?"

"Until I figure out why I stole two glasses and don't feel guilty about it, yes."

***

Maile made a jailbreak for the exit as soon as she paid, and never looked back. She hurried home, got a few things in a knapsack, and went right back out again. Catching a cross-town bus, she watched for her stop. Getting out, she went into a crack seed store and got a packet of dried fruit. Stuffing that and a couple bottles of water into her knapsack, she crossed the street and started hiking up hill.

After the long weekend and not getting much sleep that day, she was dog-tired. But she had something important to do, and that evening would be perfect. One murder had been solved, and the police were closing in on finding the culprit of another. It was time to move on from the Girl Scout campout at the beach two weeks before.

Gus was gone forever as far as Maile was concerned. He was as close to a relationship as she'd had in years, but it was time to leave him behind.

Her career was back on track with her new job as a flight nurse, and good money would be coming in. Her tour business was still on its feet, and maybe even growing a little. With a little more effort, it might turn into something.

She wasn't sure, but she might actually be a homeowner, with the recent discovery about the Manoa House. She wasn't banking on that, and was going to do whatever David Melendez suggested to thwart someone from stealing it.

Things were going well since she'd come home; not perfectly, but good enough. Keeping that idea in her mind, she went into the rest of the day with renewed energy.

She'd have to hurry if she wanted to get to where she needed to go before it was too dark. Taking to the steep sidewalk at a jogging pace, she wound her way up the steep Wilhelmina Rise until she got to a trailhead at a nature preserve. That led her to a narrow dirt trail.

Wet leaves and branches swept her body as she climbed, at times running, at other times barely making progress. It took an hour before she got to the cutoff trail that led to the next valley over. She was up in the lush, green slopes of the Ko'olaus now, two thousand feet above the city. She couldn't hurry on the narrow goat trail she was following, even though the sun was getting low. One misstep and she'd plunge hundreds of feet.

Once the sun started kissing the horizon, she got out the battery headlight. Fitting it to her head and turning it on, she continued on to a spot she hadn't been to in over a decade.

Maile needed to scramble along a razorback ridge, with steep drop-offs on both sides, often proceeding on all fours. It was a solid hundred yards long, and seemed like it went on for miles as the steady wind tugged at her body. With only the light from the stars and her headlight, she finally got to where she wanted to go. It had taken three hours to travel only a few miles, but she got there without dying in the process.

She used a second flashlight to check out the inside of a little cave. It was outside opening of the end of an old lava tube, a natural tunnel that lava had flowed through during the birth of the island. Only a few feet in, it was filled with moss, ferns, and dripping water. She'd never had the nerve to go any further.

"Someday, I'm coming back with a brighter light and find out where this goes."

On a half dozen earlier visits, she'd never found any bones of signs of human use at all. Strange, since the ancient Hawaiians often used caves and lava tubes as gravesites for the bones of the departed. The more difficult the better, and the hardest ones to get to were secretly reserved for royal ali'i. Because there was no indication anyone else had ever been there, Maile thought of the place as her own.

"Not a bad place to hide my bones, when the time comes," she said, dropping her knapsack to the ground. She removed her shoes and socks, along with her shirt, which she used to wipe water and mud from her legs and arms. It hadn't been her longest, but it had been the most fun run she'd been on in a long time.

There was a rock ledge for her to stand on, and she crept her toes forward. That was a lot easier than it would've been during the daytime, since she couldn't see the sudden drop below of a thousand feet or more. She opened a bottle of water and took a long swig.

Using her flashlight, she dug an envelope from the bag and opened the flap. It was the same envelope that Kaia had given her at the salon, the one with a lock of her hair in it. Turning off her lights put her in near-complete darkness.

She eased forward toward the front of the stone ledge. When her toes felt the rounded edge, she stopped.

Maile pinched the lock of hair between her fingers and held it out into the wind. Flicking her fingers a few times, she let the hairs blow off into the wind.

"E 'olu'olu e mālama pono iā mākou."

Once the simple offering was made and her prayers complete, Maile pulled on a hoodie and sweat pants. She sat on the ledge and watched the lights of the city below her twinkle.

Interrupting the sedate mood that was descending was her phone ringing with a call.

"Why didn't I turn this stupid thing off," she muttered. Ready to jab her finger on the *On/Off* button, she noticed the call was from an unknown number. Since getting home a few weeks earlier, almost all of her calls were coming from unknown numbers, friends and relatives with new phones, or new contacts about work. She couldn't ignore something that might be important.

"Hello, Aunt Maile?"

The voice was familiar. "This is Maile Spencer. Can I help you?"

"This is Nancy."

Maile wondered if someone was pranking her. "Okay."

"Nancy Miller."

"Nancy! Hi, how are you?"

"You remember me?" the girl asked.

"Of course I do. Happy New Year. Are you using the phone you got for Christmas?"

"You're my first call."

"I'm your first? You haven't called anybody before this?"

"My dad said I can't make dumb calls to people. He's right here. Do you want to talk to him?"

Maile smiled, wondering if the girl was trying to play matchmaker again. "I'd rather talk to you."

"Me?"

"Yeah, you. Tell me what you and your dad did on New Year's."

More from Kay Hadashi

Thanks for reading about Maile's return home to Honolulu! The fun continues on the Big Island when she takes a small group on a tour of chocolate factories, the rainforest, and a few places that shouldn't be visited in a van that has seen better days and drier roads. The real trouble starts when she waits a little too long in the driver's seat at a downtown Hilo curb.

But anything is better than being back in Honolulu, where she'd have to deal with too many sexy blonde Hawaiians, a brother that needs a loan in a hurry, a mother summoning the powers of Lono, and her home being on the silent auction block.

Travels and Travails of Maile Spencer

Almost Home—Maile takes herself on an around the world journey

Beach Bummed—Maile takes a group of Girl Scouts on a hike and one or two things go wrong

Cocoa Nuts—Trouble brews when too much caffeine is consumed by chocolate lovers

Double Trouble—Two weddings on Maui at the same time is too much trouble for everyone

Fool's Gold—All she wanted was to say goodbye to any old friend at his funeral

Going for Broke—Hiding in plain sight has never been so much fun, or dangerous

Hooray for Haolewood—When Hollywood comes to Hawaii, they bring trouble with them

And more!

§

Made in the USA
Las Vegas, NV
30 April 2023